PRAISE FOR
THE INCORRIGIBLE CHILDREN OF ASHTON PLACE

"It's the best beginning since *The Bad Beginning* by Lemony Snicket and will leave readers howling for the next episode."
—*Kirkus Reviews* (starred review)

"How hearty and delicious. Smartly written with a middle-grade audience in mind, this is both fun and funny and sprinkled with dollops of wisdom (thank you, Agatha Swanburne). How will it all turn out? Appetites whetted."
—ALA *Booklist* (starred review)

"With a Snicketesque affect, Wood's narrative propels the drama. Pervasive humor and unanswered questions should have readers begging for more."
—*Publishers Weekly* (starred review)

"Jane Eyre meets Lemony Snicket in this smart, surprising satire of a nineteenth-century English governess story. Humorous antics and a climactic cliff-hanger ending will keep children turning pages and clamoring for the next volume, while more sophisticated readers will take away much more. Frequent plate-sized illustrations add wit and period flair."
—*Sch___ ___ ___ ___ Journal* (starred review)

Also by Maryrose Wood

THE INCORRIGIBLE CHILDREN OF ASHTON PLACE

The
INTERRUPTED
TALE

by MARYROSE WOOD

illustrated by ELIZA WHEELER

BALZER + BRAY
An Imprint of HarperCollins *Publishers*

Balzer + Bray is an imprint of HarperCollins Publishers.

The Incorrigible Children of Ashton Place Book 4: The Interrupted Tale

Library of Congress Cataloging-in-Publication Data
Wood, Maryrose.
The interrupted tale / by Maryrose Wood ; illustrated by Eliza Wheeler. — 1st ed.
p.   cm. — (The incorrigible children of Ashton Place ; bk. 4)
Summary: Miss Penelope Lumley assuages the disappointments of her sixteenth
birthday by accepting an invitation to speak at her former school, the Swanburne Academy
for Poor Bright Females, which will be closed if she cannot prove the academic progress
of her incorrigible charges.
ISBN 978-0-06-179123-9 (pbk.)
[1. Governesses—Fiction. 2. Feral children—Fiction. 3. Orphans—Fiction. 4. Ashton
Place (Imaginary place)—Fiction. 5. Incorrigibles (Fictitious characters)—Fiction. 6.
Lumley, Penelope (Fictitious character)—Fiction. 7. Children's stories. 8. England—
Fiction.] I. Title.
PZ7.W8524 Int 2013   2013953787
[Fic]—dc23   CIP
                                                                                  AC

Typography by Sarah Hoy and Dana Fritts
15 16 17 18 19   CG/OPM   10 9 8 7 6 5 4 3 2
❖
First paperback edition, 2015

For Andrew and Joe, with whom I shared an unforgettable (and unescapable) walk through the ferns

The
INCORRIGIBLE CHILDREN
of
ASHTON PLACE

BOOK 4:

The
INTERRUPTED TALE

THE FIRST CHAPTER

*A Swanburne girl thinks
of home.*

AT THE SWANBURNE ACADEMY FOR Poor Bright Females, birthday parties were cheerful but brief affairs. They took place at breakfast, in the dining hall, over bowls of hot porridge. (It was customary to offer the birthday girl an extra helping, which was generous but hardly necessary, as porridge is rather filling to begin with.)

Small gifts were permitted as long as they were of the humble sort that the girls could make themselves, such as knitted neck scarves and monogrammed handkerchiefs and, of course, the ever-popular pillows embroidered with the sayings of the school's founder, Agatha Swanburne. But after the porridge had been eaten, the presents opened, and a round of "For she's a credit to Swanburne, for she's a credit to Swanburne, for she's a credit to Swah-han-burne! And so say all of us!" had been rousingly sung, the party was done, and all the girls, including the birthday girl herself, were shooed off to their lessons straightaway.

"Remember, a sound education is the very best present of all," Miss Charlotte Mortimer, the headmistress, would say, clapping her hands to signal an end to the festivities. "Off you go, now. Don't forget to clear your plates." *Clap clap clap!*

Nothing unkind was meant by the brisk efficiency of these celebrations. There was simply a great deal to learn, and limited hours in which to learn it. As Agatha Swanburne herself once remarked, "So many cupcakes, so little time"—an unfortunate mathematical ratio that remains in effect to this very day.

Miss Penelope Lumley no longer lived at the Swanburne Academy, of course. She had graduated more than a year earlier, and was now a professional governess in the grand house known as Ashton Place, currently the home of Lord Fredrick Ashton and his excitable young wife, Lady Constance. (The historically minded among you have doubtless heard of the Ashtons; in Miss Lumley's day, they were known for their immense wealth and sprawling estate, including a vast and mysterious forest in which some unusual things had been known to happen—but more on that subject later.)

With its manicured gardens, countless elegant rooms, and a fleet of servants tending to the house and its residents, Ashton Place was a far more luxurious setting than the Swanburne Academy for Poor Bright Females could ever hope to be. Even so, on this particular autumn morning, Penelope found herself feeling rather homesick for her alma mater. She missed the hard wooden benches and chilly classrooms in winter (for there was rarely enough wood to keep more than a modest fire going in each hearth, even on the coldest days). She missed the long march from the dormitories to the dining hall every morning, during which the girls bellowed the school song with great feeling and even greater volume, in order to wake themselves up. She even missed the porridge, which, to be frank, was sometimes lumpy, especially if one let it get cold.

Most of all, she missed the birthdays. For although the parties were short and lacked cake, and the presents were homespun and predictable (to Penelope's knowledge, never had any Swanburne girl received a golden locket from a secret admirer on her birthday, or a magic lamp with a wish-giving genie inside, or even a sweet-tempered pony to spoil and train and make one's best friend forever and evermore)—still, at Swanburne, when it was your birthday everyone knew it. The day began with gifts and a song, and there were friends close at hand to share jokes and make a fuss. Even the sternest teachers and the brash older girls with whom you hardly dared to speak smiled at you in a special, knowing way your whole birthday long.

"Nevertheless, it is my birthday, even if no one knows it but me," Penelope confided to her bedchamber mirror, as she readied herself for the day ahead by brushing her hair into its customary neat bun. "I am sixteen years old, at last."

Curious, she examined her fingers and wiggled her toes. At sixteen they seemed no different than before. Nor did the mirror show any evidence of transformation. Her drab, dark hair, her clear gray-green eyes, her brow that was prone to furrowing in deep concentration, especially when there was a mystery to be solved—all seemed unchanged by the momentous nature of the day. Yet a page on the calendar had turned, and here she was, sixteen! To Penelope it sounded quite grown-up, never mind that she spent most of her waking

4

hours in a nursery full of toys (which was understandable, since she was, in fact, a governess).

Now, some of you may be tempted to feel sorry for Penelope, for what could be sadder than to have a birthday that no one knows about? Recall that she was not without companions at Ashton Place. She was on cordial terms with Mrs. Clarke, the head housekeeper, and was equally fond of Margaret, the good-hearted and squeaky-voiced housemaid. There was no question that Penelope was liked and admired by all the household staff.

Even so, in Miss Lumley's day, to be the governess in a grand estate was a lonely job. She was not counted among the servants, for she was an educated person and had no household duties other than tending to the children. Yet she was in no way the equal of her employers. She was rudely ordered about by Lady Constance and could be dismissed from her position with a word.

In short, in a world where a person's place in society was either high or low, Penelope was somewhere in between. It made it difficult to feel real friendship with anyone, at least in the free and easy way she had once had with the girls at Swanburne, where one Poor Bright Female was no better or worse than any other.

For this and perhaps some other reasons, the people to whom she felt closest at Ashton Place were her pupils: Alexander, Beowulf, and Cassiopeia Incorrigible, the three wards of Lord Fredrick Ashton. The children had been found barking and yapping in the forest during one of Lord Fredrick's frequent hunting expeditions. Their puppyish behavior was a consequence of having been raised by wolves, although, as Penelope had discovered, they may have had some human help as well.

The Incorrigibles adored their Lumawoo, as they called her (little howling *ahwoo*s often snuck into the children's way of talking, due to the wolfish influence of their early years). But they were still children, which was not quite the same as Penelope having friends her own age. In any case, she was much too kindhearted to have told the Incorrigibles about her birthday, for one simple reason: She did not know when the children's birthdays were, and neither, she assumed, did they, and she would never want to hurt their feelings by drawing attention to that fact.

"After all, an uncelebrated birthday is not nearly as bad as never having a birthday at all," she thought. "Poor Incorrigibles! It would be terribly unkind of me to make a fuss about turning sixteen, given the circumstances." Still thinking, she closed the door of her bedchamber behind her and headed toward the nursery. "Anyway, presents can be such a nuisance. All those bits of torn wrapping paper to tidy up! And if one does not get presents, one does not have to bother writing thank-you notes, which saves both time and ink."

As you can see, it was Penelope's nature to try to cheer herself up when feeling glum. "No birthday cards means no danger of paper cuts. No cake means I will have a good appetite for supper. And no birthday candles greatly reduces the risk of accidental fire. Really, I am quite lucky to be spared all that bother. If there is anyone for whom one ought to feel sorry, it is the children. Even if they did know when their birthdays were, I am quite sure the wolves in the forest would not have had the slightest notion of how to throw a decent party. . . . Eureka!"

(For those of you unfamiliar with the term, "Eureka!" is what to exclaim when you have discovered something worth shouting about. It was an ancient Greek scholar named Archimedes who first shouted "Eureka!" He was in the bathtub when it happened; coincidentally, his discovery had to do with how water in a bathtub rises when an ancient Greek scholar is bathing in it, and how measuring this "displaced" water would be a foolproof way to find the volume of said scholar, should anyone need to do that. Bear in mind that this is advanced mathematics; most of us will never need worry about the volume of old Greek men in the bath. What is important is that shouting "Eureka!" is both enjoyable and a spur to productivity. Try it for yourselves: You will discover how peppy it makes one feel to do one's math homework when there is a bracing cry of "Eureka!" to look forward to at the completion of each problem.)

"Eureka!" Penelope exclaimed again, for her idea was truly an excellent one. "I will organize a birthday party for the children! Since there is no way of knowing when their true birthdays are, I shall simply declare today to be the Incorrigible Birthday and do all of them at once, one, two, three. It will be a wonderful surprise for them, and pleasant for me as well. For this way there will be cake and singing anyway, and I doubt I will miss being given any more handkerchiefs, as I already have so many."

With her lip quivering only a little (for the thought of those sweet monogrammed handkerchiefs made her even more homesick for Swanburne than before), Penelope opened the door to the nursery. "Children, rise and shine! You will never guess what today is—"

"Tuesday?" Alexander jumped up and blocked her way into the room. Still, she was able to get a glimpse of Beowulf at his desk, chewing on some object that he quickly hid in his pocket.

"No, it is Thursday," Penelope replied, squeezing past. "Where is your sister?" The boys looked down at the floor, up at the ceiling, and sideways at each other, everywhere but at their governess.

"Owwwwwwooooooh!"

The howl of pain came from the back nursery, where Penelope found Cassiopeia in her bed, whimpering and thrashing to and fro. "Cassiopeia, what is it? Are you ill?"

"Very ill." The girl squeezed her head with both hands and waggled her tongue from side to side. "Tummy ache."

"And I have a headache," Beowulf added, crossing his eyes.

"We are all sick. I am dizzy, see?" Alexander tottered about the room, spun in a circle, and fell to the floor. Then he gazed up at Penelope and croaked, "Highly contagious! Plague, perhaps?"

Penelope helped the boy to his feet. "I doubt it is plague. But I hope it is not the chicken pox."

"Chicken pox!" Beowulf strutted around the room and flapped his arms like wings, until his brother shot him a look. "I mean, *ahhhhhhh! Ahhhhh!*" He clutched his leg and moaned in agony.

Penelope frowned. "I thought you had a headache?"

"In my leg I do," Beowulf explained. "From chicken pox." He hopped on his one good leg and made chicken noises. *"Buck-buck, buck-buck!"*

"Tummy ache!" Cassiopeia wailed. "In my nose! Ahhh!" Then she buried her head under a pillow, from which some sort of unidentifiable, repetitive, smothered sound—weeping? sneezing? giggling?—could be heard.

Penelope looked around the room and considered this unexpected turn of events. The children were acting strangely, to be sure. But perhaps it was because they were sick. In any case, it was obviously not the right day for an Incorrigible birthday party.

No party! Her disappointment swelled, and she permitted herself one small, melancholy sigh before saying, "Our topic of study for today is poetic meter, but there is no point in doing lessons when you are all so sick. I presume you do not feel well enough for breakfast?"

The children's eyes gleamed with hunger, but all

The children were acting strangely, to be sure.

three shook their heads.

"That is too bad, for I believe the kitchen baked fresh biscuits this morning." Penelope waited for some sort of reaction, for the children dearly loved biscuits, but three stoic faces avoided her gaze. "Very well," she said, not wholly convinced. "Stay in bed, all of you. I shall go ask Mrs. Clarke to summon a doctor."

PENELOPE FOUND MRS. CLARKE IN the pantry, inspecting bags of flour for beetles. "The children are not feeling well," she said, trying not to look, for the thought of bugs in the flour threatened to put her off her own breakfast. "Alexander is dizzy, and Cassiopeia is in bed with a tummy ache. Would you be so kind as to have the doctor called?"

Mrs. Clarke dug into each bag with a tin flour scoop and a sieve. "The doctor? For a child's tummy ache? Nonsense. I'll send up Margaret with a hot-water bottle, some castor oil, and a nice big spoon. Hold the bag open, would you, dear, while I snoop around for weevils."

Penelope obliged, although she was not wearing an apron and the flour made white streaks on her skirt. "Beowulf is also ill. He claims to have a headache in his leg."

"In his leg? Well, that's peculiar. Got one!" Mrs. Clarke crushed the bug between two fingers and flicked it to the ground.

Penelope winced. "Highly peculiar, I agree. That is why I would like the doctor to examine them—"

"A sip of brandy will dull the pain. Anyway, it's not the end of the world to let them suffer. Builds character! Look, there's another weevil right there." She squinted at the tiny intruder. "We'll have to sift this whole batch."

To suggest that sick children ought to be left to suffer in order to improve their characters seemed quite unlike Mrs. Clarke, whom Penelope knew to be thoroughly kindhearted. Then again, Penelope had never asked her to summon a doctor before. Perhaps there was more to it than she realized.

"If you say so, Mrs. Clarke," she replied cautiously. "But if they get any worse, I will have to insist that you reconsider. And while I am thinking of it . . . when the children are feeling well again, perhaps in a few days, or next week, I would like to have a small party in the nursery for them. Could I trouble the kitchen to provide a cake for the occasion?"

Once more, Mrs. Clarke's response seemed to lack her usual warmth. "Oh, cake's an awful bother. A plate of buttered toast and sugar will be more than enough."

"Toast and sugar!" Penelope could not hide her dismay. Even at Swanburne, a birthday girl might sometimes get a spoonful of jam in her porridge.

The housekeeper clucked disapprovingly. "Plenty of children would be grateful for a piece of toast, Miss Lumley, even without the sugar. You can see for yourself, we're short of good flour. I'll speak to the kitchen and find out what can be done. No promises, though."

Sick children. No party. Toast instead of cake.

Sixteen years old, and nobody cared!

Penelope's mood was grim. In fact, she felt things could hardly get worse, which is a dangerous way to think, and not only because it makes one the sort of miserable, dissatisfied person whom no one wants to sit next to at parties. Just as an excess of optimism (also known as optoomuchism) can cause one to act without considering what might go wrong, so can an excess of gloom incite one to recklessness. For if things truly cannot get any worse—and alas, this is rarely the case—why bother being careful?

It was in just this sort of rash and foolhardy mood that Penelope decided not to go straight back to the nursery. Instead, she took a detour that brought her to the entry hall of Ashton Place. There she found the housemaid, Margaret, energetically polishing the already gleaming brass door handle.

"Good morning, Margaret." Penelope tried to sound cheery. "Lovely day, isn't it? By any chance, has the mail come?"

"It surely has, Miss Lumley. Just look on the mail tray," the girl replied in her piercing mouse squeak of a voice. "Any special reason you want to know?"

"No! No special reason." Penelope leafed idly through the unopened letters. Ashton, Ashton, Ashton—those were for Lord Fredrick. They were all from his gentlemen's club or from various banks, except for one thin, stained envelope with no return address but which bore many colorful postmarks and exotic stamps from distant lands.

There was also a small, square envelope of heavy, cream-colored paper addressed to Lady Constance Ashton. It looked like a party invitation, Penelope thought with a pang. How unfair it was that some people were invited to parties for no good reason (other than being a Lady and young and fashionable and very rich, of course), while other people, whose actual birthday it was, could scarcely beg a piece of toast from the kitchen!

There were no more letters on the tray. She had hoped a card might come from Cecily, at least. Cecily was a clever, round-cheeked girl with wildly curly hair that she kept in two thick braids. She and Penelope had been the best of friends at Swanburne; they were assigned to the same dormitory and had even shared a cot when they were small. Like Penelope, Cecily had graduated early. Now she worked as a companion and translator for an elderly Hungarian lady who lived in the town of Witherslack. Cecily had always been a whiz at languages; no doubt she could say "happy birthday" in at least four or five, although Penelope would have settled for one.

And what about Miss Charlotte Mortimer? Surely Penelope's former headmistress would never have forgotten her sixteenth birthday! Apparently, she had. Apparently, Miss Mortimer's attention was now wholly fixed on her current students, and she had no time at all to think of Penelope—why, she had not even replied to the last letter Penelope had sent, even though Penelope had marked it *Urgent: Alarming News Contained Within*, underlined twice. The alarming news concerned a shady character who had recently joined the Swanburne board of trustees. He went by the name of Judge Quinzy, and Penelope had reason to fear he was

16

up to no good. Such a dire and clearly marked warning ought to be worth a reply. But, apparently, not.

As for her parents, whom she had not seen for many a year and whom she had come to think of as the Long-Lost Lumleys, "Not a card, not a letter, not even a picture postcard," Penelope whispered to herself. A tear might have begun to roll down her cheek, but if it did, she brushed it aside so quickly that no one was the wiser.

PENELOPE'S RESOLVE TO THROW A party for the Incorrigibles was now twice as keen as before, even if it meant she would have to bake the cake herself. She marched with purpose to the nursery. Outside the door all seemed quiet, but the moment she entered, each of the children assumed a pose of distraught misery, accompanied by moans and feverish gibbering. Penelope shooed them into the night nursery and ordered them to nap or read in their beds until Margaret arrived with the hot-water bottle. (Even in her unhappy state, Penelope was much too kind to mention the castor oil and large spoon that Mrs. Clarke had threatened. If the children did not already know that castor oil was the most vile-tasting substance ever invented, they would find out soon enough.)

Finally alone, she collapsed into her usual armchair and stared at the clock. Eleven o'clock in the morning! The whole long, partyless, presentless, friendless, cardless birthday loomed before her. Was it possible that time had actually stopped? She knew the Latin phrase "tempus fugit," which means "time flies," like a bird—but there were flightless birds, after all: ostriches and emus and dodos and so on. Could some days be made of flightless time?

Her thoughts were interrupted by a dreadful scuffling noise from the back nursery, followed by a cry.

"Lumawoo, come quickly! Beowulf's leg is worse." It was Alexander, calling in a highly dramatic voice. "Alas, it is *much* worse, woe is he!"

Penelope hurried to look. Beowulf writhed on the bed while his brother and sister stood by. "Leg*awoooo*!" he howled in pain.

"How about a peg leg instead?" Alexander suggested, offering a wooden pointer that seemed about the right length. "Will be good for playing pirates." But Beowulf only whimpered and moaned.

"Poor Beowoo." Cassiopeia took Alexander's hand. "He was nice. But at least we will still have each other."

Penelope did her best to examine the miserable child, but he would not stop thrashing. "Beowulf, I can

18

see nothing wrong with your leg. Why are you making such a fuss?"

Bang!

Bang bang!

Bang bang bang!

Someone was pounding on the nursery door, which was odd, as Penelope could not recall locking it. "Who is there?" she cried, at her wit's end. "Margaret, is that you?"

"Open the door, Miss Lumley. It's Mrs. Clarke! I've fetched the doctor."

"The doctor, thank goodness!" Penelope ran to the door and flung it open. "You are not a moment too soon. Beowulf is worse, and I cannot tell why . . . what?"

Just outside the door was a serving cart, upon which rested a large covered tray. Behind the cart stood Mrs. Clarke, Margaret, and nearly a dozen other members of the household staff.

"Surprise!" they yelled as one.

"Surprise?" Penelope did not know where to look.

Mrs. Clarke lifted the cover off the tray to reveal a decorated cake, edged with marzipan flowers and iced with the words *Happy 16th Birthday Miss P. Lumley.*

"Surpris*ahwoooooo!*" the three perfectly healthy

children cried as they raced to their governess and threw their arms around her.

AND A SURPRISE IT SURELY was. It took Penelope a full minute to recover the power of speech, and when she did, all she could blurt was, "How did you know?"

"It was the cards that tipped us off. 'Something must be up with Miss Lumley,' I said to Cook, 'to get so many cards all at the same time.' So we did a bit of investigating." Mrs. Clarke rubbed her hands together and laughed. "Oh, I do love a good mystery!"

Cook shrugged apologetically (doubtless she had a name, but everyone called her Cook, and therefore so shall we). "I tried, but I couldn't fit 'Penelope' on the cake. Sorry 'bout that!"

Under normal circumstances, Penelope might have offered some educational remarks on the topic of abbreviations (for an abbreviation is what Cook had made by putting "P." instead of "Penelope"), but the birthday girl was still reeling from the shock of her unexpected party. "The cards?" she repeated in a daze. "What cards?"

"The birthday cards! We hid them as part of the surprise." Margaret held out a thick packet of correspondence, tied in a ribbon. There was a card from

Miss Mortimer right on top, and another from Cecily in Witherslack. At least two dozen cards had a return address of the Swanburne Academy for Poor Bright Females in Heathcote—but Penelope had no time to look further, for her party guests had already lit the candles. Now they sang.

"For she's a credit to Ashton Place,
For she's a credit to Ashton Place,
For she's a credit to Ashton Place!
And so say all of us!"

The cake was cut into slices and gobbled up without delay. Everyone agreed that Cook had outdone herself with the marzipan flowers, which were both lifelike and delicious. Even Mrs. Clarke treated herself to a slice, although she had been watching her figure in recent months. After her last forkful, she announced, "And now your present."

"A present!" Penelope could hardly believe it. But it was true. Even on their modest incomes, the servants had managed to pool together enough money to buy Penelope an absolutely spectacular gift. It was a new type of pen called a "fountain pen," which could write line after line without having to be dipped into the inkwell. Penelope could not stop marveling at it and thanked them all repeatedly.

"Aw, Miss Lumley! We all know how much you like to write letters," Margaret squeaked, and the rest of the servants smiled, because it was clearly a well-chosen gift.

The Incorrigible children each had presents of their own to give, not as fancy as the pen, perhaps, but they had been handmade for the occasion, and that made them all the nicer, everyone was quick to note.

Alexander had drawn a map of the nursery, tinted with watercolors and oriented according to the compass, with all the furniture drawn to scale, down to the last footstool.

Beowulf had gnawed a perfectly usable letter opener out of a piece of wood. That the wood looked suspiciously like the remains of a ruler Penelope had searched for in vain just the other day was a fact she chose to ignore.

As for Cassiopeia: "Here, Lumawoo." The girl sounded uncharacteristically bashful as she offered her gift. It was a small, hand-sewn pillow, with one word embroidered crookedly on its front.

Loveawoo, it said.

The stitching was far from expert, and the pillow

was uneven in shape. The fabric, Penelope recognized at once, was cut from an old blanket that had been retired from use in the nursery after Beowulf had chewed off the corners, but still—who would have thought little Cassiopeia could manage such a thing?

"Fluffy," Cassiopeia said, and gave the lumpy pillow a squeeze to demonstrate. "Bertha made the feathers." (Bertha, as you may already know, was a sweet but dim-witted ostrich who had been left at Ashton Place by a recent visitor, and who was being cared for by Penelope and the children until a qualified person could be found to accompany the large bird back to Africa, where she rightly belonged.)

"Lumawoo likes pillow?" she nudged, for Penelope was still staring wordlessly at her gift.

"I do." Penelope thought of the window seats at the Swanburne Academy, which were so full of embroidered pillows that one could scarcely find a place to sit and read. "It is the fluffiest and loveliest pillow I have ever seen."

The girl lifted her hands and revealed tiny bandages of gauze tied about three of her fingers. "Sewing is hard," she said. The sight of those dear pricked fingers made Penelope's eyes fill with tears, and the children jumped over one another to reassure her that

Cassiopeia was not seriously injured. Cassiopeia proved it by using her fingers to do sums on her abacus, and flicked the beads up and down with nary a wince.

But Penelope's heart remained full to bursting. "Thank you all, so very much," she said, and gazed with affection on each of her three pupils, and on all of her guests as well. "This is the nicest birthday I could possibly imagine."

THE SERVANTS SOON HAD TO get back to work, but Penelope was used to quick parties, so she did not mind. It was only after Mrs. Clarke, Cook, Margaret, and the others had made their farewells that Beowulf suddenly remembered.

"One more present!" he cried, running to the windows. "Almost forgot Nutsawoo."

Nutsawoo was the twitchy and half-tame squirrel who spent his (or her) days in the branches of the elm tree just outside the nursery, performing amusing antics and begging for treats. At Beowulf's chirruping call, the little rodent scampered into the nursery and offered Penelope a great prize indeed: a single perfect acorn, carried with pride in those tiny, monkeylike paws. She (or he, for it is hard to tell with squirrels) dropped the acorn neatly into Penelope's hand before skittering back outside. The creature's bushy gray tail flicked to and fro with satisfaction.

Now, for a squirrel to sacrifice even a single acorn in autumn is a profound act of generosity, as Penelope well knew. For some reason this was what pushed her "over the edge," as they say nowadays, and she began to cry in earnest. The children were alarmed by her outburst and offered to cheer her by staging a *tableau vivant* of either "The Wreck of the Hesperus" by Henry Wadsworth Longfellow or "The Raven" by Edgar Allan Poe, or another poem they had recently begun reading, called "The Tyger," by Mr. William Blake, which began like this:

> *Tyger, Tyger, burning bright,*
> *In the forests of the night;*
> *What immortal hand or eye*
> *Could frame thy fearful symmetry?*

But Penelope shook her head, blew her nose (luckily, she was well stocked with handkerchiefs), ate a second piece of cake, and quickly regained her composure.

"Time to get back to our lessons," she said, clapping her hands briskly three times, just the way Miss Mortimer used to do to signal an end to a birthday party.

The children scurried to obey, and Penelope could not help thinking that the eagerness and good cheer of her students was the very best present of all. For whether she was six, sixteen, or (unimaginable as it might now seem) even sixty, Penelope would always be a Swanburne girl, through and through.

THE SECOND CHAPTER

*Lady Constance takes a leap of
the imagination.*

PERHAPS IT WAS THE EXCITEMENT of the party, or the several slices of cake topped with sugary marzipan flowers that each of the Incorrigibles had eaten for breakfast—whatever the cause, that afternoon the children were even friskier than usual. They could not settle down for lessons and kept popping up from their chairs for various reasons: to fetch an unneeded book from the shelf, or to switch one dull pencil for another that was no sharper, or to call Nutsawoo in from the elm tree for a scratch behind the ears. This was particularly time-consuming, for no matter how long the children scratched, the greedy squirrel always demanded more.

Needless to say, little was getting done in the way of schoolwork. But Penelope could hardly be cross with the children, after all their kindness and generosity. Too, she still felt the tiniest bit guilty about having a sixteenth birthday when her three pupils had yet to have one—and oughtn't she have some time off on her special day as well?

"Lessons will resume tomorrow; outside we go," she announced, to the children's delight. Under the changing leaves of the trees near the house, she entertained them with some vigorous skipping and dancing games that she had recently invented. The games were meant to show the various types of poetic meter: iambic pentameter, for example, which William Shakespeare used to marvelous effect in many of his poems and plays. (Scholars have written lengthy books on the subject of iambic pentameter, a topic of great complexity that can only be mastered by experts, geniuses, college professors, and the like. Fortunately, Penelope did not know this; she thought iambic pentameter sounded like five strides of a gallop—*ta-TUM, ta-TUM, ta-TUM, ta-TUM, ta-TUM*—and could easily be learned by pretending to have a pony race, after which anyone might read the works of Shakespeare with far greater enjoyment than before.)

But Shakespeare would keep for another day. For now, her plan was to tire out the children with all the poetic meters she could think of and then set them to work on some quiet activity. In this way she hoped to gain herself a few peaceful moments to sit and examine her precious stack of birthday cards. She taught them the five *ta-TUM*s of the iambic gallop, followed by the anapestic skip (*biddle-BUM, biddle-BUM*), and even the dactylic waltz (*OOM-pa-pa, OOM-pa-pa*). At last the exhausted Incorrigibles were ready to stumble back to the nursery and be still. Beowulf and Alexander stretched out on the rug next to each other, with paper, pencils, and watercolor paints nearby. Beowulf drew fanciful tygers that were inspired by Mr. Blake's poem, while Alexander made a map of places where such creatures might be found (so far he had come up with Tygerland, Tyger Island, Tyger Mountain, and the Spooky Grotto of Tygers).

Cassiopeia, the youngest, had taken a Giddy-Yap, Rainbow! book from the shelf to look at the pictures and had promptly fallen asleep in the rocking chair. Now she was sweetly snoring, the book nestled beneath her chin.

At last—the birthday cards! Penelope scooped them up and retired to her comfortable chair near the hearth. "Oh, how glorious to be a postal worker!" she thought as she spread her treasures across the ottoman, so as to have the satisfaction of seeing them all at once. "To be the bearer of such joyfully anticipated correspondence! To bring warm greetings from distant friends and deliver long-awaited news of family . . . long-awaited . . . news . . . family . . ." But after going through the stack twice, it was clear that there was nothing from the Long-Lost Lumleys, and Penelope had to swallow hard to make the lump in her throat go away.

Luckily, the card from Cecily cheered her a great deal. It contained comical descriptions of life in Witherslack, as well as a tasty-sounding recipe for Hungarian goulash that called for vast amounts of paprika. Dear, funny Cecily! Her ear for languages made her a brilliant mimic of all types of sounds. Her animal calls could fool even Dr. Westminster, and her creaky-door noise would set anyone running for an oilcan. The younger Swanburne girls had lived in terror of her bloodcurdling scream, which was put to good use every autumn

30

at Heathcote's annual Haunted Hay Maze festival.

Penelope tucked the goulash recipe in her pocket, so she might show it to Cook next time she passed by the kitchen. She hugged Cecily's letter before putting it back in its envelope and felt a pang of regret. What with all her responsibilities as governess, not to mention the endless parade of mysterious events that seemed to crop up willy-nilly at Ashton Place, she had not written to her friend nearly as often as she should. Why on earth not? It was an oversight she resolved she would soon remedy, and with her new fountain pen, too.

Next she opened the many cards from the girls at Swanburne. They were friendly enough, and the penmanship was, of course, superb, but there was something odd about them. For one thing, not one of these cards mentioned Penelope's birthday. "We are inspired by your success!" one girl enthused. "You do the name of Swanburne proud," wrote another.

"It is flattering, to be sure, but a simple 'Happy birthday!' would have done just as well," she thought. Carefully, she put these cards aside. "Still, it was kind of the girls to write. I shall send each one a lengthy thank-you note, perhaps in iambic pentameter, if the mood strikes." Once again she felt excited at the prospect of using her new pen.

She had saved Miss Mortimer's card for last, precisely because it was the one she was most eager to read. "As Agatha Swanburne once observed, 'Peas first, biscuits last, makes for a happy meal,'" she said to herself as she used the letter opener from Beowulf to slit the envelope. She unfolded the letter within (for it was a letter, not a card, and a rather long one at that, running many pages), and leaned back in her cozy armchair to discover what loving words and pearls of wisdom her former headmistress might offer on this never-to-be-repeated event, the very special occasion of Penelope's one and only sixteenth birthday!

> *My dear Penny,*
>
> *Greetings! How are the children faring? Please send an update on their progress, particularly regarding their grasp of multiplication. The ones are no great challenge, and counting by twos is easily mastered, but I do hope they have figured out those tricky sevens and eights. . . .*

The letter went on to discuss the finer points of the multiplication tables, in precise and painfully dull detail.

Penelope raced through the next few paragraphs, and then turned to the next page, and the one after that, but it was simply more of the same. "'Twelve times three is thirty-six, and so is half of twelve times two times three' . . . all quite true," she thought, puzzled. "And sixteen is two times eight as well as four times four, but that is hardly the same thing as saying 'Happy sixteenth birthday!'" Flummoxed, she dropped the letter into her lap. "I wonder if Miss Mortimer received my most recent correspondence? In it, I told her of my disturbing suspicions regarding Judge Quinzy, yet she does not mention it here at all."

Indeed, Penelope suspected that Quinzy might actually be Lord Fredrick Ashton's father, Edward Ashton, who had long been presumed dead after meeting a gruesome end in a medicinal tar pit during an otherwise pleasant spa vacation. Many unanswered questions remained. Could Quinzy be the real, live Edward Ashton? If so, why would he fake his own death and assume a false identity? And why had he recently maneuvered his way onto the board of trustees of the Swanburne Academy?

"But first things first—back to the letter," she thought, for at the moment she was trying to solve an altogether different mystery: Had Miss Mortimer forgotten her birthday, or not?

Penelope skimmed paragraph after paragraph, page after page. "Multiplication, multiplication, long division, geometry . . . Eureka! Here it is, at last."

> *But that is quite enough about isosceles triangles. I have a particular reason for writing to you, for very soon it will be time for the CAKE.*

"See? She did not forget!" she thought, but her excitement was dashed in the next sentence.

> *CAKE is something new at Swanburne. It is the Celebrate Alumnae Knowledge Exposition. We plan a day of festivities and a delicious dinner, followed by speeches that I hope will be both pithy and wise, as Agatha Swanburne herself would wish. Would it be possible for you to attend our CAKE on 12th October to speak about the value of your Swanburne education? The Swanburne Path to Success, or something of that ilk?*
>
> *Penny dear, you must say yes; your alma mater needs you. I confess I have already let it slip to the girls that you would be coming, and they are rather too excited. Many asked if they might write to you.*

You are one of our more accomplished graduates, you know.

"So they were not birthday cards, but simply ordinary, everyday correspondence." Penelope felt somewhat deflated by this, understandably. And CAKE had nothing to do with birthdays either; it was only an acronym. Was it possible that Miss Mortimer *had* forgotten? But the letter was not over yet.

I have also taken the liberty of writing to your mistress, Lady Constance Ashton, to ask if she would consider adding our school to the list of charitable institutions she supports. Who would know better than Lady Ashton just how capable a Swanburne girl can be? She has placed her wards in your hands, after all.

And speaking of the children, I so long to meet them! Please bring them with you, for my sake, and for the trustees' sake, too. For it is the transformation you have wrought in your three remarkable pupils that best proves the worth of all you have learned here.

After that there were more paragraphs about multiplication, followed by a brief review of cave geology

35

(stalactites grow down, stalagmites grow up, Penelope was grateful to be reminded). The letter concluded with a long list of various types of ferns, complete with their distinguishing characteristics.

"The upholstery fern? The Winnebago fern? I believe Miss Mortimer made those up; at least, I have never heard of them. And I fear she is being much too optimistic about Lady Constance." Penelope looked fondly at the Incorrigibles: the boys with their sketching and mapmaking, and Cassiopeia napping peacefully with her book still open upon her chest, the pages fluttering to and fro with each childish snore, like tiny sails in a changeable wind. Who could fail to see the charms of these three? Alas, Lady Constance could, and did. She disliked the children with a passion and was often harsh with their governess. There was little chance that the spoiled young mistress of Ashton Place would become a benefactor to Swanburne—or Swansong, as she sometimes glibly called the school.

As for the children being proof of the value of Penelope's education . . . well, the Incorrigibles' best behavior was very good indeed, but their less-than-best could be positively hair-raising. "As is true of most young people," Penelope thought, feeling suddenly protective. But then she reminded herself that the Swanburne Academy was a place where all children were treated with understanding and respect. At Swanburne, even three children who had been raised by wolves would be appreciated for their unique qualities. Of this she felt quite sure.

"*Grrrrr!*" Cassiopeia awoke with renewed energy. Before long she had corralled her two brothers into an energetic game of tygers, complete with snarls and pretend biting. It was mostly pretend, anyway. Soon Alexander's teeth were sunk into Beowulf's pant leg, and the two were having a devil of a time getting untangled.

Penelope called from her chair. "Careful, children! If the trousers get torn, you will have to mend them yourself, Alexander."

"Not children. Tygers!" Cassiopeia corrected. At the moment she clearly had the advantage over her brothers, and she readied herself to pounce. One . . . two . . . *three—*

Penelope sighed. It was time to get back to work, but at least she had read her mail, or most of it, anyway. As she refolded Miss Mortimer's letter, her eyes fell upon the last few lines.

Oh! Happy birthday, dear Penny. I hope you did not think I had forgotten. I wish you many happy returns of the day, from all your loved ones, near and far.

Yours in hope,
Miss Charlotte Mortimer

P.S. There is no need to reply by post. In fact, it is better if you do not; the mail delivery at Swanburne is less reliable than it once was, and I might not receive your answer. All will be explained when we speak in person, here, within these ivy-covered walls. Remember, twelve times eight is ninety-six!

The birthday greeting was much appreciated, of course, but it was that last bit about the "ivy-covered walls" that kept Penelope awake and thinking long past her usual bedtime. She knew very well that the Swanburne Academy was kept spit-spot; nary a shred of ivy was allowed to grow anywhere near the walls. "Bad for the stonework," the groundsmen would say. They always pulled it up by the roots.

Ivy-covered walls and an unreliable postal service? Was Miss Mortimer trying to tell her that something was amiss? If so, why not just come out and say so? Penelope lay in the dark with her eyes wide-open.

"Perhaps Miss Mortimer was making a joke about the ivy, as she surely was about the ferns. But Judge Quinzy on the board of trustees is no joke. It seems Miss Mortimer never received my warning about him. What can he be plotting? How fortunate that this invitation to speak at the CAKE gives me an excuse to go to Swanburne and put things right."

Sleepy as she was, her mind would not stop flitting from one worry to the next. "But, dear me, a speech! Thank goodness I took that class on Great Orations of Antiquity. It ought to come in useful as I prepare my remarks. And the twelfth of October is only a week away. . . ."

Clickety-clack, clickety-clack . . .
Whoo-hoo!
Whoo-hoo!

Penelope awoke the next morning thinking of trains—or train tickets, to be precise. She had recently used all her savings to pay for the services of Madame Ionesco, a Gypsy soothsayer of spooky reputation. It was Madame Ionesco who had eerily suggested that Edward Ashton might not be dead at the bottom of a tar pit, but still alive, although she did not explain how or why that might be. This unexpected news from

Beyond the Veil had been worth every penny, but now Penelope had not a cent to her name with which to buy tickets to Heathcote.

True, her salary was generous, but Lady Constance rarely thought to pay it unless asked. This Penelope seldom bothered to do, for she only spent money on books, presents, and the occasional soothsayer, and how often did the need for a soothsayer arise? Not often, in her limited experience. Yet now the urgency of making such a request could not be denied, unless she and the children intended to walk to Swanburne.

"Which would take many months, given the shortness of Cassiopeia's legs," she reasoned. "We would miss the CAKE completely. And who knows what mischief the Person Who Calls Himself Quinzy But Whom I Suspect Is Really Edward Ashton, Long Presumed Dead, may have accomplished by then?"

Therefore, after sharing breakfast with the children and setting them to work dusting the nursery bookshelves (this chore always took a good long while, for the children could not help being distracted by the books they were supposed to be dusting), Penelope went in search of Lady Constance. She found her outdoors, in the cutting garden.

"But I ordered flowers!" Lady Constance sounded

petulant. She carried a frilly parasol against the sun, and twirled it to and fro in irritation. "These are nothing more than knobby, ugly, dirty turnips. I asked for beautiful and frightfully expensive tulips."

The gardener, a young, plain-spoken fellow, gestured toward his wheelbarrow. To Penelope's eye it seemed to be full of small, misshapen potatoes. "These *are* the flowers, ma'am. At least, they will be in the spring, if I put them in the ground now."

Penelope curtsied. "Lady Constance, good morning. May I have a word?"

"Not now, Miss Lumley." Lady Constance covered her mouth with one hand as if she did not want the gardener to hear, although she spoke just as loudly as before. "This man seems to think these unattractive lumps are tulips, rather than turnips. I fear he is not well."

Penelope peered into the wheelbarrow for a closer look. "Tulip bulbs, how exciting!" she exclaimed. Indeed, tulips were wildly popular in Miss Lumley's day, particularly "broken" tulips, which were not really broken at all. It simply meant that the tulips were striped in different colors, rather like Mr. Blake's tyger, although one could no more mistake a tulip for a tyger than a tyger for a turnip.

The gardener sighed and leaned on his spade. "No offense, m'lady, but if I don't plant them soon they'll rot. Now, where would you like them?"

"Nowhere! Who would want such unattractive things lying about?"

The poor fellow scratched his head. "Once they're planted you won't see the bulbs, m'lady. They'll be under the dirt."

Lady Constance poked at the tulip bulbs with her parasol's sharp tip. "My dear man, if I will not be able to see these awful 'bulbs,' as you call them, what difference does it make where you put them?"

Penelope felt sorry for the frustrated gardener, who had a great deal of work to do and no parasol to shield him from the sun, either. And she had business of her own with Lady Constance, so the sooner this confusion about the tulips was settled, the better. "My lady, perhaps I can be of some help," she interjected. "I believe this situation calls for a leap of the imagination."

Lady Constance turned to her. "Miss Lumley, do I look like a Russian ballerina to you? I am in no mood for leaping."

"It will not require any exertion, I promise. But if you could imagine that it were spring right now . . ."

"Nonsense. Look at the leaves on the trees. They are falling like . . ." Even as Lady Constance gazed upward, a leaf landed on her pert, doll-like nose. "Why, like leaves in autumn."

"So they are, my lady. But if you would close your eyes for just a moment, perhaps you could *imagine* that it is spring."

"Close my eyes! Very well. I will humor you, but only out of boredom." With a skeptical snort, Lady Constance squeezed her eyes shut, whereupon she brightened immediately. "I see it!" she exclaimed in surprise. "It is just as you say, Miss Lumley. April crocuses everywhere I look."

Pleased, Penelope went on. "And now that it is spring, imagine that there are pretty tulips blooming as well, so that all your friends might come for a garden party and admire them."

Lady Constance squealed with delight. "A garden party! Yes, of course. There is the punch bowl, and the wrought-iron garden chairs arranged just so. And look at the guests! Lady Partridge and Lady Peartree are wearing the same hat. How humiliating."

"Quite embarrassing, I agree. Now, where are the tulips?"

Lady Constance gestured blindly around her with

"It is just as you say, Miss Lumley.
April crocuses everywhere I look."

the parasol. Penelope and the gardener had to jump out of the way.

"Over here, and around the fountain. And sprinkled in and around these other plants on the right. And in a large clump over there, near that shrubby thing, the whatsit. Lilac. Oh! And look what else is here in the garden, come springtime. . . ." Her voice trailed off, but her expression grew dreamy and soft.

The gardener gave Penelope a grateful look. "Around the fountain, in the flower beds, and near the lilac. Very good, my lady. That is just what you will see, come April." At last the poor man was able to get to work. There were hundreds of bulbs to be planted; Penelope grew weary thinking of all the holes he would have to dig. And yet she too could imagine how lovely the tulips would look come springtime, and was glad for his efforts.

WITH HER MOOD CONSIDERABLY LIGHTENED, Lady Constance twirled her parasol and began to stroll through the garden. "Come April, he says! Who can think that far ahead?" She smiled to herself; it was the smile of a person who has an important secret but no intention of telling it. "Truly, Miss Lumley, those tulips cost a shocking sum. But Fredrick bought them for me without any complaint. What a dear and generous man he is."

Lord Fredrick Ashton was hardly what Penelope would call a "dear and generous man," but it was not her place to offer an opinion, so she said nothing.

They stopped under the shade of a beechnut tree. Lady Constance lowered her parasol and shut it with a snap. "It is pleasant here, but there is no bench. Would it be perfectly uncivilized of us to sit upon the ground?"

It seemed out of character for Lady Constance to propose anything that Penelope herself would enjoy, and she wondered if it were a trick of some kind. "Not at all, my lady, but you might ruin your dress," she answered cautiously.

"I have many other dresses, Miss Lumley. Anyway, this one scarcely fits me anymore. I think I am getting plump!" With a light laugh, Lady Constance settled herself comfortably upon the ground.

Lady Constance's strange behavior made Penelope think of how Mrs. Clarke and the children had acted so oddly the previous day, when they were trying to conceal their party preparations from her. Was Lady Constance also hiding something? If so, was it the sort of deception that was harmless and short-lived (for example, a surprise birthday party)? Or was it the kind that was cause for worry (for example, a person faking his own death and assuming a new identity as a judge for dark purposes as yet undiscovered)? There was no way to tell.

On the other hand, she could think of nothing nicer than to sit upon the ground and enjoy the autumn dance of copper-colored leaves in the branches over-head. Nor did she have any special concern for her own dress, which was a plain brown worsted and easy enough to wash if it got dirty. So she sat.

The earth was springy with moss, and a white-throated warbler chirped merrily from somewhere nearby. It was almost as if she were out on the lawn at Swanburne being reduced to giggle fits by Cecily (for no one could imitate the teachers as well as Cecily could). The moment was so agreeable, and so unexpected, that she nearly forgot the reason for her errand—but not quite.

"Pardon me for raising the subject, Lady Constance," she began, "but due to some unforeseen expenses, I find I am in urgent need of my—"

"Miss Lumley!" The words burst from Lady Constance in much the same tone of voice that a person might use to shout "Eureka!" "I have thought of something clever! I shall have the gardeners move the flower garden right here, beneath this tree." She patted the mossy ground beside her. "This way, during the summertime, I can sit among the flowers in comfort, in the shade, and not have to carry a parasol everywhere I go."

"But the flower garden cannot be moved here, my lady," Penelope blurted. Immediately, she wished she had not been so direct, for Lady Constance's expression looked suddenly brittle, like a soft bread roll gone stale and hard. "That is, you are quite right. It is cool and shady here. But flowers need sun. They will not grow and bloom without it. On the other hand, ferns will grow quite nicely in the shade, and there are so many different kinds."

The moment of imagined friendship was gone and seemed unlikely to return, but still, Penelope went on. "Why, this would be a lovely spot for a fern garden!" she enthused. "If I close my eyes I can see it: the graceful fronds waving in the breeze. . . ."

Lady Constance pouted and tore the fallen leaves into strips. "I suppose you are right about the ferns. But it seems wildly unfair that one cannot grow tulips in the shade, after paying so much money for them. What is the point of having money, then? If one can be overruled by a gnarled, grubby little bulb? Don't *they* realize what Fredrick paid for them?" She turned to Penelope, clearly expecting an answer.

"I think . . . I assume . . . that is, I would imagine that the tulips do not know what they cost," Penelope began, but then stopped herself. For who could say what tulips knew? Only the tulips, and they were not talking.

Lady Constance let out a sharp laugh. "According to you, they know whether it is sunny or shady; surely they might know their own price. But never mind. You said you had urgent need of something, Miss Lumley. What is it?"

Relieved to be able to get to it at last, Penelope spoke in a rush. "My salary, Lady Constance."

"But you were paid only last month. Or perhaps it was the month before. Where has your money gone, Miss Lumley? Surely you have not spent it on tulips!" Lady Constance seemed to find this amusing and chuckled at her own remark.

"I have spent it on . . . gifts," Penelope replied. (This was true in a way, for it was Madame Ionesco's gift for communicating with spirits Beyond the Veil that had caused her services to be required in the first place.)

"Gifts! Miss Lumley, I am disappointed in you. 'Charity begins at home.' That is what I tell Fredrick, anyway, and as you see from my new tulip garden, he listens. And that is precisely what I shall say in response to *this*." Lady Constance reached into her reticule and extracted the same square, cream-colored envelope that Penelope had spotted on the mail tray the previous day. "This letter is from that school of yours, the Sunburne Academy. From a Miss Charlotte Mortimer. I believe she is the same person who wrote your letter of recommendation when you applied for your position here at Ashton Place."

She held the envelope between two fingertips, as if it were something unsavory. "What nerve! Asking me for a donation to support the Sunburne School. It is a short letter, thank goodness, and her handwriting is very neat. But really! If one wants money, one ought to inherit it from one's parents, as I did, or failing that, one ought to marry a rich person, as I also did. That is the proper way to get money, Miss Lumley. One does not simply go around asking for it."

Penelope's cheeks reddened as if she had been slapped. Had she herself not just asked for money? And was working for money also shameful in Lady

50

Constance's eyes? She suspected it might be, although she could not imagine why.

"I am sure you are correct, my lady. Yet some people do give small amounts to charity," she said haltingly. "Especially for hospitals, and schools, and the poor. Some of the girls at Sun—Swan—at my alma mater . . . are penniless orphans who would have no place to live if not for the school, and no chance to better themselves. Why, they are rather like your tulip bulbs," she said on impulse. "Grubby at first glance, but if planted properly and given some sunlight and time to grow, they can blossom quite nicely."

"Yes, yes, paupers and grubby orphans; it is all quite tragic." Lady Constance sounded impatient. "Miss Lumley, if I decide to pay you your salary, are you going to squander it on gifts, or hide it in a piggy bank somewhere? Or will you be sensible with it, and spend it on something worthwhile?"

"No more gifts, my lady. In fact, I intend to buy . . ." Penelope thought hard about what sort of purchase Lady Constance would approve of. "A new dress! And shoes. And a hat. And some train tickets, to take the children on a short and educational trip to Sunburne . . . Swanburne . . . I mean, Heathcote." She mentioned the trip in order to be truthful, but it did not matter, for Lady Constance had heard all she needed to hear.

"A new dress! Miss Lumley, that is the first sensible thing I have ever heard you say. For a moment I was afraid you intended to give your money to the Sunburne school." She slipped the letter back in her reticule. "Well, you do put up with those dreadful children, and so you shall be paid your salary. You must give the steward a note of instruction from me. Write it and sign my name; you know better than anyone what you are owed."

Lady Constance leaned back on her elbows and dismissed Penelope with a wave of her tiny foot. "Off you go, then. Oh, it will be a relief to be rid of the wolf children for a time! I can barely sleep at night knowing they are under the same roof, barking and drooling and baying at the moon. As for your new dress, Miss Lumley, try not to look so much like a governess. All that brown worsted pains the eye."

Penelope climbed to her feet and brushed the leaves off her skirt. "Thank you, my lady. I will take care of it at once."

"But remember your station! Nothing too flashy. I would not have people saying the Ashtons' governess was pleasant to look upon. It would be most unseemly to draw attention to yourself in that way."

"I shall remember, my lady." Penelope curtsied and backed away as quickly as seemed polite. As if it were possible to forget one's station around Lady Constance Ashton!

The Third Chapter

*At last, Penelope makes use of
her new fountain pen.*

PENELOPE'S EMBARRASSMENT BLEW HER BACK to the house like a skiff caught in a hurricane. "Now I shall have to waste part of my salary on clothes, which I hardly need," she fumed, although it was not really true, for the elbows of her sleeves were worn rather thin. "And what objection could any reasonable person make to brown worsted?" Brown was not the sort of festive shade a spoiled lady might wear to a party, perhaps, but it was a cozy color that made Penelope think of pleasant things: antique woodwork, or a chestnut-colored pony, or the chocolate layers of a Black Forest cake.

She marched to the front parlor, where Lady Constance's personal stationery was kept in an antique writing desk worth more than a whole fleet of governesses could earn in a year. It was not the first time she had helped with her mistress's correspondence, for Lady Constance received a great many invitations, all of which had to be accepted or declined in courteous handwritten notes. Lady Constance rarely had the patience to write these herself, and her cursive letters were loopy to the point of being illegible. Fortunately, Penelope had the same excellent penmanship that every Swanburne girl was expected to learn. (As Agatha Swanburne once said, "The most eloquent letter says nothing if it cannot be read.")

"If not brown worsted, then what? I suppose I could get a blue worsted instead. Or would she consider blue to be 'too flashy'? And how am I to look less like a governess when that is precisely what I am?" Penelope's cheeks warmed again with shame; firmly, she pushed away the feeling. "But never mind that. First, the letter to the steward."

She perched on the delicate chair and helped herself to a sheet of stationery and a matching lilac-scented envelope. Resignedly, she dipped a quill pen into the inkwell. She had used this same quill many times before without complaint, but the mere thought of the gleaming new fountain pen made it seem hopelessly old-fashioned, like a prop from a play set long ago. Penelope's imagination was no stranger to leaping, and she decided to rid herself of any leftover bad feelings by pretending, just for a moment, that she was not a drab governess in a plain brown dress who was in need of money, but the well-to-do lady of a grand house all her own.

"My dear Mr. Harley-Dickinson," she wrote, addressing a playwright friend of hers who had briefly and memorably visited Ashton Place some weeks before, and who was never very far from her mind. "The great . . . no, the enormous . . . no, the *titanic* pleasure of your presence is requested at my tea party, to be held Tuesday next."

What else ought she say? "Formal attire requested"? "There will be dancing on the terrace"? "Regrets only"? Then she sighed and put down her pen, for the spell of pretending was broken. If she were a real Lady, she would know all about tea-party invitations, and which colors were flashy and which were not, and a host of other things, too. All at once her Swanburne education felt woefully incomplete.

"It is Lady Constance's notepaper, in any case, which I ought not to waste on letters not meant for sending. If it were mine, it would have an L for 'Lumley,' right here. . . ." She traced a finger over the cursive capital A engraved at the top of the page. The A stood for "Ashton," of course, but she had seen similar initial As elsewhere: on a mysterious letter received by an acting troupe hired to entertain at Lady Constance's holiday party last Christmas, to give one example. Or as the signature on a dust-covered painting in the British Museum, to give another.

"All those As! It is an A-mazing coincidence," Penelope thought. She crumpled her pretend invitation to Simon and put a fresh sheet of paper on the blotter. "Then again, A is a very common letter. With only twenty-six letters in the alphabet, they are all bound to turn up sooner or later. Although, come to think of it, one hardly ever sees a J. Why, Js are even rarer than Zs."

(Many years later, a popular word-making game would be invented that assigned points to letters based on how scarce they were: The scarcer the letter, the more points it was worth. If Miss Lumley's mind had not already been so thoroughly occupied, she might well have invented such a game herself at this very moment, and thus changed the course of history forevermore. Alas, her attention was fixed on the task at hand, and that invention, like so many others, would have to wait awhile longer.)

Her quill hovered over the paper as she considered how to begin. *Dear Esteemed Steward, Keeper of the Household Accounts and Other Mathematical Necessities,* she wrote. The letter need not be long, for it was simply intended to let the steward know how much salary she was owed. But Penelope longed to shore up her spirits after that humiliating conversation with Lady Constance and the failed pretend-letter to Simon, and so she decided to indulge herself.

"*Ta-TUM, ta-TUM, ta-TUM, ta-TUM, ta-TUM,*" she murmured, to remind herself how the rhythm of the words ought to sound.

> *Miss Lumley labors hard to earn her pay,*
> *And so you must disburse her funds today.*

"Iambic pentameter, and a rhyming couplet, too," she said, pleased with her effort. Then she wrote the amount, whimsically added *Yours in both sun and shade,* and signed Lady Constance's name with a flourish.

The steward cocked an eyebrow when he saw the

note, but made no remark. Penelope half hoped he would notice and perhaps even admire the jaunty, galloping rhythm of the words, but he simply counted out the money and went back to his budgets.

HER GOOD MOOD RESTORED AND ample money for train tickets in her apron pocket, Penelope climbed the stairs back to the nursery. "How lovely it will be to introduce my three pupils to Swanburne, and show them my own childhood haunts," she thought, taking the steps two at a time. "We shall have to pay a call on Dr. Westminster, the Swanburne veterinarian. However, I must be careful not to leave the children unsupervised near the chicken coop." The sight of all those plump, delectable, *buck-buck-buck*ing chickens might be too much for the children to resist, especially if it was getting close to lunchtime.

Inside the nursery the Incorrigibles marched in circles, waving their feather dusters (as you recall, they had been instructed to dust the bookshelves while their governess was out, but Penelope had been gone for half the morning, and that chore had long since been finished). As they marched, they recited.

> *"Tyger, Tyger, burning bright,*
> *In the forests of the night;*

What immortal hand or eye
Could frame thy fearful symmetry?"

Even without the full benefit of Penelope's lesson on poetic meter, the children had discovered that Mr. Blake's poem naturally fell into a strong marching beat. "Hup, hup, hup!" Alexander directed his siblings. "Tygers, halt!" They began to tickle one another with the dusters.

"Trochaic tetrameter, more or less," Penelope announced brightly, pushing her way past the waving feathers. "Children, I have excellent news. We are going on a trip, to the Swanburne Academy for Poor Bright Females." Even saying the name made her voice catch with feeling. What a joyful homecoming it would be!

"Poor Bright Females," Cassiopeia gloated to her brothers. "No boys. Bye-bye!"

The boys looked crestfallen, and Penelope rushed to explain. "It is true that the students at Swanburne are all girls, and that the teachers are nearly all women—but there are some men there as well, like my old friend Dr. Westminster, who cares for the animals. And boys are certainly welcome as visitors. In fact, all three of you children have been specially invited by

Miss Mortimer. I am sure everyone will make a fuss over you."

Penelope pulled a spare suitcase out of the closet and began to plan what to pack for the trip. Meanwhile, the thought of being fussed over by a whole school full of girls had struck fear into Alexander. He ran and stood in front of the mirror with a wet comb and slicked his hair around in different ways, but it always reverted to its natural upright position.

"Why are we going to Swanburne?" Beowulf asked. His hair was just as unruly as his brother's, but he felt no similar urge to comb it. This may have been yet another sign of his artistic nature, or perhaps he was just too young to think of it. "Is Cassawoof going to school?"

Now it was Cassiopeia's turn to look worried. The question gave Penelope pause as well, for Cassiopeia was about the same age Penelope had been when she was first delivered to Swanburne—had she really been that young? She had no clear memory of the day; it was all in bits and pieces, like many different pockets emptied carelessly into the same drawer.

She had traveled to Swanburne by train, of that she was certain. If she closed her eyes, she could still hear the *clickety-clack* of the wheels. She assumed that her parents had brought her, but she could not actually picture them at Swanburne. Instead, she remembered the firm grasp of Miss Charlotte Mortimer's hand, leading an absurdly tiny version of Penelope to the dormitory to put away her things before supper.

Had she wept openly to say farewell, or bitten her lip to keep the tears inside? Had she strained to look over her shoulder for one last good-bye? Or did she march bravely into her new home without a backward glance? Penelope had tried to conjure the scene so many times that she no longer could tell what was memory and what was simply her own imagined version of the day. Yet if she concentrated hard, she could still summon the feeling of that warm grown-up hand enveloping hers, the sound of Miss Mortimer's heels clicking along the wooden floors, and the sight of pillows everywhere—in the chairs and window seats, embroidered with sayings she was not yet old enough to read.

"Surely a place with so many pillows is bound to be pleasant," the little girl had chirped bravely to the tall, strange lady at her side.

"I hope you will find it so," Miss Mortimer had replied, with a tender and welcoming smile.

Her reverie was broken by a whimper. Its source

was Cassiopeia, whose large, sea-green eyes brimmed with tears at the thought of being shipped off to school, far away from her brothers and her beloved Lumawoo.

Penelope sat in her armchair; the girl jumped in her lap and curled up in a protective ball, like a startled hedgehog. "Cassiopeia has a private governess and is the ward of one of the richest men in England. She has no need of a school for poor bright females." Penelope patted her littlest pupil reassuringly. "We are taking a trip to Swanburne because I have been asked to give a speech at the CAKE."

At the word "cake," Cassiopeia stopped whimpering. Her brothers perked to attention.

"However," Penelope continued, "please note that CAKE is only an acronym, describing a particular, special day that Miss Mortimer has planned."

"Like a holiday?" Alexander asked.

"Yes, I suppose so. But it has nothing to do with—"

"Cake Day! Cake Day! The best day of the year!" The boys interrupted before she could explain further. Cassiopeia uncurled, grabbed her feather duster, and joined the celebratory parade around the nursery as the children chanted the names of every kind of cake they could think of: "White cake, yellow cake, angel cake, Gypsy cake, Black Forest cake . . ."

63

Penelope did not bother to correct them. Their impromptu Cake Day parade was enough to distract the Incorrigibles from asking more questions, and this suited her perfectly, for she would rather keep her concerns about Judge Quinzy and Miss Mortimer's strange letter to herself for now. Besides, their excitement about cake had reminded her of an important task that she would have done at once, except that the urgency of Miss Mortimer's summons had knocked it out of her mind: She needed to write a thank-you note to Mrs. Clarke for organizing that wonderful surprise birthday party.

At last she could try out her new fountain pen! Truly, it was a marvelous invention. Penelope could scarcely believe that it did not run out of ink after a few words, as a quill pen always did. Simply holding this fine pen made her feel poetically inspired, and she wrote:

Dear Mrs. Clarke,

I thank you for the party yesterday.
It made my birthday full of joy and cake.
Hooray, hooray, hooray, hooray, hooray!
Three cheers for Cook as well, for she can bake!

"More iambic pentameter, *ta-TUM, ta-TUM, hooRAY, hooRAY*," she said to herself as she signed her name at the bottom. "And two rhymes this time! Penny old girl, you have outdone yourself." She was well aware that the "hoorays" made five cheers, not three, but there was no need to split hairs. After all, with thank-you notes, as with so many other things in life, it was the thought that counted.

Gently, she blew on the ink, but it hardly needed any time to dry. She folded the letter crisply, slipped it inside an envelope, and sealed it with a drip of wax from a candle. Feeling playful, she used the edge of her thumbnail to press an L for "Lumley" into the soft wax, just as if she had her own personal seal.

"Who is ripe for an adventure?" she called out gaily. The Incorrigibles jumped up and down, waving their dusters so vigorously that the loose feathers wafted down like snow. She held up the sealed envelope. "I have a letter here addressed to Mrs. Clarke, and it must be delivered."

"Post office! Post office!" the children cried.

Penelope smiled at their eagerness to go to town; she hoped they would be as cheerful about traveling all the way to Heathcote, a far longer and more exhausting trip. "Under normal circumstances, the post office is exactly the right place to bring a letter to be sent," she replied. "However, as Mrs. Clarke's bedchamber is just upstairs, I see no need to put this particular letter in the post. Shall we deliver it ourselves?"

How GLORIOUS IT WAS INDEED to be a postal employee! After a brief recess for luncheon (Penelope had long ago learned her lesson about skipping meals; a hungry Incorrigible was prone to mayhem, and must be avoided at all costs), the children quickly fashioned costumes for themselves out of their dress-up trunk. They turned their pillowcases into mailbags full of letters. They even carried slingshots loaded with very hard acorns, in case they met up with dangerous mail bandits along their postal route. This was unlikely, as they only needed to go up a flight of stairs. But they were not ready to stop being tygers yet, or to end their Cake Day parade, so they quickly dubbed themselves the Cake-Eating Postal Tygers of Ashton Place, complete with marching song:

> *Our tyger feet*
> *Are quieter than most.*
> *We can't be beat*
> *Delivering the post.*

We eat our peas,
But cake we like the best.
We say, "More, please!"
And gobble up the rest.

The tune for this ditty was suspiciously like a tune from *Pirates on Holiday*, the nautical operetta whose first act Penelope and the children had witnessed while visiting London some months earlier. (Sadly, they had been forced to flee halfway through the performance with the entire cast and even some of the audience in hot pursuit, amid many cries of "Harrr!" and "Avast, ye hearties!" and other piratical turns of phrase. The experience had left all three Incorrigibles, and especially Cassiopeia, with a strong dislike of pirates, although, luckily, not of operetta, which is rarely dangerous unless a piece of heavy scenery falls upon the singers during a performance.)

Neither Penelope nor the children had ever seen Mrs. Clarke's room, so their planned excursion felt like a true adventure. With their pillowcase mailbags slung over their shoulders and jaunty postal helmets perched upon their heads (these were actually bowls left over from the soup at luncheon, wiped clean with a dish towel), Penelope and the Cake-Eating Postal Tygers headed upstairs to deliver their letter, singing all the way.

They found Mrs. Clarke's room without difficulty. It was at the end of the narrow, low-ceilinged hallway and had a rag-rug welcome mat woven from the same fabrics as Mrs. Clarke's trademark floral print dresses. Cassiopeia did the honors of slipping the note beneath the door, as she was closest to the ground.

"A job well done," Penelope declared. "What say you, Postal Tygers? Shall we return to the Nursery General Post Office and draw some stamps? Each one featuring a different sort of cake, perhaps?"

A few more choruses of their marching tune brought them back to the stairwell. In one direction, the steps led downstairs to the third floor. In the other was a much narrower and steeper flight of steps that led upward, to the attic. These stairs were dark even in daytime, for there was no window anywhere near.

"Lumawoo, wait." Alexander tipped his head to the side, a pose that Penelope knew meant he was listening extra hard.

Ba-bump—ba-bump—ba-bump—ba-bump—
Thump!

"Someone is upstairs, in the attic," Penelope said

in a low voice. "Stay here, children. I am going to see who it is."

"Maybe ghost?" Beowulf asked, sounding hopeful.

"Or mail bandits." Alexander brandished his slingshot.

"Or pirates!" Cassiopeia growled dangerously.

"It may be a lost bird caught in the rafters," Penelope said, although she too feared something worse. At that the children insisted on coming, and would hear no argument, so to the attic the four of them climbed, step by unseen step.

Penelope willed her heart not to race as she led them up the lightless stairs. It had been many months since the first time she and the children had ventured to the attic and discovered the ominous landscape that had been painted there, then hidden beneath layers of wallpaper. On that occasion, too, they had heard something unexpected, a mysterious howling sound that came from behind that very same wall.

Without matches or a candle, she had to walk with her hands stretched in front of her, so she might feel the door at the top of the stairs as they approached. She groped for the knob; she found it and gave it a twist. The door was stuck and would not budge.

She put her shoulder to the door. "Heave-ho!" she

grunted, and pushed. As she did, the door was flung open from the other side, and she tumbled forward. The children were right behind her. Now the four of them lay in a heap in the pitch-dark.

"Owwwwwwww!" A spooky howl came from someplace nearby.

"Ghost bandits!" Alexander yelled. "Slingshots, up! Load acorns! And—fire!"

"Aye-aye, Captain!" his siblings cried. All three children rapidly fired their slingshots into the void.

"Ow, ow!" the ghost cried. "Stop, I say! Don't shoot! Blast, can't see a thing up here; it's dark as the inside of a boot. Hold on, my candle's gone out, what?" A match was struck, and a candle lit. "Blast, I say! Who's attacking me? In my own home, no less!" For there, in the unsteady light, was Lord Fredrick Ashton himself, tangled in cobwebs that he tried in vain to bat away. Red welts on his face showed where the acorns had hit.

"It is Miss Lumley and the Incorrigible children, my lord," Penelope replied in a shaky voice.

He squinted in their general direction. "Well, well, well—the wolf children and their governess. What are you doing up here, then? Other than pelting me with nuts, I mean?"

"Apologies for the attack, my lord! We are delivering

"Blast, I say! Who's attacking me?"

the mail." Alexander bowed low. His manners were really quite excellent, thanks to his governess's careful training. "Postal Tygers, at your service." On cue, the children began to sing.

"Our tyger feet
Are quieter than most.
We can't be beat
Delivering the post."

Lord Fredrick pulled anxiously at his collar. "Tigers? What nonsense. Go back to your books and globes and whatnots, what? The attic is no place for singing."

"It is for howling, though," said Beowulf sagely.

Lord Ashton's jaw clenched in anger, which made his almost-pointed ears quiver in a frankly canine way. "Trying to catch a fellow in the act of howling, is that it? Well, let me tell you something, young pup. If there's any howling coming from the attic of Ashton Place, it's none of your beeswax. Anyway, you've done a fair share of howling yourselves, haven't you?"

The children nodded, for it was true, and they were not ashamed of it.

"Some people have howling fits now and then, that's all. They're entitled to their privacy, just like everyone else. Now, off with you, and don't come back! And I'll thank you not to tell anyone about this little adventure, either."

"Yes, sir. Very sorry to intrude, my lord." Penelope curtsied as best she could with shaking knees, and the children gazed at Lord Fredrick with understanding—they, who happily scratched and howled and barked, indoors and out, in sun and shade and in the moonlight, too.

Cassiopeia let her mailbag slip to the floor. She stepped forward and took Lord Fredrick's hand. "It's all right to howl," she said, full of sympathy. But the master of Ashton Place became angrier still.

"Off with you, I said! Go downstairs to the nursery, and stay there!" His eyes gleamed yellow in the dark, and the children stepped back in fear. "Except for you, Miss Lumley. You are to come see me in my study at five o'clock, precisely one hour from now. I would have a word with you. In private."

"Yes, my lord," Penelope answered with a gulp. A private word with Lord Fredrick did not bode well, for her or for the Incorrigibles. "I shall be there at five, on the dot."

THE FOURTH CHAPTER

*Penelope acquires a new
student.*

Ga-dong! Ga-dong! Ga-dong! Ga-dong! Ga-dong!

With solemn authority, the tall ebony clock in the corner of Lord Fredrick's study struck five. Penelope was far too preoccupied with worry to notice how the five *ga-dong*s made a perfect line of iambic pentameter, which only goes to show how extremely worried she was.

"Why," she thought, "why, oh why did we not simply bring the letter to the post office as we should have, rather than trying to deliver it ourselves? Then none of this would have happened, and I would be at my writing desk this very minute, drafting my speech for the CAKE with my new fountain pen! A valuable lesson has been learned: Delivering the mail is a job for skilled professionals, and ought not to be attempted by amateurs. Dear me, Lord Fredrick looks very cross! I wish he would speak, though I dread what he might say."

Lord Fredrick Ashton was in his chair by the hearth. He took a long time lighting his cigar, and with each passing minute, Penelope grew more convinced that she was about to be dismissed from her job. "It would be poor timing if so," she thought morosely, "for I can hardly make a speech about my successful career as a governess if I have just been fired in disgrace." Her triumphant homecoming to Swanburne seemed ready to unravel before they had even boarded the train—and all because of a thank-you note!

"Well, well, well," Lord Fredrick began. He took a puff on his cigar. "Miss Lumley. Your snooping or mail delivering or whatever it was seems to have been a bit of bad luck, for both of us. Now my little secret is out."

"What—what secret, my lord?" she stammered.

"Don't play dumb. Those wolf children of yours understood straightaway." The lord of Ashton Place leaned forward in his armchair and fixed her with his blurry gaze. "Let me put it to you in a nutshell, Miss Lumley. I howl, my father howled. From what I've been told, his father did, too. When I asked why, Father always said it was our family legacy and he'd explain when I was older. Then he met a gruesome end in a gooey tar pit, and that was the end of that. Blasted mystery, wouldn't you agree?"

"A mystery indeed, my lord." The eyes of the ancestral portraits in Lord Fredrick's study seemed to stare at her accusingly. Each of the three Ashton forebears had met a gruesome and untimely end: Admiral Percival Racine Ashton, killed in a hunting accident (whether he had been torn to bits by bears, wolves, or some other fierce animal had never been determined, for there was too little of him left to tell). Judge Pax Ashton, pecked to death by furious pheasants. And finally, Lord Fredrick's father, Edward Ashton, said to have drowned in a tar pit but whose body had never been found.

She lingered on the portrait of Edward and thought of Judge Quinzy. The stocky build had dwindled to slimness, the thick silver hair tinted black, and the distinctive Ashton nose altered with putty, but those dark and penetrating eyes would be impossible to mistake. Perhaps it was why Quinzy always concealed his behind thick glasses.

"Howling, scratching, barking—you can't imagine what a nuisance it is. Only happens when the moon is full. When it's at its worst, I lock myself away in the attic. I've a set of rooms up there, ever since I was a boy." Lord Fredrick's bitter laugh pierced the air. "Other lads got tree houses and velocipedes. I got my own private attic for baying at the moon. No complaints, mind you. I'm glad to have it. It's a cozy spot. Nicely furnished. Old Timothy brings up my meals. Sometimes I go up there on my good days, just for a bit of quiet. Usually I tell Constance I'm at the club. Last thing I need is her lurking around, full of questions, watching me paw at my own ears. I'm no danger to anyone, mind you. It's just . . . well, it's embarrassing, that's all."

Whether an avid hunter with poor eyesight posed no danger to anyone was debatable, in Penelope's view. "I am sorry for your difficulties, my lord," she said. "But if you cannot help it, surely you have nothing to be ashamed of. Perhaps your true friends, and even Lady Constance, would understand better than you think, if they only knew the truth."

Lord Fredrick snorted. "It's all right to howl, isn't that what the littlest pup said? Hah! Easy for her to say. The Incorrigible children were raised by wolves in a forest. Of course they howl. Anyone would, under those conditions. It's an ironclad excuse. I was raised by wealthy Ashtons. Good manners, the best schools, blasted hunting parties every week. My father made me go. I like to hunt, don't get me wrong. That is, I learned to like it, over time. But I've always been a dreadful shot. Imagine being the only boy in the county who couldn't hit a serving tray at ten paces." Indeed, Lord Fredrick's eyesight was very poor. "And when the other lads found out what came over me at the full moon . . . If you were me you'd be a bit secretive too, I'd expect."

"I am sorry, Lord Ashton," she said again, for she was.

"Not as sorry as I am. My own mother's ashamed of me. 'Poor Freddy, how's your tragic condition? Poor Freddy, you must have inherited it from your father. Make sure you don't have children! They'll turn out just like you!' Miss Lumley, I ask you: Did your parents ever warn you not to have children so they don't turn out like you?"

Of course, Penelope would have been grateful to have any conversation at all with her parents in recent years, but now was not the time to say so. She shook her head. "No, my lord. My parents never said anything like that to me—at least, that I can recall."

"Lucky you, then. Well, no matter what Mother thinks of me, she had no business blabbing my personal business at dinner. After all the trouble I take to hide it! Now Constance won't leave me alone about it."

Penelope sat up extra straight in her chair, much the way Miss Mortimer did when she was reminding the girls at Swanburne not to mope and complain. She, too, had a strong inclination to tell Lord Fredrick to buck up and look on the bright side. After all, was he not a very rich man, still young, and in reasonably good health twenty-seven days out of every twenty-eight? But she knew this advice would not be well received. When people feel sorry for themselves, the last thing they want is to be reminded how fortunate they really are. "A misery contest is not worth entering, for one only wins by losing," as Agatha Swanburne once observed, and yet there are many who insist on holding such competitions, even to this very day.

"My lord, the children and I have no desire to intrude upon your personal affairs," she said, hoping to put an end to the conversation. "I apologize for our accidental meeting in the attic, and for the acorn attack as well. I assure you, it will never happen again."

He leaned forward in his chair. "Never mind all

that. Miss Lumley, I summoned you here for a reason. There's something I've wanted to discuss with you for some time, but there was no way to do it without letting my embarrassing secret slip. Now that you know, it doesn't matter." He paused and drummed his fingers on the chair arm. "How do you stop the children from acting like wolves?"

"How?" His question took her by surprise, for neither Lord Fredrick nor his wife had ever expressed any interest in the children's education before. "It takes patience, I suppose, and a great many reminders, and we must be careful to avoid temptation, especially if the children are hungry. Treats are also useful, as a reward for good behavior."

"Patience? Treats? That's not going to work with me, I'm afraid." He held up a hand to stop her interjecting. "Yes, me. Why do you think I'm so interested in having the wolf children live here? I've been keeping an eye on their progress. Not directly. Through Old Timothy."

Old Timothy! It was true that the enigmatic old coachman of Ashton Place had a habit of lurking nearby. Penelope had often suspected that he was watching her and the children. She had come to think it was out of friendship, for he had been distinctly helpful to them on several occasions—but had he merely been spying on them all along?

Lord Fredrick rose and paced the length of his study. "The moment I laid eyes on those three, barking and running wild in the forest, it came to me. 'Eureka!' I thought. Three children raised by wolves. If they can be taught to stop scratching and howling, then maybe . . . well, maybe so can I." He gestured with his cigar. The trail of smoke seemed to form letters in the air that disappeared before they could be read. "I had Constance place the advertisement, though I put in the bit about 'experience with animals strongly preferred.' Then you showed up. And you do seem to have a knack for handling them, Miss Lumley. They've never bitten you, have they?"

Penelope's mind clickety-clacked like an abacus, trying to sort out this new information, but Lord Fredrick's question demanded an answer. "No, my lord. They have not," she said meekly.

His study was filled with taxidermy, and Lord Fredrick wandered from one lifeless creature to the next, idly petting their sawdust-filled heads. "The truth is, Miss Lumley, I'm sick of it. Sick of missing Christmas parties and openings on the West End, just because they fall on the full moon. I try to keep track, but that blasted almanac won't stay put." Nervous, he glanced out the window of his study. "The moon is always catching me unawares."

Penelope was no astronomer, of course, but she understood enough to know that the moon had been keeping a rather predicable schedule for countless thousands of years. She resisted the urge to point this out to Lord Fredrick. Instead she replied, "My lord, are you suggesting that I try to teach you to stop acting so wolfishly, just as I have taught the children?"

"Why not? But my condition only comes upon me when the moon is full. So there won't be many chances for lessons. You'll have to work quickly. And you can't tell a soul, of course. Will you do it?"

What a plot twist this was! Not only was she not being fired, Lord Fredrick Ashton himself wanted to become one of her pupils! It would make a thrilling conclusion to her CAKE speech, if only she were not sworn to secrecy. Yet at the same time Penelope feared Lord Fredrick was being optoomuchstic (that is to say, he had taken his optimism much, much too far) in thinking she could help him.

After some consideration, she replied, "Sir, if you wish to proceed with lessons, of course I will oblige, but I should warn you—the children's circumstances

are different from yours. They have some wolfish hab-
its, true, but the moon plays no part. It has more to do
with their upbringing among the animals of the forest,
as if they spoke English with a charming accent left
over from their native tongue. In your case, I believe it
would be helpful to know more about this family legacy your father spoke of." She paused, and recalled the
warning words of Madame Ionesco. "Have you ever
considered that the Ashtons might be under some sort
of a curse?"

He flinched at the word. "Curses? Poppycock! And
what if there were such a thing? Everyone's cursed one
way or another, what? One fellow has bad eyesight and
howls at the moon. This one suffers heartburn; that
one's a terrible dancer."

As he spoke, Lord Fredrick rested his hand on the
head of a stuffed tiger. The glass eyes flickered yellow in the firelight. "'It's what you do with the curse
you're under that counts.' That's what Father always
told me, anyway. He was full of pithy sayings like that."
He paused. "Blast, Father did use to say that! I wonder
now if he was giving me some sort of clue? Pity he died
so unexpectedly. He could have told us all about it, and
then the mystery would be solved."

"But what if he is not dead?" Penelope nearly

blurted—yet she stopped herself, for she had no proof that Quinzy was really Edward Ashton, and she knew Lord Fredrick would never believe her without proof.

It was only a trick of the light, of course, but the lips of the taxidermy tiger seemed to pull back into a snarl. Uneasy, Penelope rose from her chair. "My lord, the challenge you present may be beyond my current abilities. However, I will soon be visiting my alma mater, the Swanburne Academy for Poor Bright Females. There one will find some of the finest educators in all of England, as well as a noted expert in animal training techniques." (By this she meant Dr. Westminster. It verged on hyperbole—that is to say, wild exaggeration—to call him a "noted expert," as he was really just a simple country veterinarian. However, some of his methods had proven quite useful with the Incorrigibles, particularly his kind manner and judicious use of treats.)

Penelope backed slowly toward the door as she spoke, and she never took her eyes off the tiger. "If anyone would know how to improve your condition, the teachers at Swanburne will. Upon my arrival, I will consult with my colleagues there, and together we shall come up with a . . ." She paused to think of a name that was both descriptive and had an easy-to-pronounce acronym, always a great boon to any endeavor. "A Howling Elimination Program, to help ease your symptoms."

Lord Fredrick chewed on the end of his cigar. "All right. But don't let anyone know it's me that needs the HEP, understood? Say it's for the children, or whatever you please. Next full moon, we start! And don't say a word to Constance about any of this, either. Blast, why did Mother have to tell her that we oughtn't have children because of my 'condition'? Constance doesn't even like babies. But tell my wife she can't have something, and soon enough it's all she wants." He slumped back into his chair. "Curses and tar pits, and children raised by wolves! Why can't I have a normal family?"

He seemed to forget all about Penelope then, and stared despondently into the fire.

"And how is the Widow Ashton, my lord?" Penelope asked, to be polite, and also to remind him that she was still there, waiting to be dismissed.

"Oh, Mother's fine." Aimlessly, he picked up a thin, stained envelope from the table next to his chair. It was the one Penelope had seen on the mail tray, with its exotic stamps and foreign postmarks. "Just got a letter from her. She's on a 'round-the-world tour with her friends from the croquet club. She says she plans to enjoy herself thoroughly while awaiting the return of her beloved Edward, now that she knows he's alive. Listen to this." He read from the letter in a mincing voice. "'My gratitude to Madame Ionesco knows no bounds. If not for her peek Beyond the Veil, I would never have known my long-lost Edward lives!' Soothsayers! Poppycock!"

It was Lord Fredrick's turn to look at Edward Ashton's portrait. "Sturdy-looking fellow, wasn't he? Bet he sank like a stone in that tar pit." Abruptly, he tossed the letter from his mother into the fire, where it crackled and quickly turned to ash. "So you're off to Swanburne, eh? You might see my friend Quinzy there. He's on the board of trustees now. Can't imagine how he finds the time for charity work, being a judge and whatnot."

Penelope kept her voice calm. "I expect I will see him, if he is there, my lord."

Lord Fredrick returned to his chair. "There's a book of mine he asked to borrow, and for the life of me I can't find it. He swears it's in the library. An old diary of a sailing voyage, with shipwrecks and cannibals and storms at sea."

He puffed again on his cigar and exhaled a slow stream of smoke. "Shipwrecks and cannibals. Does that ring any bells, Miss Lumley? I know you filch books from my library sometimes; don't deny it."

Penelope's face grew hot at the accusation, for she did sometimes take books from the library. How could she not, in her line of work? Even worse, the very book Lord Fredrick described was in her possession. *An Encounter with the Man-Eating Savages of Ahwoo-Ahwoo, as Told by the Cabin Boy and Sole Survivor of a Gruesomely Failed Seafaring Expedition Through Parts Unknown: Absolutely Not to Be Read by Children Under Any Circumstances, and That Means You,* it was called.

She knew precisely where the book was, too. At first she had kept it in her bedchamber so as not to alarm the children with its potentially disturbing contents, but she worried that the housemaids might find it while cleaning her room and return it to the library. Now it was hidden on the nursery bookshelves, behind Mr. Edward Gibbon's six-volume masterpiece of historical narrative, *The History of the Decline and Fall of the Roman Empire,* where no one was likely to come across it anytime soon.

"I—I may have seen it, my lord," she half lied. "I will keep an eye out for it, to be sure."

"If you find it, deliver it straight to Quinzy,

understood? He's keen to read it, for some reason. Blasted books! They never stay where I put them. First my almanac wanders off, then this cannibal tale. Can't imagine why Quinzy wants it. Rather an unappetizing topic, to my taste. I'd rather go hunting than read a book, anyway."

His study was proof enough of that. Together they gazed upon the dead tiger, with its ferocious teeth and flaring nostrils. Nearby, a bear stood taller than even a tall man would, furred arms outstretched for a deadly embrace. And there was the poor stuffed wolf, its head thrown back in a howl that knew no end.

Thoughtfully, he twirled his cigar between thumb and forefinger. "I wonder if cannibals keep trophies of their prey, the way I do of mine? That'd be a gruesome end, what?"

"Yes, my lord," Penelope replied, with a shiver of horror. "It would be gruesome, indeed."

IMMEDIATELY UPON RETURNING TO THE nursery, Penelope ran to the bookshelf. "Gibbon, Gibbon, *Decline and Fall*," she muttered, pushing the books out of the way. "And—what? Where is it?"

The cannibal book was not there.

Penelope froze. She was certain this was where it

had been hidden. She had put it there herself, at that exact spot on the shelf.

"Blast," she muttered, as Lord Fredrick so often did when he could not find his almanac. "Where could it have gone?"

"Look, Lumawoo! We are packing for our trip." Alexander and the other children had laid their clothes out on the beds for Penelope's inspection. The Postal Tyger uniforms were included, as were some other imaginative outfits.

"Toothbrushes, too," Penelope mumbled absently. Shelf by shelf she looked, but *An Encounter with the Man-Eating Savages of Ahwoo-Ahwoo, as Told by the Cabin Boy and Sole Survivor of a Gruesomely Failed Seafaring Expedition Through Parts Unknown: Absolutely Not to Be Read by Children Under Any Circumstances, and That Means You* was nowhere to be found.

She took one of the deep, calming breaths that all Swanburne girls were taught to practice before exams. "No panicking," she reminded herself, "and no crying over spilt milk, either. The book may yet turn up, and if not, it is no great loss. After all, the pages were so faded and sea stained they could scarcely be read, by me, Quinzy, or anybody else. But blast! It is very unsettling to have something disappear like that. And I was so hoping to show the book to Simon, too."

This, of course, was the reason she had kept the cannibal book in the first place. Simon Harley-Dickinson! Quick of mind, loyal of heart, with a knack for navigation and a keen appreciation for a good plot twist. It had been nearly two months since Penelope had bid her friend farewell at the train station. He was off to see his great-uncle Pudge in the old sailor's home, in Brighton. Pudge had been a cabin boy in his youth and, coincidentally, had served on a ship captained by the famed Admiral Percival Racine Ashton himself. Simon and Penelope suspected that the unreadable diary of the ill-fated trip to Ahwoo-Ahwoo might have described the same voyage taken by Pudge and the admiral, and might even have been written by Pudge himself. Simon had promised to find out.

But there had been no word from Simon since his departure—not a letter, not a scrap of dramatic verse, not even a picture postcard from the beach at Brighton. Penelope thought it odd that Simon had not yet written to tell her what he had learned from his great-uncle. On the other hand, she was so accustomed to not receiving mail that she had simply put it out of her mind, and trusted that he would be in touch when the opportunity arose. (But really, would a small seashell be too much to ask? Penelope had never been to the shore, and she longed to know if it were true that one could hear the ocean simply by pressing a conch to one's ear.)

In the meantime, three tired children had to be put to bed, which meant it was time for their governess to read aloud. The children wanted tygers and only tygers, and so Penelope read them their new favorite poem, the one by Mr. William Blake. It was not a very long poem, so she read it through twice.

"Do tigawoo," Cassiopeia insisted, rolling over in her bed.

So "Tyger, Tyger, burning bright," Penelope began again, this time in a whisper, for the children were beginning to yawn. As she said the words, she thought of that snarling stuffed tiger in Lord Fredrick's study. For some reason she pictured the animal wearing Judge Quinzy's thick and distorting glasses, which made its glinting amber eyes appear larger and more menacing than they already were. It was a disturbing image, and one she could not put out of her mind for a good long time, even after the children were asleep.

THE FIFTH CHAPTER

*The journey has many stops
and starts.*

WHEN LORD FREDRICK ASHTON TOLD Penelope he
would explain his predicament "in a nutshell," he was
not talking about acorns. Rather, he meant that he
would be brief, concise, and to the point—in a word,
pithy.

As any Swanburne girl could tell you, a knack
for pithiness is well worth acquiring. Beginners are
advised to start with the larger nuts, such as the Bra-
zil nut, and then work their way downward in size,
through the pecan, the cashew, and the hazelnut. With

practice, one soon discovers that even the most profound ideas can be packed neatly inside the shell of a pistachio, with room to spare.

Speaking of packing, it was two more days before Penelope and the Incorrigible children began their journey to the Swanburne Academy, but to tell all that happened would take nearly as long, for there is always a great deal to do in preparation for a trip. In a nutshell, then: Penelope had hoped to organize suitcases for herself and the children, then write up her CAKE speech and practice it in front of a mirror so that she might find the perfect dramatic gestures to go with the words. She also planned to spend a relaxed afternoon shopping for the new dress she had promised Lady Constance she would buy.

Alas, none of these hopes unfolded according to plan. Take the shopping trip, for example. There was no one available to drive her to town, not even Old Timothy, and so she had to leave the children in Margaret's care and beg a ride in the back of a hay wagon. She ran into the dress shop with wisps of straw stuck to her legs and only minutes to choose, for the wagon could not wait long. Luckily, the first dress she saw seemed to fit the bill; it was the right size and not exactly brown, although it was not exactly not-brown, either. "I would say the color is halfway between bark and russet," she decided, and brought it to the cashier.

At the milliner's shop, she chose a bonnet to match the dress, and at the shoemaker's, a pair of sturdy oxfords that would do nicely for the fall weather. "As Agatha Swanburne once said, 'If both of your shoes are shined, your best foot will always be forward,'" she reminded herself. She made it back to Ashton Place just in time to do afternoon lessons with the children, who had already convinced poor Margaret that, yes, Miss Lumley always gave them cake for both breakfast and luncheon, as long as they each ate a single pea first.

The night before their departure was equally fraught. Instead of lining up their suitcases by the door and tucking in for an early bedtime, the children wanted to play Swanawoo School. Cassiopeia's notion of a Poor Bright Female was slightly off. She felt that Poor meant hungry and lacking shoes, and Bright meant she must speak only in Latin. Barefoot, she ran around the nursery begging for treats and spouting Virgil.

Meanwhile, the boys wrapped blankets 'round themselves as dresses and tiptoed here and there, speaking in high voices and pretending to be Swanburne girls.

When they grew tired of that, they assumed the roles of Dr. Westminster and his equally qualified assistant, Dr. Eastminster, and attempted to perform medical examinations on Nutsawoo. Fortunately, the frantic little squirrel was much too busy with his (or her) autumn preparations to sit still for this sort of thing.

At last the overexcited children were persuaded to sleep. Feeling worn-out herself, Penelope checked to make sure the straps on each piece of luggage were tightly fastened, and the coats and jackets for the journey laid out, for the weather grew cooler and the winds brisker by the day. By the time she sat down to collect her thoughts about her CAKE speech, she was already yawning, and all she could think of was, not CAKE, but cake—cheesecake, ginger cake, carrot cake, plum cake. . . .

"Luckily, it is a long journey to Heathcote. I shall have more than enough time to prepare my speech on the train," she told herself. "All I need do is bring my notes from orations class, some paper, and my new fountain pen." (You see how optoomuchism can sneak its way into even a sensible person's logic. This is especially true when that person is tired and would rather go to bed than face unpleasant facts—for example, the fact that she, or he, must shortly give an important speech for which he, or she, is woefully unprepared.)

And so, the next morning, not long after sunrise, wearing an itchy new dress, stiff new shoes, and a bonnet that tipped over her eyes whenever she turned her head, Penelope and her three bleary-eyed pupils finally began their trip. Old Timothy drove them to the train station in the landau carriage with the roof up, as the sky threatened rain. When the boys put on their Dr. Westminster and Dr. Eastminster voices to discuss the condition of the horses' teeth, he chuckled. Then he fell silent until they were nearly at the station.

He stopped the carriage and fixed Penelope with his cockeyed glare. "It's a long way there, and a long way back. And heaven only knows what'll happen in between. Are you sure you want to go?"

"Of course we shall go." For the hundredth time, Penelope adjusted her new hat. "We are expected, and I am to give a speech."

"Bought fancy new clothes for the occasion, too, I see. Be a shame to cancel now, eh?" The way he said it suggested that to cancel now would be a prudent thing to do. Yet what harm could befall them at Swanburne? To Penelope it was the safest place in the world, a place where she would be surrounded by old friends and beloved teachers, and where everyone would have the Incorrigible children's best interests at heart.

Unless the school had changed, that is. Miss Mortimer had hinted as much in her letter. But surely the new board of trustees could not have altered things so much, so quickly? Like ivy twining up a wall, a tendril of fear snaked 'round Penelope's heart.

"The tickets have already been purchased," she said.

He snorted. "Do what you must, then. But keep an eye on those children, Miss Lumley. And if anything goes amiss, remember . . . you can always bring 'em to the vet." He looked one way and then the other, as if afraid of being overheard. "Sure, if there's any trouble, young Westminster'll sort things out."

"The children will be well cared for, have no fear," Penelope replied crisply. As if she would bring the children to a veterinarian! And how dare he try to frighten her with vague warnings, when the train ride was bound to be taxing enough as it was, with three children to entertain and a speech to write, too.

She ignored the coachman's offered hand and climbed out of the carriage herself, dropping lightly to the ground. "Will you get our luggage down, please? It is nearly time for our train."

The children carried their own bags, for it made them feel like sophisticated world travelers, but Old Timothy took Penelope's suitcase to the platform himself. He nodded a silent farewell to her and the Incorrigibles. Then his rolling gait retreated into the fog as the great red Bloomer engine huffed into the station, billowing steam. Its lonely, hooting whistle pierced the air, until the children winced and pressed their hands over their ears.

Whoo whoo!

Whoo whoo!

"Whatever adventures our journey holds, we are safer together than apart," Penelope thought as the conductor helped them one by one onto the train. "And I have no choice but to go. Swanburne needs me! Still, I wonder how Old Timothy knew Dr. Westminster's name?"

THE TRAIN RIDE TO HEATHCOTE was a long one, lasting a day and a night and most of another day after that, and the train made many stops along the way. Penelope had explained this to the children several times. She had reminded them to bring books to read, and extolled the virtues of patience while traveling, and the importance of taking naps.

They were only half an hour into the journey before Alexander tugged on her sleeve and asked, "How much longer, Lumawoo?"

"Why, we have only just begun!" she exclaimed. "Remember what Agatha Swanburne said: 'A journey of a thousand miles is best spent napping.' Nap, everyone! Take as many naps as you can." But the Incorrigibles could not stop climbing on the seats to look out the windows. Sheep-dotted meadows were hardly a novelty to three English children who lived on a country estate, but seeing the landscape flick by through the windows of a fast-moving train certainly was, and they were captivated.

Meanwhile, Penelope kept smoothing the skirt of her new dress and adjusting it beneath her so that it might not wrinkle overmuch during the journey. Alas, it was already beginning to crease. "Perhaps I ought not to have worn it to travel in," she thought resignedly. "But it will be near nightfall when we arrive, and no one is likely to notice. In the morning I shall give it a good shake and, if necessary, borrow an iron from the housekeepers at Swanburne."

Cassiopeia noticed her fussing with the skirt. "Nice dress," the girl remarked. "Nice and brown."

Penelope looked aghast. "It is not brown, is it?"

"So brown. Ask Beowoo," Cassiopeia suggested, for her brother was a talented artist with a keen eye for color.

Fearing the worst, Penelope extended her arm so that he might examine the sleeve. "Do you think so too, Beowulf?"

He eyed the fabric and nodded. "Brown. Brown like acorns."

Alexander disagreed. "Brown like mud," he said.

"Halfway between acorn and mud," Beowulf conceded.

This was disappointing news, to say the least! To Penelope's way of thinking, halfway between bark and russet was nowhere near as brown as halfway between acorn and mud. But in the dim light of the train compartment such distinctions were useless, and it was time to face facts: She had bought a dress that was brownish, if not actually brown, no matter what the shade might be called.

"You are quite correct, Beowulf." She pulled the front of her jacket closed to conceal as much of the dress as possible. "I prefer brown myself. It is a perfectly fine color, no matter what some people think. Oh, dear, look at the clock! According to my pocket watch, it is well past time for all the children on board to nap."

"Train has nap time?" Cassiopeia asked, confused.

"Certainly. I believe it was printed on the tickets." Penelope quickly hid the tickets in the pocket of her jacket so the children could not check. "Now hurry. Be quick, before the conductor comes!"

Obediently, all three Incorrigibles leaned their heads on the seats and closed their eyes. In her mind Penelope counted slowly to a hundred, to make sure she gave her ruse enough time to work. Soon the children were still.

"What a relief," she thought, stealthily taking out her pen. "At last I can work on my CAKE speech! With luck I shall have the whole thing written before the next stop." She began by reviewing her notes from the Great Orations of Antiquity class she had taken at Swanburne. In the margins were little drawings that she and Cecily had made to amuse each other when the teacher was not looking. (Nowadays we would call this "doodling." But rest assured, both Penelope and Cecily had earned very high marks in the class and had only let themselves doodle after achieving a firm grasp of the lesson at hand.)

What glorious speeches people gave in days of old! Ought she model herself after Demosthenes, who spent months locked in an underground room with a mouthful of pebbles, practicing elocution and dramatic gestures in order to become one of the ten official orators of ancient Greece?

Or was she more of a Cicero? The greatest of the Roman orators, Cicero was known for his long and carefully plotted sentences that did not reveal their full meaning until the very last word. Cicero's elegant style was much to Penelope's liking, although it did set a high standard. This was only her first speech, after all. Then again, who knew if she would ever be asked to give another?

"Whether it is my first speech or my last, I might as well give it my all," she decided. "As Agatha Swanburne once said, 'Doing one's best is never cause for regret.' For rhetorical style, I shall look to Cicero. Now I need only think of what to say."

She referred to her notes once more, for there were many types of speeches to choose from. Was she arguing for war, or against? Was she trying to sway an election? Incite revolution? Raise taxes? There was even a type of speech called the filibuster, whose sole purpose was to waste time. In the margin, Cecily had drawn a hilarious picture of a Roman senator named Cato the Younger who was famous for his filibustering. He would talk on and on, from morning until night, in order to prevent the senate from voting on laws that he did not want to see passed. (In Cecily's drawing, Cato the Younger looked suspiciously like the Great Orations of Antiquity teacher in a toga. An endless stream of gibberish poured from her oversized mouth, like smoke from a bake-house chimney.)

Penelope stared out the window and let her mind wander. "Strange how things work out for the best. If I had found that cannibal book where I was certain I had put it, I would have been honor-bound to give it to Judge Quinzy, as Lord Fredrick told me to do. But since the book is lost, I cannot, which is a happier outcome for all, in my opinion. For that book is no business of his, and I am sure whatever purpose he has in mind for it is a wicked one—though what use could anyone have for a book that cannot even be read?"

She found a blank page in her notes. "Sway an election comes closest, I think," she decided, turning her thoughts back to her work. "When Shakespeare wrote a speech in the Roman style in his tragic play about Julius Caesar, he began it thus: 'Friends, Romans, countrymen, lend me your ears.' Perhaps I can try something along those lines. . . ."

Inspired, she began to write. Soon she was so lost

in her task that she did not even notice the children stirring. Try as they might, they could not nap, for it was still morning, and although they had arisen well before dawn, they were much too excited to sleep. After checking to make sure the conductor was nowhere near, and seeing their governess deeply engaged in her work, all three Incorrigibles quietly took out their books to read.

"I come to bury Caesar, not to praise him," Penelope murmured under her breath. She tried to think of something half as catchy, but it was difficult. How on earth did Shakespeare manage it? And in iambic pentameter, too!

"Shakespeare!" Alexander cried in recognition. He turned a page in his own book. "'Shall I compare thee to a summer's day?'"

Penelope looked up. "'Thou art more lovely and more temperate.' Sonnet Eighteen, if I am not mistaken." The book of Shakespeare's sonnets had been a gift from her to Alexander at Christmas. She was so pleased to see him take an interest in it that she hardly minded discovering that the children were awake. "*Ta-TUM, ta-TUM, ta-TUM, ta-TUM, ta-TUM!* That was well spoken, too. I could hear the iambic pentameter galloping right along."

"I will read from *my* book now," said Beowulf eagerly, for all of the children dearly loved praise. He opened his volume and began to read, rapid-fire.

"'In the second century of the Christian era, the empire of Rome comprehended the fairest part of the earth, and the most civilized portion of mankind. The frontiers of that extensive monarchy were guarded by ancient renown and disciplined valor—'"

"Beowulf, what book is that?" Penelope interrupted.

"Mr. Gibbon," he announced, and held up the first volume of Mr. Edward Gibbon's masterpiece of historical narrative, *The History of the Decline and Fall of the Roman Empire*. He patted the cover approvingly. "I found it when I dusted the bookshelves. Is long but full of fighting."

Not to be outdone, Cassiopeia stood on the seat and waved her book in the air. "I found mine dusting, too. 'Ahwoo-Ahwoo!'" she proudly read off the front.

"Ahwoo-Ahwoo?" Penelope's bewilderment was short-lived, for there it was: *An Encounter with the Man-Eating Savages of Ahwoo-Ahwoo, as Told by the Cabin Boy and Sole Survivor of a Gruesomely Failed Seafaring Expedition Through Parts Unknown: Absolutely Not to Be Read by Children Under Any Circumstances, and That Means You.*

"The cannibal book!" Penelope cried, and all three children gave a delicious shiver of horror, as if the book itself might gobble them up with its toothy covers.

"Long title. Nothing inside," Cassiopeia said, showing off the sea-washed pages as she balanced precariously on the seat.

"If there were words inside, you would be too young to read them. The title says as much. Now, sit down, everyone, please. Surely it is time for another nap." Inside, Penelope was aflutter. The hypothetical problem of whether or not to give the cannibal book to Judge Quinzy had suddenly become all too real. What should she do? "If only Lord Fredrick had never mentioned it!" she fretted. "If only I knew when I might hear from Simon! If only I knew why that impostor Quinzy wanted it so badly! If only I had finished writing my speech earlier! Now I shall never be able to concentrate."

"I will read *my* book," Cassiopeia stubbornly declared. She opened the illegible volume. "Once upon a time, cannibals ate everybody. No one left. Yum, yum! The end."

"But who ate last cannibal?" Alexander asked.

"Himself!" Cassiopeia cried with glee. All three children pretended to devour their own limbs. Passengers

All three children pretended to devour their own limbs.

in nearby seats began to clear their throats in disapproval, for the children's game was noisy and, frankly, disgusting.

Penelope lifted a stern eyebrow and held out her hand. "Let me hold that book, if you please. It belongs to Lord Fredrick, and I do not want it going astray again."

Cassiopeia handed it over with reluctance. In sympathy, Beowulf put down his book as well. "*Decline and Fall*, too depressing," he said, and sighed heavily.

"Sonnets, too lovey-dovey," Alexander agreed, for he and his siblings tended to stick together, like cubs in a litter, one might say.

Books closed, three bored children gazed out the window, where one sheep-dotted meadow had begun to look very much like another. They kicked the seats until their toes hurt. Before long they began to poke one another.

"Lumawoo?" Cassiopeia tugged on her governess's nut-brown sleeve. "Lumawoo? Are we there yet?"

"*Shhh.*" Alexander gestured at Penelope, who had closed her eyes in despair. "Nap time for Lumawoo."

"*Clickety-clack!* GIVE THE BOOK BACK!

"*Clickety-clack!* Give the book back!"

It is strange what guilt will do to a person's imagination. This Penelope had learned from reading the stories of Mr. Edgar Allan Poe, who wrote wonderfully spooky tales about people driven mad by their own secret wrongdoings, to the point where they begin to imagine the beating of dead hearts and even worse things, too.

But Penelope was not about to be unhinged by the clicking of train wheels. She had plenty of other worries to unhinge her. "As far as Lord Fredrick knows, the cannibal book is lost," she thought. It would be easy enough to keep it hidden away and not say another word about it. However, that would be dishonest. And, in a nutshell, dishonesty was not the Swanburne way.

"Yet Quinzy's request was dishonest to begin with, for he is not who he says he is. Surely, it would be wrong to assist him in deceiving Lord Fredrick," she reasoned. And what if it turned out that Simon's great-uncle Pudge really was the author of the cannibal book? Would that not make him its rightful owner? In that case, she ought to save the book for Simon's return, for once Quinzy got hold of it, there was no telling whether they would ever get it back.

She looked out the window, but night had fallen; if

there was a sheep-dotted meadow out there to keep her mind off her troubles, she could not see it. "A Swanburne girl is loyal and true . . . most of the time," she decided uneasily. "But it is not always clear to whom one should be loyal. I wonder what Agatha Swanburne would say about that?"

THE HOURS PASSED, THE MORNING turned to afternoon, and the train stopped at one town after another, bringing Penelope and the Incorrigible children ever closer to their destination. During one of these stops, Penelope was able to pass some coins out the window and purchase a copy of *Heathcote, All Year 'Round (Now Illustrated)* from an urchin boy on the platform.

The children begged for the cartoon and puzzle pages, and Penelope was happy to oblige, for even she had grown weary of hearing Beowulf read aloud from *A History of the Decline and Fall of the Roman Empire*, as he had been doing in a loud voice since breakfast. Most of the nearby passengers had since moved to compartments well out of earshot.

From the newspaper she learned that the opening of the traditional autumn hay maze had been postponed due to excessive rain. Several new calves had been born, and a dispute involving the ownership of a plow had been peaceably resolved, once both parties realized that plowsharing would grow more crops than fighting ever could.

One announcement in particular caught Penelope's eye—in fact, it made her feel rather excited. The monthly meeting of the Heathcote Amateur Pteridological Society would take place the following Wednesday, with a special talk on "Ferns Under Glass: Tips and Techniques for Indoor Growing." Alas, she would be on her way back to Ashton Place by then, but she would have dearly liked to attend, especially when she read that Wardian cases would be available for purchase, "with all proceeds to benefit the society." (As fans of ferns know, Wardian cases are nothing more than glass boxes in which one can grow ferns indoors. They were invented by the famous fern expert Dr. Ward, who made a fortune selling what was admittedly a rather simple item. Evidently, when it comes to ferns, some people will spare no expense.)

The conductor rang his bell up and down the aisle and called in his singsong voice, "Heathcote! Heathcote station will be next!"

Penelope stood up so fast she nearly bumped her head on the luggage rack. "Here we are," she said, although the children were already on their feet and letting out excited yips and barks. "Suitcases in hand, please." Together the four of them sidestepped their way down the aisle. The children giggled as the movement of the slowing train made them sway and wobble into one another, as if they stood on the deck of a storm-tossed ship.

The conductor came up behind them, still clanging away on his bell. "All off for Heathcote and the School for Miserable Girls!"

"I believe you mean the Swanburne Academy for Poor Bright Females," Penelope corrected with a smile. "We are on our way there right now."

"They're about to change the name, though," he said, squeezing past. "The sign painter made new signs for the station already. I've seen 'em. As soon as it's official, we're supposed to hang 'em up."

"But—but . . . that is nonsense! Poppycock! There are no miserable girls at Swanburne," Penelope said, now quite flustered.

"Well, you sound pretty unhappy yourself, miss," he retorted, and went on with his ringing.

FROM THE STATION THEY BOARDED the stagecoach that stopped at the crossroads nearest to Swanburne. From there it would be only a short walk to the school, no more than a mile. The passengers piled their luggage in the compartment beneath the coach, but Penelope kept her carpetbag in her lap, for in it was the cannibal book (as well as her favorite book of German poetry in translation, which had been a gift from Miss Mortimer and which she always carried with her). It also held the notes for her speech, and her new fountain pen, too. These treasures she would not let out of her sight.

"The School for Miserable Girls! What a comical name." She tried to make a joke out of it, for the Incorrigibles had looked worried and sad ever since the conductor's remark. "That is a worse name than the Sunburne Academy, as Lady Constance calls it. I am sure it must be some sort of mistake."

Cassiopeia pouted. "Do not like Mizawoo School," she said.

"Names change," Alexander observed philosophically. "Istanbul is Constantinople. Same place."

"Constantinople! Named after Constantine the Great, Emperor of Rome." Excited, Beowulf looked for the relevant page in his book. "Mr. Gibbon says—"

Kindly but firmly, Penelope stopped him. "I am sure this confusion about names will soon be cleared up. For now, the only school you need worry about is

Miss Lumley's Academy for Incorrigible Children."

That made them smile, and they were all in better spirits by the time they reached the crossroads. The stagecoach rumbled off, and the four of them stood and gazed upon the verdant meadows of the valley of Heathcote, now spread before them like a lush green blanket laid out for a picnic. Autumn-painted trees and hillsides of sheep-dotted meadows ringed the valley. The sky was streaked with spiraling ribbons of smoke that rose from farmhouse chimneys and disappeared into the orange blaze of the sunset.

Nestled in the heart of this happy scene was the familiar outline of the Swanburne Academy. Penelope could only stand and stare. It was like seeing the face of a long-lost loved one appear unexpectedly in a crowd, shocking and yet so very familiar, as if the person in question had never been lost at all.

There was the main building where classes were held, the dormitories and dining hall, the observatory tower, the barn, the chicken coop—

"Let us run!" Penelope called, for she felt merry but also as if she might cry, and she much preferred merry. "Let us gallop, brave ponies, *ta-TUM, ta-TUM*!" Suitcases swinging by their sides, Penelope and the children half skipped and half tumbled down the grassy slopes, only stopping when they were winded and could no longer catch breath enough to laugh.

After that they walked, and Penelope pointed out the school buildings as they got close enough to see them clearly (she left out any mention of the chicken coop for the moment, for it was past dinnertime; the children were in need of a meal, and she strongly preferred it be one they did not catch themselves).

"When we arrive, you will see my favorite thing of all, written just above the door, in letters that are each one as tall as Cassiopeia." Her voice throbbed with pride. "It is the Swanburne motto: 'No hopeless case is truly without hope.'"

"What is hopeless case? Is it a kind of suitcase?" Alexander guessed, holding his up.

"A hopeless case is a person whom others think is doomed and beyond help. Or a situation where an unhappy ending is thought to be unavoidable." She put down her carpetbag and flexed her stiff hand, for suddenly the bag seemed quite heavy. "Hopeless is the opposite of optimism. Hopeless is what people feel when they give up."

"*Decline and Fall,*" Beowulf observed. "Rome, hopeless case."

"'No panicking, no complaining, no quitting!'"

Cassiopeia said in answer. It was one of Agatha Swanburne's catchier sayings, and the children knew it by heart, since Penelope said it often enough.

"An excellent point, Cassiopeia. If the ancient Romans had only had the benefit of your good advice, and Miss Swanburne's, their empire might still be around today." Penelope shielded her eyes against the glare of the setting sun. They were nearly at the entrance to the school, and already she could see that something was not quite right.

"Is this the Swanawoo School?" Alexander asked, confused. "Looks more like a cave."

"That is because of these ivy-covered walls." Penelope gazed upward, amazed. The front wall of the building was completely overgrown with vines. She pulled at one, but only succeeded in tearing off a leaf. "It looks more like a jungle than a school. Why has no one cut down this greenery?"

"Hopeless case!" Cassiopeia pointed.

"Do not be dramatic, Cassiopeia. Perhaps the gardener is on vacation. Ivy can grow very—ugh!—quickly." Penelope tugged harder, but still it would not come down.

"But, Lumawoo, look. No motto." Cassiopeia pointed with both hands this time, high above the door. Instead

116

of carved letters bearing noble sentiments, there was only ivy.

"The motto is . . . gone!" Penelope could scarcely believe it. "At least, it has been hidden by all this shrubbery. Where is it?" She grunted, pulling hard on the vines. "Where is the motto?"

"Maybe in the motto grotto?" Alexander suggested. No doubt he was still thinking of the Spooky Grotto of Tygers.

Beowulf shook his head. "Not even a spotto of a motto."

"Motto, notto," Cassiopeia concluded sadly.

"It is still there. It has to be. They would never have removed the school motto." Penelope yanked at the overgrowth, but the vines were as thick around as her wrist. "Help me, children! Together we can manage it. Heave-*ho*!"

The four of them struggled and pulled, but the ivy would not budge. Incensed, Penelope rang the door-bell, first once, then twice, then a third time. "Never fear, children. We will not be outwitted by vegetation. I will speak to Miss Mortimer, and all will be made well. If the gardeners are away, the girls themselves are more than capable of forming a work party. I will organize it myself if need be. We shall require a ladder, and some shears, and a broom to sweep up the mess. . . ."

The door swung open. "Good evening, Miss Lumley," said a deep, melodious, and all-too-familiar voice.

"Quinzawoo!" Alexander gasped. The children recoiled. Penelope felt as if the temperature had dropped twenty degrees.

Judge Quinzy stepped out from the shadows. "And the Incorrigible children, too. What an unexpected pleasure to find all four of you huddled on the doorstep like a litter of abandoned kittens—almost as if you had been left here by unfeeling parents whom you would never, ever see again."

Quinzy smiled, and the last ray of flame-colored light glinted off his glasses as the sun disappeared over the valley's edge. "But let us not think of unhappy things. I bid you welcome." He opened the door fully and gestured for them to enter. "Welcome to my school."

"Quinzawoo!" Alexander gasped.

The Sixth Chapter

*Proof that Penelope is not a
princess in disguise.*

MANY YEARS INTO THE FUTURE, and in an entirely different country than the one in which Miss Penelope Lumley and the Incorrigibles had their adventures, a book titled *You Can't Go Home Again* would be published to great acclaim. (As it happens, the book was written by a Mr. Thomas Wolfe. However, the wolfiness of his name is purely coincidental to our discussion.)

At first glance, to say "You can't go home again" seems absurd, for most of us go home every day, assuming we have left our houses in the first place. But let us take a leap of the imagination. Say that you have not merely gone out to walk your prize Pomeranian, or ridden your velocipede to the corner store to purchase a doughnut and the newspaper, or hopped on the omnibus to bring soup and some headache lozenges to an ailing neighbor.

Instead, imagine that you have actually moved away, to a distant city in a faraway land, and had to make your way among strangers. With crampons and pickax you have scaled the slippery summits that life has placed in front of you, and now here you stand, weather-beaten and freckled by the sun, with impressive biceps and dressed in a parka. Your friends might recognize you if they saw you, but you are not so sure you recognize yourself. That is the moment when the words "You can't go home again" toll their sad bell of truth. You leave your home in Constantinople; by the time you return, all the signs read ISTANBUL, and there is no going back to the way things were before.

So it was for Penelope. An overgrowth of ivy could be trimmed away with garden shears, but to see Judge Quinzy, Edward Ashton, or whoever he was looming in the doorway to her beloved Swanburne made her feel like a marionette whose crucial strings had just been cut. She could not move; she could scarcely breathe. Where was Miss Mortimer? Where were the Swanburne girls?

The Incorrigible children had a different reaction.

"Tygawooo!" Cassiopeia yelled as she and her brothers hurtled through the door.

"Ahhhhh!" Quinzy cried, reeling backward, out of sight.

"Children, remember your manners!" Fearing the worst, Penelope dashed inside. Quinzy had his back pressed against one wall, but there were no signs of bloodshed or torn clothing. Indeed, the children paid him no mind. Their attention was fixed a few yards farther on, down the long, dim hallway that led to the first-floor classrooms.

"Quiet, please!" Penelope clapped her hands for attention. "Children, what on earth are you barking at?"

As if in answer, a horrible hissing sound issued from the hall. The children stopped yapping and turned pale.

"King cobra!" Alexander whispered. "Native to India. Far off course."

"Or Burmese python," Beowulf hypothesized. "Unusual for Heathcote."

Cassiopeia, who was tired and cranky from the

long day of travel, cupped her hands to her mouth and hissed right back. "*Sssss!* What do you say to that, snakey?"

"*Meowwwwwwwwww!*" A pair of eyes glinted in the dark, quite low to the ground.

"It is Miss Mortimer's cat, Shantaloo!" Penelope darted ahead of the children and sank to her knees, one hand extended toward the shadows. "Come, Shantaloo. It is me, Penny Lumley. Remember all those afternoons we sat in the window seat, me reading among the pillows and you in my lap, purring? How we both loved the tales of Edith-Anne and her pony friend, Rainbow! I used to call you my Rainbow kitty sometimes. Don't you remember?"

"*Meow!*" Blinking, the creature inched forward into the light. It was quite a small cat, as cats go, with a white ruff under its neck, and orange and black stripes everywhere else. Delicately, it touched the tip of its nose to Penelope's outstretched finger.

"Tiny tygawoo!" Cassiopeia cried in delight.

"*Ah-choo!*" Quinzy sneezed, and his hands flew up to his face. "*Ah-choo!*"

Alexander and Beowulf searched their pockets for clean handkerchiefs, but they had used all theirs on the long journey from Ashton Place. The boys shrugged apologetically, but Quinzy turned away.

"Clever kitty! She is always first to know when visitors arrive. Ah, my dear Penny, at last!" Miss Mortimer came rushing out of the hallway into the light and threw her arms tight around Penelope. "Thank goodness you are here," she whispered in Penelope's ear as they embraced. "Safe and sound, and the children, too."

The kind headmistress stood straight. "Welcome to Swanburne, Incorrigible children! I am Miss Mortimer, and you have just met my little lap cat, Shantaloo. She is infallibly shrewd. See how she already thinks of you as friends?"

Indeed, now that the cat had recognized Penelope, there was no more hissing. The arch of her back softened, and she rubbed up against the children's legs, demanding to be petted. Naturally, they were happy to oblige.

"Tyger, Tyger, burning bright," Cassiopeia recited, for in addition to that attractively striped coat, the cat had gleaming amber eyes that burned bright as candles.

That made Miss Mortimer smile. "You may call her Tyger if you like. She will not mind. In fact, she is very fond of poetry, just as a Swanburne cat should be."

"Ah-choo!" A snuffling, wheezing sound came from the corner.

Miss Mortimer turned. "Are you all right, Judge Quinzy? It sounds as if you have come down with a dreadful cold."

Quinzy's hands covered the lower part of his face, and his eyes bulged behind his glasses. He stayed hunched against the wall and spoke in a muffled voice. "Forgive me. I have a strong . . . *aversion* . . . to cats. They make me quite ill. I happened to be passing by when I heard the door chime. I meant only to welcome our guests. Now that Miss Mortimer is here, she will see to your comfort." Head down, he scuttled away like a nervous crab and disappeared into the shadowed hall.

Miss Mortimer scooped the cat into her arms and tickled it behind the ears. "Imagine having an aversion to cats! Poor fellow, we shall have to ask the girls to embroider an extra supply of handkerchiefs for him. Look how tall and grown-up you are, Penelope! And the children, too—my, my." Her expression grew soft and dreamy. "How easy it is to imagine you as you might have been some years ago, when these two strapping fellows were tiny boys in short pants . . . and baby Cassiopeia! If I close my eyes, I can just picture you as a bright-eyed infant, with scarlet hair that stood

125

up like a plume in a lady's hat."

Still cradling the squirming cat, she knelt before the children and gazed at each face in turn. "Yet even if a person had not laid eyes on you in all the years since, no matter how much they might have wished to see you and to know that you were safe . . . even after all this time, I am quite sure that person would never, ever mistake you three for anyone but who you really are. How dusty it is in here!" Miss Mortimer dabbed her eyes with a handkerchief. "It seems I have something in my eye."

The children were hypnotized by her words, but Penelope felt uneasy. Could she be jealous of all this tender attention lavished on the Incorrigibles, who, despite their adorable eccentricities and mysterious background, were really perfect strangers to Miss Mortimer? She had always enjoyed being the kind headmistress's favorite, but now she felt rather pushed to the side. "Like a big sister who everyone ignores when cooing over the new baby," she scolded herself sternly. "A sentiment that is hardly appropriate to the occasion!"

She shook off the feeling as best she could, for there were other, more important things to think about. Indeed, Penelope had so many questions she hardly knew which to ask first. "Miss Mortimer, why did Judge Quinzy say Swanburne was his school? Why are the walls overgrown with ivy? And is it true that the name of the school will be changed?"

"I hope you have not been reading the newspapers, Penny! They seem to print all kinds of inaccuracies nowadays." Miss Mortimer stood once more, the cat squirming in her arms. "Tomorrow we shall discuss your concerns. Tonight is for happy homecomings only. First you must unpack your suitcases and get a good night's rest. The dinner hour is over, but I will have a bedtime snack brought to your room. In the morning you may have breakfast in the dining hall, with the Swanburne girls."

"Birthday parties! Porridge and jam!" the children cried happily, for of course Penelope had told them all about it.

Shantaloo would not stop wriggling. Miss Mortimer sighed and let the cat hop to the ground. "There might be jam, unless we have run out. But there will be porridge, without fail. After breakfast I will expect you in my office. Children, follow me, please. You will be staying in our guest quarters. The accommodations are humble, but 'The warmer the welcome, the grander the palace,' as Agatha Swanburne used to say."

Miss Mortimer held out her hand to Cassiopeia. The little girl took it without hesitation and gazed up at the kind headmistress with a trusting smile. The two of them led the way, with Alexander and Beowulf following eagerly behind. Shantaloo blinked a silent farewell and slipped off the way she had come.

Flustered, Penelope grabbed her carpetbag and scurried after the children. "But . . . Miss Mortimer! What about the motto?"

Miss Mortimer answered without breaking her stride. "'No hopeless case is truly without hope.' Remember it well, Penny, dear. It may be precisely the advice we need at present."

Miss Mortimer was wise to show them to their room, for Penelope had rarely visited the guest quarters (she had been woefully short on visitors during her school years, and especially so on Parents' Day), and she might well have made a wrong turn. They swiveled around corners, marched up flights of stairs and down again, and passed through doors that creaked as if they had not been opened in years.

The children thought it all a great game; by turns they pretended they were moles in dark tunnels, or explorers charting an unmapped jungle, or Postal

Tygers delivering the mail along an unfamiliar route. Miss Mortimer was charmed by their talent for make-believe and praised them for the fine condition of their imaginations.

But to Penelope it was no game, and no happy homecoming, either. The well-worn stones of Swanburne were beneath her feet, but everything felt wrong. This was not the school she knew and loved. It was an impostor, like Quinzy; a labyrinth where a blood-thirsty minotaur might leap out from every shadow. "It is because of the new shoes," she told herself uneasily. "They are bound to make even familiar ground feel strange."

Or perhaps it was the sight of Miss Mortimer leading Cassiopeia through the halls that made her feel so unsettled. The tiny hand nestled firmly inside the kind headmistress's comforting grasp, the way Miss Mortimer inclined her head to hear the little girl's observations—why, it was as if Penelope had traveled back in time to witness her own arrival at Swanburne! The sensation was so strong she had to resist the urge to look over her shoulder, to see if she could catch a final glimpse of her parents. If only she had known that they would not be coming back for her! She would have certainly taken a good long look, and imprinted it on her memory for safekeeping.

"Here we are," Miss Mortimer announced at last. "It is off the beaten path, I know. Few people even know this wing of the school exists, so it ought to be nice and quiet." She fitted a key in the lock and gave a hard twist.

Penelope forgot her worries and laughed out loud at what she saw inside: four freshly made-up cots, lined up in a row. "Those are the beds all the Swanburne girls sleep in. It seems Miss Mortimer has given us our own Incorrigible dormitory," she explained when the children wanted to know why she had laughed. She sat on the edge of one cot; the thin, lumpy mattress and pained squeak of the old springs made her sigh with contentment. This, at least, was exactly as she remembered.

"No doubt you have become used to sleeping in a soft feather bed, and all the other luxuries of Ashton Place," Miss Mortimer teased. "I hope our cots do not keep you up all night, as in the story of the princess and the pea."

The mere mention of peas caused the children to voice heartfelt objections, but Miss Mortimer smiled and assured them that something much tastier was on its way. A moment later the promised snack arrived: a basket of apples from the orchards, fresh-baked biscuits, and a pitcher of cream-topped milk from Swanburne's very own cows. After they had eaten, she showed them where to put away their things and helped everyone find their nightclothes. Soon the children's heads were nodding, but still Miss Mortimer's hand lingered on the doorknob. "Look at you all," she said softly. "What a joy to see you again."

"But, Miss Mortimer, you have never met the Incorrigibles before." Penelope stifled a yawn. She, too, was more than ready for bed.

Miss Mortimer paused. "It must be your letters, Penny. They are so vividly written, I feel as if I have met the children a hundred times. I know all about you three: Alexander the navigator, and Beowulf, with your skill for drawing and fine, strong teeth. And you, Cassiopeia, with your sweet little squirrel pet. Remind me, what is that furry scamp's name again?"

"Nuts*ahwoo*!" the children howled sleepily from their beds.

Miss Mortimer laughed so hard that tears formed in the crinkles of her eyes. "*Ahwoo*, indeed! Your wolf family did a fine job raising you. They even provided musical training. How I would love to stay and read you a bedtime story! But a headmistress's work is never done, and there is much for me to attend to before my own bedtime comes. Miss Lumley will see that you have a story, of that I have no doubt. Our library is closed at this hour, but tomorrow you may help yourselves. Did you bring any books with you from Ashton Place?"

"Of course," Penelope said quickly, for no Swanburne girl would be caught out and about without something interesting to read tucked into her pocket or purse. Miss Mortimer nodded approvingly and left.

Alas, the only books Penelope had close at hand were the cannibal book, her own book of melancholy German poetry in translation, Alexander's book of Shakespeare sonnets, and Mr. Gibbon's tome about the Roman Empire. None of these seemed quite right for bedtime. Yet a story was needed, so Penelope made up a tale on the spot. It was about a princess in disguise whose true identity is revealed when she cannot make herself fall asleep in a lumpy bed. Penelope called it "The Princess and the Very Tiny Biscuit," and the children much preferred it to any story involving a pea.

"MORNING MAY NOT PUT ONE'S problems in a new light, but at least it puts them in a new day," as the wise founder of the Swanburne Academy liked to say. And it was true. By morning Penelope's list of problems had in no way diminished, and yet they seemed more manageable, somehow, as if she might simply put them in a list and tick them off, one by one. There were her suspicions about what the impostor Quinzy (or the IQ, for short) was doing at the Swanburne Academy, and her misgivings about the cannibal book, which was now hidden in the bottom of the armoire, beneath her rolled-up stockings. There was her mounting anxiety about her unwritten CAKE speech—and what on earth was she to do about Lord Fredrick's howling? In hindsight she realized she ought to have checked the almanac for the date of the next full moon, so she might be prepared to begin the HEP, as promised. Too late now, though. It would have to wait until she returned to Ashton Place.

Yet despite all her worries, waking up in the deliciously familiar discomfort of a Swanburne cot made Penelope feel positively giddy. The sharp tips of feathers poking out of the pillow and the bracing smell of bleach from the sheets flooded her senses until they erased every bit of trouble and care that had cropped up since the day she left school. Rolling over, she half expected to get tickled across the face with the tip of one of Cecily's long braids.

"Who remembers the words to the Swanburne song?" she called out gaily as she swung her legs over the edge of the cot and gave her arms a good stretch. The Incorrigibles groaned and shook themselves awake. All three looked creaky and stiff as they climbed out of their cots, which goes to prove that even children who were raised in a forest by wolves will soon become accustomed to soft feather beds in a luxurious mansion, if given the chance. (Perhaps this is why some storytellers insist that a true princess would never be able to sleep in a lumpy bed. But it is not so. Princesses of even the most delicate sensibilities have been known to enjoy a rugged camping trip, with melted marshmallows and spooky tales told 'round the fire. Indeed, princesses are often far pluckier than given credit for, and can manage their sleeping bags and mountaineering equipment as well as the next person, and while wearing sparkly tiaras, too.)

The children dressed and combed their hair, and Penelope quizzed them once more on the words to the song, in case they wanted to join in when all the girls came marching and singing into the dining hall. Unfortunately, the children had learned the words according to the way they sounded, rather than what they actually meant, so that "All hail to our founder" became "A pail full of flounder" and so on. But it only made Penelope smile, for the Swanburne girls did exactly the same thing.

"Perhaps I am making too much of this business with the impostor Quinzy," she thought as she herded the children out the door. "Surely, one person, no matter how devious, is no match for all of Swanburne! I will deliver my warning about the IQ to Miss Mortimer after breakfast, and then I can turn my attention to happier pursuits—like preparing my CAKE speech, although there is no need to rush. After all, I have until tomorrow to get it done. . . ."

And so, with Penelope's merry mood veering dangerously close to optoomuchism, the four young people marched to breakfast, singing all the way. The words to the Swanburne school song occasionally got mixed up with those of the Postal Tygers marching song, but as long as the children sang with conviction Penelope did not bother to correct them. "Better to make mistakes with gusto than squeak like mice so no one can hear you at all. Hmm! I wonder if there will be a birthday party this morning?" She said it to entice the children to walk faster, but she too was excited at the prospect.

They reached the empty dining hall just before eight o'clock, and settled themselves at a table at the far end, nearest the kitchen, so that they might get the best view of the girls' arrival and also be first in line for porridge once it was brought out. As the clock began to strike the hour, Penelope could barely contain herself. "Here they come," she said excitedly. "Listen! You will hear them coming, loud and clear—any minute now. . . ."

But there was only silence. After a moment, the doors swung open, and the Swanburne girls marched in two quiet rows to their seats. A few gave curious, sidelong glances to the strangers in the hall, and their eyes grew wide at the presence of the boys, but none dared break rank to offer a greeting. When the girls sat down, they did so all at once, and landed on the benches with a unified *thud*.

Taking that as her cue, Cassiopeia climbed up on the bench, threw back her head, and began to sing: "A pail full of flounder, Agatha!"

But no one joined in, and Penelope gently guided her littlest pupil to sit down again. "Perhaps they have changed things so that the singing comes after the meal," she whispered. "Let us wait and see, and do as the others do. But be ready. When it comes time to stand in line, you will have to scurry to the front to get porridge while it is still hot!"

The children nodded and braced themselves to take off from their seats like sprinters at the starting blocks. But apparently that, too, had changed. The girls did not rise up and jostle themselves into a happy, wriggling line to get their breakfasts, as Penelope remembered. Instead, two giant vats of porridge were brought out from the kitchen on wheeled carts and pushed 'round the hall by blank-faced kitchen maids, who stopped once at each table. Wordlessly, the seated girls passed their bowls to the end, where the eldest girl ladled in the porridge and passed the bowls back full. In this way it only took minutes to serve the entire school.

Penelope and the children were also served in this way. Alexander did the ladling, as no one had joined them at their table. It was efficient, one had to admit, but lacked the sense of adventure and cardiovascular exercise that dashing to get a good spot on line had always provided.

Cassiopeia stuck her spoon in the bowl to see how long she could make it stand up on its own. The steaming porridge was thick as glue, and the boys were able to count to five before the spoon tipped over. She licked it and made a face. "Where's the jam?"

"They must have run out," Penelope answered casually, as if it did not matter. But, honestly, jam! How hard could it be to keep enough on hand for breakfast? A mere spoonful would be enough to lift anyone's spirits.

Beowulf scanned the hall for signs of levity. There were none. "Where are the birthday parties?" he asked.

"Perhaps it is not anyone's birthday today," Penelope replied, but she found it surprising as well. With so many girls on hand, it seemed that every day was likely to be at least one person's birthday.

"*Shhhh!*" The shush came from another table. There had never been any shushing at Swanburne before.

"Jam. Jam jam *jam*!" Cassiopeia complained, her voice rising.

"Don't worry. Will be plenty of cake at Cake Day," Alexander reassured her.

"Maybe even jam cake," Beowulf added wistfully, and began to drool.

"Actually, the CAKE has nothing to do with cake," Penelope tried to explain once more, for she did not wish there to be any further misunderstandings. The children had already been led to expect singing, jam, and birthday parties at breakfast, and had been disappointed each time. To then expect cake and get none could be a recipe for disaster.

"*Shhh!*" The shush came again, louder, this time from several different sources. Chagrined, Penelope gestured for the children to eat in silence.

No singing, no jam, no birthday parties—but at least there was still porridge, and it was warm, too, with a dusting of cinnamon on top. The four of them filled their tummies, and while they did, Penelope puzzled over how much had changed. The dining hall even looked different. But how?

She put down her spoon. There were the same long wooden tables, the same hard benches, the same tall windows through which light streamed onto the wide-planked wooden floor. And there were the same bright and earnest girls, their glossy, well-combed heads bent over to the serious task of eating.

"Eureka!" she cried, and then clapped her hand over her mouth, for the word rang through the hall like a gong. Each girl's head swiveled momentarily to stare, then turned back to her bowl.

The swiveling heads made Penelope's realization all the more obvious. It was the hair! When Penelope had been a student, all the girls had dark, drab hair. This was the result of the Swanburne hair poultice that was applied on a regular basis, to repel lice and fleas and encourage healthy scalps, according to school policy.

Penelope had never thought one way or the other about this practice, which the girls dutifully lined up for every six weeks or so. None of the girls questioned it. After all, having the same color hair simply made their uniforms look more, well, uniform. And there had not been an outbreak of fleas in quite some time.

But now the shining sea of girl heads in the dining hall boasted hair of all different colors, from pale wheat-gold to inky black, and everything in between, including many different shades of brown: from acorn and mud to russet and bark. Some were flecked with gold; others were dark as rich chocolate. Even so, the Incorrigibles' lustrous auburn locks stood out vividly from the rest, like bright red poppies in a grassy field.

Penelope's hand flew to her own hair then, dark and drab as it still was, for Miss Mortimer had insisted she continue to use the poultice even after graduating, and had even extracted a solemn promise from her to that effect. Yet the Swanburne girls themselves appeared to have given it up. And, she realized with a start, in all the letters she had received from Cecily since they both left school, her friend had not once mentioned receiving the same instruction from Miss Mortimer. Nor had she reported receiving the packets of poultice that Miss Mortimer sent Penelope every few months, like clockwork.

Penelope stood and clapped her hands briskly, *clap*

*But now the shining sea of girl heads in the dining hall
boasted hair of all different colors. . . .*

clap clap. The sound echoed nakedly through the hall. "Come, children. Put away your bowls," she instructed. Her voice was level and strong. It was just as a Swanburne graduate ought to sound, and this time she did not care who shushed her. "It is time to go see Miss Mortimer."

The Seventh Chapter

*Miss Mortimer's office is filled
with ghosts.*

PERHAPS THE STRANGELY SILENT BREAKFAST had lit a
fuse of rebellion in Penelope's heart, or perhaps the
thrill of her discovery made her feel like making noise.
Whatever the reason, she decided there was no time
like the present to lead the children in a spirited and
exceedingly loud performance of the Swanburne
school song. The four of them sang it over and over
again as they marched through the eerily quiet halls,
all the way to Miss Mortimer's office. Penelope's own
clear soprano carried above the rest.

"All hail to our founder, Agatha!
Pithy and wise is she.
Her sayings make us clever,
And don't take long to tell.
When do we quit? Never!
How do we do things? Well!

"We strive to be like dear Agatha.
Cheerful and brave are we.
Our hard work makes us lucky.
We're optimistic, too.
How do we feel? Plucky!
We're Swanburne, through and through!"

They sang and they marched, and all the while, Penelope thought of her hair. The one time she had stopped using the poultice, her hair had soon begun to reveal its true color: a striking reddish brown, quite like the color of the children's hair, and wonderfully shiny, too. But Penelope took her promises seriously, even when they doomed her to a head of dark, drab locks that did nothing to flatter her complexion. Why had Miss Mortimer insisted that she keep using the poultice when even the Swanburne girls themselves had stopped? Penelope was determined to find out.

The final go-round of the song reached its climactic end. A bemused Miss Mortimer opened her office door to find the Incorrigibles taking mock bows and curtsies before an imaginary audience, as if they had just concluded a successful opening night on the West End.

"Bravo, one and all!" the headmistress exclaimed as she beckoned her visitors inside. "And such lovely harmony on the last note, too. I never tire of hearing 'A Pail Full of Flounder,' as the girls like to call it, especially when sung with so much feeling. Did you know that the song was written by one of our earliest graduates? She grew up to be quite a talented poet, as I recall." (Only a very observant sort of person would notice how Miss Mortimer smiled a small, secret smile as she said this. Under normal circumstances Penelope was precisely this sort of person, but her mind was already so crammed with urgent and mysterious matters that it is possible even she may have missed it.)

The children wriggled themselves into the straight-backed chairs that faced Miss Mortimer's desk and swung their legs excitedly, for to be ushered into a headmistress's office was wonderfully school-like, and that was a great novelty to them.

Penelope settled in a chair as well, but she glanced with longing at the window seat. It was scarcely a year since the last time she had curled up there among the pillows, a Giddy-Yap, Rainbow! book in her lap and Shantaloo draped across her legs, purring like a miniature steam engine. Tempus fugit, indeed! Those simple, mostly happy days would never come again. "That is, unless there was some sort of machine that could let one travel back and forth through time," she thought. "A time machine, you might call it. I wonder if such a thing could exist?"

(She had no way of knowing this, of course, but some years later, a book titled *The Time Machine* would be published in England. It was written by a Mr. H. G. Wells, who also wrote books about invisibility potions, alien invasions, and other subjects that continue to fascinate readers to this very day. As for time machines, perhaps you too have longed to live among the ancient Romans, practicing elocution like Demosthenes with your mouth comically full of pebbles. Or you might prefer to peek over the shoulder of Shakespeare as he composed his sonnets, and make helpful suggestions regarding the poetic meter. And who could fail to enjoy a quiet afternoon in the days when Victoria was queen, sipping a nice, restorative cup of tea? Alas, despite its many practical uses, the time machine has yet to be invented, although a library card and a leap of the imagination have been known to do the job nearly as well.)

"Ghosties! Boo, *woof*!" Cassiopeia yapped in excitement, and then poked Beowulf, for her exclamation had sounded rather like his name.

"You must forgive the mess." Miss Mortimer gestured around. Except for the desk and chairs, all the furniture in the office was covered with white sheets, and the rugs were rolled up and propped against a wall. "My office is soon to be painted, and everything is in a jumble."

"'Jumble' means 'chaos.' Boo!" Beowulf agreed, for all the white sheets did make the office seem full of ghosts.

"Pandeminimum . . . pandemaniac . . . oh, havoc!" Cassiopeia covered her face in shame at forgetting how to say "pandemonium," which, to be fair, is not an easy word to pull off without practice.

"Now, now. A little mayhem never hurt anyone," Alexander said, and patted his sister on the shoulder.

"The children have a knack for synonyms," Penelope explained modestly, although she took great pride in her students' accomplishments, as all good teachers do. "Miss Mortimer, before you say anything more, there was an urgent matter that I wrote to you about, regarding the board of trustees. But I fear you may not have received my letter of warning, as you did not mention it in your correspondence. Of course, you included a great deal of other useful information, for which I am grateful. Nine times eight is seventy-two!" she added, suddenly uneasy. She missed being able to see the portrait of Agatha Swanburne that hung on the wall behind Miss Mortimer's desk. The founder's calm gaze had always been a comfort to her, but the portrait, too, was draped in a sheet. And was it not the case that Agatha Swanburne's hair was also a distinctive shade of auburn? That was how she remembered it from the painting, at least, but now it was hidden from view.

"A warning about the trustees?" Miss Mortimer frowned. "I received no such letter, though we ought not to blame the postal service. The Defense of Definitude Office reads all the incoming and outgoing mail to check for spelling errors, neatness, the proper use of the apostrophe, and so forth. Their corrections are most helpful, of course, but not every letter meets with the DODO's approval. Those that do not tend to disappear."

Penelope was about to protest, for her penmanship was nothing if not neat, and she was positively meticulous in her use of the apostrophe—but at the word "dodo," the children leaped up from their chairs and waddled clumsily around the office. Occasionally, they attempted to fly. Naturally, these efforts did not succeed.

Penelope turned to Miss Mortimer. "What on earth is the Defense of Definitude Office?"

"It is another innovation by the new trustees." Miss Mortimer addressed the Incorrigibles, who now lay wheezing on the floor. "Can it be nap time already? I hope you slept comfortably on your cots, despite the lumps. Or were you kept up all night, like that poor princess with the pea?"

The children politely explained that they had slept perfectly well, but that their species was in the midst of going extinct and would soon be no more.

"Maybe peas will go extinct," Alexander said to his siblings, who squawked faintly but approvingly.

Miss Mortimer had no answer for that, and turned to Penelope. "Save your urgent news until later, when we can speak privately; I would not want to alarm the dodos at such a sensitive moment. And how did you enjoy breakfast in the dining hall? I trust things were as you remembered, more or less."

"Rather less than more, I should say," Penelope

replied, frowning. "It was much too quiet for my taste. And I could not help noticing the difference in the girls' hair. Unless I am mistaken, it seems they no longer use the hair poultice. I was hoping you might tell me why."

"The new way of serving the porridge keeps it nice and hot, did you notice?" Miss Mortimer replied, after a pause. "It is a vast improvement, I think. Change can be for the better, Penny, dear. One must remember that."

Penelope squirmed in her chair, which suddenly seemed uncomfortably small. "Of course. But about the hair poultice—"

"Jam!" Miss Mortimer abruptly cried. "Was there a little jam, at least?"

Still on the floor, all three Incorrigibles sadly shook their heads.

The headmistress sighed. "Pity. I am afraid that jam is simply too expensive, given the new and rather strict budgets prepared by the trustees. But I will tell you a secret: Dr. Westminster occasionally smuggles jars of honey into the dining hall, straight from his own beehives. Those are happy mornings indeed. Children, have you made plans to see Dr. Westminster yet? I know he will be delighted to make your acquaintance. And what veterinarian would miss the chance to examine three not-quite-dead dodos? It is a rare opportunity, to say the least."

The children squawked, even more faintly this time, as they drew ever nearer to the brink of doom. Truly, it was a pathetic sound. *Skwah-ahhhhhk! Skwah-ahhhhhk!*

"Miss Mortimer!" Penelope had to fight the urge to raise her hand in hopes of being called upon. "*Why* have the girls stopped using the hair poultice?"

Miss Mortimer adjusted her posture until her back was straight as a yardstick. With one hand she smoothed her dark blond hair, which was arranged in an elegant chignon at the nape of her neck. "That was another budget-cutting measure," she said at last. "The trustees have deemed the application of the poultice an unnecessary expense, although I am quite sure they themselves would not enjoy being bitten by fleas." She gave Penelope a wan smile. "Still, a little itching and scratching is hardly a tragedy. Remember when you had the chicken pox, Penny, dear? And there was one time that poor Shantaloo was absolutely tormented by fleas—"

"But what of the color?" Penelope blurted. Miss Mortimer looked at her blankly, so she went on. "Surely you are aware that the poultice gives all the girls the same hair color?"

Miss Mortimer's face remained impassive. "Does it really?"

"Why, yes! The poultice makes everyone's hair the same drab dark brown." Penelope stretched out her arm and offered the sleeve of her new dress as an example. "Without it, the girls' hair is a whole paint-box of different colors. I noticed it in the dining hall this morning. It made me curious. If I may ask bluntly, why do you feel it is so urgent that I continue to use the poultice?"

Graceful as a ballerina, Miss Mortimer rose to her feet. "A healthy scalp is a happy scalp, Penelope! There is no harm in using the poultice, and it may do some good. Personal vanity ought not to factor into it. Now arise, dodos! I believe I promised you a tour of the school. Classes are not in session this morning, as the girls are busy preparing for tomorrow's CAKE, but perhaps you will be able to sit in on a class or two this afternoon."

The children clambered to their feet and lined up eagerly at the door, but Penelope would not give up so easily.

"Then why not ask the same of all Swanburne graduates? Why only me?"

Miss Mortimer tucked her chair in its proper place

behind the desk before walking to the door. "The Incorrigibles have very strikingly colored hair," she said thoughtfully, gazing down at the three tousled heads. "An unusual, rich auburn. Not quite brown, not quite red, and it catches the light like a mirror. If they were in danger and wanted to disappear unnoticed in a crowd, disguising that hair would be a clever first step."

Miss Mortimer spoke quietly and evenly, as if planning how to hide from one's enemies was a usual topic of conversation one might have after breakfast. Then she clapped her hands briskly, as if bringing a lesson to a close. *Clap clap clap!* "Now, that is all there is to say on the subject of hair. Shall we begin our tour?"

As THEY WERE LEAVING THE headmistress's office, the children got the idea to costume themselves as ghosts. With Miss Mortimer's permission, they used scissors to cut eyeholes in some extra sheets they found. Then they had to decide whether to call themselves the Cake-Eating Postal Ghostie Dodo Tygers, or the Cake-Eating Ghostly Dodo Postal Tygers. Either way, there would be cake, they reasoned, which was precisely why it was so hard to choose.

In the end they decided it did not matter, and the

tour of Swanburne began. Along the way there was much spooky moaning and more than a few collisions, for even with the eyeholes it was not easy for the Ghostly Postals to see where they were going. Luckily, the children had keen senses of smell. In short order they found the gymnasium by following the scent of gym shoes. Then, with sheets hoisted up above their ankles for safety, the children daringly climbed the spiral stairs that led to the observatory, which they located handily, they explained, by following the scent of the sky.

Alexander in particular greatly enjoyed looking through the telescope, all across the farm valley of Heathcote. There was a comical incident when he turned the focus knob and unwittingly brought the face of a distant woolly sheep into close-up view. After some initial confusion over how a sheep had suddenly materialized in the observatory, the children jostled for turns to look through the lens at the unsuspecting creature. No matter how the children called to it and waved, the faraway sheep only blinked and chewed its cud.

Back down the spiral stairs they went. Penelope and Miss Mortimer walked at a safe distance behind the three sniffing, careening, sheet-clad children. Miss

Mortimer could not stop marveling at their navigational skills—"Who knew the sky even had a scent?" she exclaimed—but Penelope was still brooding about the poultice. Had Miss Mortimer meant to imply that Penelope herself was in danger, and that her distinctive hair color had been camouflaged by subjecting the entire student body to the gooey ordeal of the poultice, every six weeks without fail, year after mousy-brown year? It was a mystery indeed, but Penelope knew better than to raise the subject again. Once Miss Mortimer clapped her hands about something, that was the end of that.

The children dashed ahead in a race to be first to the laboratory, a marvelous place full of test tubes and beakers that sizzled and smoked and gave off such foul odors that anyone with a nose would be able to find it in the pitch-dark, and blindfolded, too. "I take it the singing of the school song every morning has also been eliminated?" Penelope asked when they were out of earshot.

Miss Mortimer sighed. "The trustees found the song too entertaining and say it is to be saved only for special occasions. What those occasions are, we have not yet been told. I have overheard the girls practicing in private, though. When the time comes, they will be ready." She paused. "And no more birthday parties, I'm afraid. The trustees feel they are too distracting." In Penelope's experience, being ignored on one's birthday was far more distracting than a few moments of friendship and a spoonful of jam would have been. But it did not surprise her that the trustees felt differently, given what she had learned of them so far.

The laboratory was locked, but Miss Mortimer produced a ring of keys to open the door. The Incorrigibles ran inside and began experimenting, while the two educators lingered in the doorway.

"And what is this urgent matter you wrote me about, Penny, dear?" Miss Mortimer asked quietly, so that only Penelope could hear.

Penelope glanced at her three pupils. Already they had found a beaker of some thick green liquid, and another of red. Now they had combined the two and were heating the resulting mixture over a gas flame, which seemed harmless enough. "I believe that Judge Quinzy is an impostor," she answered. "He is not who he claims to be. And I think I know his true identity, too."

Miss Mortimer allowed one eyebrow to rise. "Who do you suppose he is?"

"None other than Edward Ashton."

"But Edward Ashton is dead."

"His body was never found." Penelope leaned close and let her voice drop to a whisper. "I believe Edward Ashton faked his own death and then, some years later, reappeared in the guise of Judge Quinzy. His appearance is much altered, true, but only in ways that would be easily achieved by careful diet, a regular exercise program, and the modest use of stagecraft."

"Eureka!" cried the children, for their bubbling liquid had turned a rich shade of brown, and the foul smell of the laboratory was rapidly giving way to a fragrance that was deliciously sweet. One might even describe it as cakelike. They called Miss Mortimer and Penelope over to admire and sniff.

After the concoction was duly praised, and the children were occupied once more, Penelope and Miss Mortimer retreated to a nearby table. Miss Mortimer lifted a flask of orange goo and gave it a thoughtful swirl. "Edward Ashton, alive. What a fascinating theory," she said after a moment. "Have you any proof?"

"Not exactly." Penelope kept her voice low. "But Fredrick's mother, the Widow Ashton, also believes the impostor Quinzy is Edward, and she swore she would never mistake her husband, no matter how changed his appearance. And there is a Gypsy fortune-teller of

"Eureka!" cried the children . . .

my acquaintance, Madame Ionesco. On a recent visit to Ashton Place, she used her powers to look Beyond the Veil, to where dead spirits dwell. She says Edward Ashton is not there."

As she spoke, Penelope found herself hypnotized by the swirling orange liquid. "You remember Madame Ionesco, do you not? I have mentioned her to you before. She was the soothsayer who claimed the Incorrigible children were under some sort of a curse. 'The hunt is on,' she said—"

The delicate beaker slipped from Miss Mortimer's hands and shattered on the floor in a spray of glass shards and orange droplets. The crash made Penelope cry out, and caused the Cake-Sniffing Scientist Postal Dodo Ghosts to look up from their experimenting.

"How clumsy I am!" Miss Mortimer exclaimed. The headmistress paused, and Penelope was surprised to see her take one of those deep, calming breaths that all Swanburne girls were trained to rely upon when anxious. "Yet soothsayers are not always reliable sources of information," she said at last. "And it still does not explain why Edward Ashton would do such a thing. Do you have a theory about that as well?"

"I do not," Penelope confessed. "But there is something . . . *unusual* about the Ashtons. Lord Fredrick has told me so himself." Briefly, she wondered if she ought to reveal the details of her employer's moonstruck condition to Miss Mortimer, but decided it was more of a medical matter and therefore ought to be kept private. "On a practical note, Miss Mortimer, if we could prove that Judge Quinzy is an impostor, surely he would have to step down from the board." There was no mistaking the eagerness in her voice. "And then—"

"And there would be jam and singing and birthday parties at Swanburne once more." Miss Mortimer took a broom from the classroom closet and began sweeping up the broken glass. "I wish it were that simple. Quinzy, as we will continue to call him for now, joined the trustees scarcely two months ago. Once sworn in, he quickly persuaded three of our longtime board members to resign."

"Persuaded? But how?"

Miss Mortimer smiled ruefully as she swept. "Whoever he may be, the man is enormously wealthy. Generous gifts were offered in exchange for those resignations. The three empty seats were filled by Quinzy's friends. That means he now controls four of the seven votes on the board."

Penelope performed a quick mental calculation. "So even if we could prove that Quinzy is a fake, it would make no difference, since he controls the majority," she said.

"Correct. That is why the faculty and I decided to organize the CAKE. We hoped that if we could demonstrate the true spirit and value of our school, perhaps we might soften the hearts of the new trustees and win one of them over, somehow . . . for we only need one."

She leaned the broom against the wall and took another deep breath. "What a promising aroma," she said, loud enough for the Incorrigibles to hear. "But that is all the inventing we have time for at present, children. Mind your step, now; there is broken glass here, and a sticky orange puddle as well. We shall have to return to the laboratory later, after the floor has been properly cleaned."

Like responsible scientists, the children extinguished the burner and put their lab equipment away, but they insisted that Penelope have a taste of their mixture before leaving. "Oh, my!" she exclaimed, after taking a spoonful. "That is a remarkable flavor. It is not quite chocolate, not quite vanilla, not quite caramel, but somehow the best of all three mixed together, and with a hint of butterscotch, too."

"Do . . . I . . . smell . . . *candy*?" A voice roared through the halls of the school. It was a furious voice, and it grew louder and more furious with each apoplectic word. "There is a *rule* about candy, and the rule is this: There is *no* candy allowed in school! None! If anyone dares to object, they ought to come see me *right now*!"

Obediently, the children bolted in the direction of the voice.

"Children—stop! Mind the goo!" Penelope cried. But it was too late; the Incorrigibles had raced out of the laboratory, leaping neatly over the broken glass but leaving a trail of sticky orange footprints behind them as they skidded into the hall. There they crashed head-long into the source of the bellowing: a tall woman in a fur cape, who now lay sprawled on the floor with three orange-splattered ghosts hovering above her.

"Boo!" they cried. All three children moaned spookily and waved their arms beneath the sheets. "Boo! Boo! We want candy! Candy candy candy!"

"Take off those ridiculous outfits at once," their victim snarled, unimpressed. "Is that any way to greet a baroness?"

"Baroness Hoover!" Penelope yelped. And indeed, that is who it was. The baroness and her husband, the baron, were close friends of the Ashtons, although even Lady Constance found the baroness a chore to be around. Penelope had met the haughty baroness on several occasions, and each time she had disliked her more than the last—a trend, she feared, that was about to continue.

"We are ghosts," Alexander explained to the capsized woman.

"'*Sheeted* ghosts.' As in Longfellow," Beowulf explained.

"He means Hespawoo," Cassiopeia added, for indeed, "sheeted ghost" was a phrase taken from "The Wreck of the Hesperus," an absolutely thrilling poem about a shipwreck that the children knew quite well.

But the baroness had no appreciation for poetry, or so it seemed. Even as the boys helped her to her feet, she sneered. "Bad manners, dreadful noises, illegal candy making! And you are out of uniform as well. It will have to go in my report."

Sheepishly, the children removed their ghost costumes.

Miss Mortimer stepped forward. "Baroness Hoover, greetings. I am afraid you are early! The CAKE is not until tomorrow. Allow me to present Miss Penelope Lumley, a Swanburne graduate of great accomplishment. These are her three students—"

The baroness waved her hand dismissively. "No

need to make introductions. I have met the wolf children and their earnest young governess before. Such strange pets the Ashtons keep!"

Ever mindful of his manners, Alexander offered a sweeping bow. "I like pets," he said gallantly. "For example, Nutsawoo."

"Also for example, Bertha the ostrich." The dignity of Beowulf's bow was marred by the appearance of Shantaloo, who had emerged from the shadows and now rubbed against his leg in a ticklish fashion. "Tygers, too," he said with a giggle, and gave the little striped cat a scratch on the head.

"My for example is *woofs*." Cassiopeia curtsied as she yapped. (By "woofs," she meant wolves. Keep in mind that wolves do not generally make desirable pets. Nor do tigers, ostriches, or even squirrels, for that matter, but the Incorrigibles' circumstances were unusual, and their taste in animal friends is in no way meant to serve as a model for others to follow. However, bowing, curtsying, and handwritten thank-you notes are always appropriate, and are as appreciated nowadays as they were in Miss Lumley's day, if not more so.)

"What about chickens?" The baroness grinned wickedly and licked her lips. "I hear there is a whole chicken coop full of tasty poultry right here on the grounds of the school. Plump and delicious, with their juicy fat chicken thighs just waiting to be devoured."

The children's eyes grew wide. A sheen of drool appeared on Beowulf's lower lip, and Alexander made a soft *buck-buck-buck*ing noise under his breath.

"Talk of chickens is best saved for lunchtime," Penelope interjected. "If you will excuse us, Baroness, the children have their schoolwork to attend to."

"Schoolwork? Sit, stay, and fetch is more like it." The baroness turned to Miss Mortimer. "I am here on board business, at the chairman's urgent request. I require access to your office. I need to see the files."

Miss Mortimer's eyebrows lifted in innocent surprise. "My door is always open, Baroness. But what files do you mean?"

"The student files, of course." The baroness flicked her cape in annoyance. "Surely you keep files on your students? Medical records, test scores, birth certificates, that sort of thing?"

"Ah, the student files! Of course, we do keep such information. But my office is about to be painted, and all the files have been packed up for safekeeping." Miss Mortimer smiled pleasantly. "They must be in storage; I do not know exactly where."

The baroness's eyes went cold. "I suggest you locate them immediately. If you cannot find them by end of day tomorrow, we will conduct a thorough search of every square inch of this school. We will pull up the floorboards and slit open every one of those ridiculous pillows. And that would be *most* tedious."

"It would make a dreadful mess, too, since the pillows are stuffed with feathers." Miss Mortimer bent low and scooped Shantaloo into her arms. "Children, do you know what sort of sound chickens make? Show the baroness, please."

"Buck-buck, buck-buck!" the Incorrigibles clucked, proud to know the answer. They flapped their arms like so many tasty chicken wings. *"Buck-buck, buck-buck!"* They flapped and *buck-buck*ed all around the baroness, until she threw up her hands in a panic.

"Keep those Incorrigible chickens away from me!" she screeched as she escaped down the hall. "Find those files! And *no candy*!"

ONCE SHE WAS GONE, THE children tried to decide which would be tastier: candied chicken, or chicken candy. They even imagined a colorful, marshmallowy sort of candy in the shape of a baby chicken. (Many years later, this last invention actually came to pass.

It remains popular with candy lovers to this very day, although the Incorrigible children are rarely, if ever, given credit for inventing it.)

"What reason could the trustees have for demanding the student files?" Penelope asked. The children were now quite sticky from all their experimenting and needed a good hand and face washing, so they had all taken a brief detour to the nearest washroom.

Miss Mortimer shrugged. "The same reason they give for outlawing singing and birthday parties, which is to say, no reason at all. The baroness is the worst of them, although I am quite sure she is merely doing Quinzy's bidding. It was she who created the Defense of Definitude Office and whipped everyone into a frenzy about changing the name of the school."

Penelope gasped. "The School for Miserable Girls! No! It cannot be!"

"Do not give up hope, Penny! It has not yet come to pass. She means to make the new name official tomorrow, after your speech. She intends for the trustees to pass a resolution at the CAKE." Unexpectedly, Miss Mortimer smiled. "Eight times twelve is ninety-six! Do you recall that peculiar letter I sent you? Filled with pages about multiplication and ferns and so on?"

The mention of her speech made Penelope feel a surge of panic. Tomorrow! How had the day come so quickly? She shook off the feeling to answer, "Yes, of course I remember. It did strike me as odd."

"Since our mail is being read by the DODO, I took pains to make my letter as boring, dull, tedious, and uninteresting as possible. I knew that only a true Swanburne girl would have the pluck and determination to find the real message within—like searching for a needle in a haystack." She paused. "That is what I suspect the baroness has been told to do. Create one distracting uproar after another."

Penelope struggled to understand. "Do you mean to say, all the baroness's meddling . . . the silly rules, the strict budgets, the meaningless demands for paperwork, the proposed name change . . ."

"Are merely the haystack. Designed to engage all our attention and make the needle within impossible to see."

"But what is the needle?"

Miss Mortimer sighed. "That, dear Penny, is an excellent question."

THE TOUR CONTINUED. BY NOW the Swanburne girls had returned to their classes, and the sight of all those

eager students with their hands in the air, \
be called upon, made Penelope feel fully at ho\
the first time since arriving at Swanburne. The girls
were charmed by the Incorrigibles and positively star-
struck by their governess. Some of them shyly asked
if she had received their letters, which, of course, she
had. She promised to reply to each one at the earliest opportunity, although with an important speech
to write and so many mysteries to ponder, who knew
when that might be?

The teachers were also overjoyed to see Penelope.
Madame Pyrénées, the geography teacher, babbled
excitedly in French and then embraced Penelope and
the children in turn until she was breathless from
planting multiple kisses on each cheek. Even Magistra
Grimsby, an angular, ageless woman who taught Latin
as if it were her native tongue, managed a brief, awkward hug.

"Little Penny Lumley, a governess! Tempus fugit,"
she said, and shook her head in wonder. "What a long
way you have come. *Per angusta ad augusta*. Through
adversity, we march onward to triumph. Remember,
Penny, even a narrow and difficult road can lead to a
high place."

Penelope was not entirely sure what Magistra

Grimsby meant, but it did not matter. Just being in a Swanburne classroom again, with dedicated teachers who dispensed nuggets of pithy wisdom like so many gum balls tumbling out of a gum ball machine, was enough to lift her spirits, and she found her optimism returning at full strength.

"Surely an hour in the library will be more than enough time for me to prepare my remarks for tomorrow," she thought as Cassiopeia proudly recited a few lines of Virgil for the delighted Magistra. "Whether the trustees will be moved by my speech, I cannot say; I can only do my part and let the rest unfold as it will. As Agatha Swanburne once remarked, 'Do your best before lunch, and your best after lunch. During lunch, have a sandwich.'" Absently, she patted her tummy, for it had been some hours and a great deal of walking since breakfast. "Now, buck up, Penny! And no more fretting. After all, how hard could it be to whip up a CAKE speech?"

The last classroom they visited belonged to Mrs. Apple, an energetic lady with full red cheeks worthy of her name. The Incorrigibles were excited to learn she was a history teacher and bombarded her with questions: Was it true that plague had determined the outcome of the Peloponnesian War? What were the real reasons for the decline and fall of the Roman Empire? Beowulf particularly wanted to know if there had been peas in ancient Rome. When told yes, he made a face. "Ancient peas," he said ominously to his siblings, and they all shuddered in horror.

Meanwhile, Mrs. Apple was delighted by their passion for her own favorite subject. She took the opportunity to show off a bit. "And that," she said breathlessly (for the bell was about to ring, and she had been talking at a breakneck pace), "is the history of England as best as I can squeeze it into a quarter of an hour. From Hadrian's Wall to Admiral Nelson! Any questions?"

After the applause died down (for truly, it had been a masterful summation), it was little Cassiopeia who shyly raised her hand. "Where is the flounder?" she asked.

Mrs. Apple was momentarily stumped. "Fishing has long played a significant role in England's economy. Is that what you mean?" she began, but the girl shook her head.

"Our cook makes a tasty fish stew," Miss Mortimer said kindly. "We can request it for luncheon, if you like."

"No," Cassiopeia insisted. "I want to see the *flounder*.

Where is she?" She turned to Penelope for help. "Is she in the pail?"

Then Penelope understood. "I believe she means 'Where is Agatha Swanburne?' Were you expecting to meet her today? And you, too, Beowulf? Alexander?"

First Cassiopeia, then her brothers, nodded solemnly. Apparently, all three had assumed that the wise old "flounder" was alive and well and could be found strolling about the school, giving sage advice.

"Agatha Swanburne?" Mrs. Apple exclaimed. "Well, I am afraid she is dead."

The children looked shocked. Then they began to cry.

"Oh, my! I am sorry to upset you." Flustered, Mrs. Apple tried to explain. "What I meant to say was, Agatha Swanburne is long dead." But that made the children cry harder, for to them, being long dead sounded even worse than being merely dead.

"Flounder is extinct!" they wept. "Nevermore, flounder!" The distraught children ran to Penelope and clung to her skirts until she thought she might cry herself.

Miss Mortimer watched them, her face full of feeling. "My dear children, what tender hearts you have. Your governess has taught you well." One by one they calmed and turned to her. She pulled up a little class-room chair, the kind used for the smallest students, and sat down in it herself, so that she might speak to the Incorrigibles face-to-face. "Agatha Swanburne was alive for a very long time, and in that time she did many marvelous things. She created this school, for example."

"Wise . . . sayings," Beowulf said, between gulping sobs.

"And pillows," Cassiopeia ventured. Her sea-green eyes brimmed with tears.

"Precisely. And the pillows help us remember the sayings, and they are quite cozy and comfortable, too. She was a great teacher and lived to be a very old lady. And then she died, as all living things must, but not until it was her proper time to do so."

"No gruesome end?" Alexander asked, in a trembling voice.

Miss Mortimer shook her head. "Quite the opposite, in fact. In her last days, she was as peaceful and well loved as a person could ever hope to be."

Cassiopeia rubbed both eyes vigorously with her fists. "That's it, then," she said, bravely accepting the truth. "We cannot meet the flounder today."

Miss Mortimer's eyes shone, but she also looked as

if she might laugh. "I am afraid not. Not the same way you can meet me, and Mrs. Apple, and the good Magistra and all the rest. But there is a spark of Agatha in all of us here at Swanburne, for a good teacher leaves a little bit of herself in all her students. As they grow up, they pass that spark on to others in turn, the way one candle is used to light another."

She looked fondly at Penelope, and then turned to the children once more. "That means the spark of Agatha Swanburne lives in each of you three. Every time you think of one of her wise sayings and use it to help muddle through your own life, it is as if you are meeting her again and again."

"Not the same." Beowulf sniffed again, loudly, and wiped his nose on his sleeve. "Decline and fall. Byebye, Rome. Is sad."

His siblings circled close to comfort him, and Penelope sighed, for although Miss Mortimer was quite right in what she had said, so too was Beowulf, and there was no use pretending otherwise. Three children who had been raised by wolves had certainly known enough of death to understand: A duck, once eaten, does not come back to paddle 'round the pond another day. The taxidermy animals in Lord Fredrick's study were proof enough of that.

Miss Mortimer, wisely, did not argue with the children. "The hands of the clock spin in one direction only, it is true. But that is the way of life, my dear children. Time flies; things change. As Agatha Swanburne herself once said—"

But then the bell rang, and it was time to move on.

THE EIGHTH CHAPTER

*Something valuable is learned
in the library.*

*"And fast through the midnight dark and drear,
Through the whistling sleet and snow,
Like a sheeted ghost, the vessel swept
Towards the reef of Norman's Woe."*

PENELOPE RECITED IDLY TO HERSELF as she wandered
through the library. The words had sprung into her
mind when the children mentioned "sheeted ghosts"
to the baroness. Now they were stuck in her head, like
a catchy tune from a nautically themed operetta that

one cannot help singing in the shower, despite having a strong dislike for the show itself. (To be fair, there are those who genuinely admire *Pirates on Holiday*, never mind all the dreadful reviews in the London papers. PIRATES ON HOLIDAY IS LOST AT SEA was one of the kinder headlines. SOMEBODY SINK THIS SHOW, QUICK was another. Those of you with hearts stony and cruel enough to grow up to be theater critics are free to imagine the rest for yourselves.)

The fact that Mr. Longfellow's poem was about a shipwreck also made Penelope think of the cannibal book. The cannibal book put her in mind of Simon Harley-Dickinson, and the thought of Simon, a playwright, made her think of Shakespeare . . . *The Tragedy of Julius Caesar* . . . ancient Rome . . . Cicero . . . orations . . . the speech! Thus, like a toy train doing endless figure eights on a looping track, her thoughts inevitably circled back to the very spot they kept trying to leave behind. But tomorrow was the CAKE, and the task of preparing her speech could not be put off any longer.

"'Finish today's work today, for tomorrow will bring its own,' as Agatha Swanburne liked to say," she thought as she removed several weighty collections of famous speeches from the library shelves and lugged them to her table. "At least the Incorrigibles are being well cared for while I work."

Indeed, the children could not be in better hands. Once the classroom tours were done, Miss Mortimer and Mrs. Apple had invited Penelope and the Incorrigibles to the faculty lounge for tea and biscuits. The children were eager, but Penelope had declined, explaining that she needed to put a few "finishing touches" on her remarks. She was too embarrassed to admit she had not yet written more than ten words.

Miss Mortimer had smiled knowingly at Penelope's request to be excused. "By all means. Mrs. Apple and I will keep the children occupied so you can work in peace. Will an hour be sufficient?"

"Oh—more than sufficient!" Penelope stammered.

"A speech, how marvelous! I do love a good oration. 'Once more unto the breach, dear friends!'" Mrs. Apple slashed an imaginary sword through the air, much to the delight of the children. "I shall be on tenterhooks to hear what you have to say tomorrow."

"Yes! Well, I hope . . . that is to say, I am looking forward to it also," Penelope had replied with a gulp.

And so it was she found herself in the library, with her new fountain pen close at hand and no time to waste. Instinctively, she settled herself at the same library table she had preferred in years gone by. It was here she had written many a term paper with great success during her student days. Perhaps it would bring her good luck one more time.

First she wrote down a list of words that she thought might come in useful when talking about the Swanburne Academy. "Education" was one. "Pluck" was another. "Tradition." "Agatha." "Friendship." "Goulash" came next, for she realized she was writing on the back of the goulash recipe Cecily had sent her. Somehow it had gotten tucked into her notebook. She doubted "goulash" would be helpful and considered crossing it out, but one never knew, and so it remained.

For inspiration, she doodled in the margin of the page. First she drew Cicero, then Demosthenes. In their flowing togas they looked a great deal alike, although Demosthenes's cheeks were puffed up because of the pebbles. That was easy for her to draw; she simply pictured Nutsawoo with his cheeks full of acorns.

She wondered what it might be like to have a mouthful of pebbles. That put her in mind of the sheep the children had seen earlier through the telescope, ceaselessly chewing on its cud. She drew that as well.

None of this was getting the speech written, of course. "With so little time left, I must make every second count," she resolved. "First I shall review, say, ten or twelve more speeches of Cicero's, to put me in the right frame of mind." She jumped up and lugged another armful of reference books to the table, which she then arranged in size order. "And what of Queen Elizabeth's rousing speech to the English troops as they prepared to do battle with the Spanish Armada in the year 1588? Mrs. Apple made glowing mention of it in her brief but thorough talk on English history. Surely, I ought to have a peek at that as well."

She found the appropriate volume and flipped through the pages. "Elizabeth, Armada . . . Elizabeth, Armada . . . Eureka! Here it is." Quietly, but with deep feeling, she read the words aloud.

"'I know I have but the body of a weak and feeble woman; but I have the heart of a king, and of a king of England, too; and think foul scorn that Parma or Spain, or any prince of Europe, should dare to invade the borders of my realms.'"

"I have no wish to invade your realms, Miss Lumley. But perhaps I might borrow a chair? The one at my table is rather wobbly in the leg."

"Impostor—I mean, Judge Quinzy!" Penelope exclaimed, but quietly, since she was, after all, in a library. "What are you doing here?"

180

"I have no wish to invade your realms, Miss Lumley."

"One does not become a judge without reading a great many books. Please forgive my appearance. It is a precaution against cats." In addition to his customary thick glasses, he wore a handkerchief tied 'round his nose and mouth, like a bandit. "I am doing what anyone would do in a library. Looking for answers."

She willed her voice to stay even. "Surely a law library would serve you better."

"My questions have to do with genealogy." The handkerchief twitched, as if he were smiling. "I am researching my family tree."

"There must be little here to interest you, then," she said, and pretended to go back to reading about the Spanish Armada.

"You are wrong, Miss Lumley. The Swanburne library is not as vast as the one, say, at Ashton Place. But it has some unique holdings. I have gone to a great deal of trouble to gain access to them. They have proven invaluable." Supple as a snake, he slid into the empty chair at her table. "For example, it was not until I consulted the special archives here at Swanburne that I discovered the existence of a diary. An extraordinary, one-of-a-kind document. It chronicles the tale of a most . . . *unusual* seafaring expedition."

The back of her neck went suddenly cold.

"A long-lost diary," he continued, "regarding a doomed voyage undertaken by Lord Fredrick Ashton's great-grandfather, Admiral Percival Racine Ashton. According to the archives, the book is part of the holdings of the Ashton library."

"But surely you were already familiar with the contents of the library at Ashton Place." She spoke slowly, for she sensed a trap being set. "You and Lord Fredrick are such good friends, after all."

"I have spent countless hours there, true. And yet it seems there were some books that escaped my notice. That diary would be a great boon to my research, but Fredrick tells me it is missing. You don't happen to know where it is, do you, Miss Lumley?"

"I am a governess, not a librarian. In any case, the diary you describe would be of use in researching the Ashton family tree, not your own." She looked him square in the face, but his glasses blurred his eyes in such a way that she could not gauge his reaction. "Unless, of course, you and Lord Fredrick are related in some fashion?"

He let out a bark of laughter. "Touché, Miss Lumley. Your years at Swanburne have given you impressive powers of observation and deduction. As it happens, the ancestry of the Quinzys and that of the Ashtons are intimately linked. As is true of many old English families, of course." He leaned closer, and his hands slid forward on the table. "Lord Fredrick's grandfather was a judge, too, you know."

"The Honorable Pax Ashton. His portrait hangs at Ashton Place." She willed herself not to stare at his hands. They were long and slim fingered, like two pale, deadly spiders crawling toward her. "I once heard Lord Fredrick's mother say that he was a most unpleasant man."

"He was stern. Uncompromising. Unswayed by emotion. Able to keep a secret to his grave, and beyond. Surely these are not bad qualities to have in a judge."

"They would be difficult qualities to have in a father, though."

"You would have to ask his son, Edward, about that. Alas, Edward Ashton is unavailable for comment." He clucked his tongue in pity. "Drowning in a medicinal tar pit, *tsk tsk*! What a gruesome way to die."

The nerve of him, to go on pretending he was not Edward Ashton! "And yet his body was never found," she said sharply.

Quinzy lifted first one eyebrow, then the other. Then he did something extraordinary. Slowly and methodically, and taking special care about his nose, he removed his glasses. He looked at her with those dark eyes, frank and unhidden. Unmistakable, the Widow Ashton had called them. Molten and frozen at the same time, deep and dark as the mouths of caves. They were Edward Ashton's eyes, lifted straight from the portrait in Lord Fredrick's study.

"Touché again, Miss Lumley." His smooth, low voice was scarcely more than a breath. "Edward Ashton was lost in the tar. Yet sometimes even long-lost things can be found. If one knows where to look."

He put his glasses back on, and in that moment Penelope had all the proof she needed. He *was* Edward Ashton. She knew it, and he knew that she knew it. Yet here they sat, toying with each other like predator and prey. But which of them was the cat, and which the wee mousie?

He pushed back his chair and stood. "Genealogy is a fascinating hobby, Miss Lumley. I highly recommend it. But perhaps my remarks are insensitive, given your personal circumstances. You hardly knew your parents, after all. Your family tree must feel as bare and cold as—well, as the trees in winter will soon be."

A rushing sound filled Penelope's ears, like an angry sea. "I do not recall discussing my personal circumstances with you, sir," she said coldly.

He gave an indifferent bow of apology. "I beg your pardon. Lady Constance must have mentioned it to me in passing. You know how she likes to gossip about the servants." With a nod, he left.

Ga-dong! Ga-dong! Ga-dong! Ga-dong! Ga-dong!

"Iambic pentameter!" Penelope exclaimed in despair. How could it be five o'clock already? But tempus fugit, as the chiming of the library clock made clear, and since Edward Ashton had left, the time had flown faster than a keen-eyed peregrine falcon swooping earthward for its prey.

The librarian rang a little bell. "The library will be closing shortly. Please come to the circulation desk and check out your books. Return all reference books to the reshelving cart."

Defeated, Penelope looked at her notes. On one page were a few lines from *Julius Caesar*. "Et tu, Brute?" she read with a sigh. (Magistra Grimsby would have pointed out that the phrase "Et tu, Brute?" was Latin for "Even you, Brutus?" These were Julius Caesar's dying words when he realized that even his dear friend Brutus had been part of the murderous plot against him. To this very day, people will exclaim "Et tu, Brute?" to point out a terrible betrayal by a friend. Latin is sometimes called a "dead language," since there is no longer a nation on earth where people speak it as their everyday tongue. But consider: If even in our own uncomfortably modern times, there are ideas and feelings that are perfectly expressed in no other way but Latin—"tempus fugit," for example, or "alma mater," or "Et tu, Brute?", to mention just a few—then surely Latin is not as dead as all that, and certainly a long way from extinct.)

On another page Penelope had made a list of the sayings of Cicero, whose knack for a catchy phrase was nothing short of Swanburnian. "There is no place more delightful than one's own fireplace," she read, and nodded in agreement, for the library had begun to get chilly now that afternoon was turning to dusk.

Otherwise, all she had were doodles. On the page that ought to have held her CAKE speech were a dozen little drawings of Edward Ashton, standing in a line. The transformation from the stocky, fair-haired Edward in the portrait that hung in Lord Fredrick's study to the lean, black-haired, putty-nosed, thickly bespectacled Quinzy was depicted step by step, with each subsequent drawing looking less like one and more like the other.

"As Cicero once said, 'The causes of events are ever

more interesting than the events themselves,'" Penelope mused. "Knowing that Edward Ashton is alive is interesting, but to discover *why* he would go to the trouble of faking his own death would be more interesting still. And to think that, all these years, Lord Fredrick has believed his father to be dead, when it turns out he never died at all!"

But then she stopped, for the shame and hurt brought on by Edward Ashton's remark about her family tree washed over her once more. His words stung because they were true. Penelope's family tree was scarcely more than a twig. There was Penelope herself, and the fading memory of two long-lost parents, and that was all. The bare and lonely fact of it made her feel like a solitary stalk of grass left waving forlornly in a field after the thresher had come and harvested all the rest for hay.

"But a library is no place for tears," she thought, wiping her nose on her sleeve (truly, the new dress was already looking rather worn), "not with so many books around that could easily be damaged by salt water. In any case, my time here is nearly up. I ought to scurry and choose a bedtime book for the children. Something soothing and familiar is in order, I think. . . . I shall have to work on my speech after they are asleep."

Out of habit she made a beeline to the favorite shelves from her girlhood, the ones where the pony stories were kept. As had often been the case in the past, the first volumes of the Giddy-Yap, Rainbow! books were already checked out. It was the later, more eccentric installments of the series that tended to gather dust on the library shelves: the one where Rainbow and Silky run away to join the French Foreign Legion, for example, or where Rainbow develops a taste for opera—

"If you are interested in the Giddy-Yap, Rainbow! books, I would recommend starting with the first one and reading them in order. Although, frankly, you might find them a bit young." The librarian appeared at her elbow. She was brisk and cheerful and not much older than Penelope, and she held a pocket watch in her hand. "Might I recommend something else? *Robinson Crusoe* is quite popular at present, if you don't mind reading about—"

"Cannibals, I know. Wait!" Penelope exclaimed, for the mere sight of a helpful librarian had caused a question to pop into her mind. "I understand the library has special archives. Could you tell me what they contain?"

The woman frowned. "You must mean our collection of the letters of Agatha Swanburne. There are thousands of them, for she was a faithful correspondent.

Luckily, her handwriting was superb."

Penelope froze. "Are you certain there are no other special archives?"

The librarian nodded.

That meant Edward Ashton had learned about the cannibal book by reading the letters of Agatha Swanburne. But how would Agatha Swanburne have known about such a book in the library at Ashton Place? What connection could there be between Agatha Swanburne and the Ashtons?

"Might I see these letters?" Penelope asked quickly. "I know the library is about to close, but it is important . . . if I might have five minutes . . ."

The librarian shrugged apologetically. "The Swanburne letters are kept locked in a safe. Even I cannot access them. Only qualified persons are permitted to request access, which is granted rarely, and only with proper permission." She looked Penelope up and down. "Are you a member of the faculty?"

"Not precisely," Penelope conceded. "But I am a professional governess. And I will be giving a speech tomorrow to the entire student body that promises to be highly educational"—although at this moment even Penelope could not say what information it might contain.

"Follow me, please." With one eye on her watch, the librarian marched back to her desk and began to search through the drawers. "I am not sure if that qualifies you or not. However, as Agatha Swanburne once said—"

"If one never tries, one never succeeds," Penelope interjected.

"Precisely. To request permission, there is a form to fill out. It is fairly simple, with only ten or twelve pages of questions, and it has to be signed by the proper authorities . . . ah, here it is."

Penelope took the pages from her. "I will have Miss Mortimer sign it at once."

The librarian shook her head. "Only the trustees can give permission. Four signatures are required: the chairman, plus three other board members."

Penelope crumpled the useless form behind her back. "I see. Thank you. You have been very helpful."

"Would you care to check out a book before you go? *Robinson Crusoe*, perhaps?" the librarian called after her. But Penelope did not answer. She was lost in thought about needles and haystacks, and all she heard was the quiet *click* of the library door closing behind her. It was the sound of one more piece of Edward Ashton's puzzle falling into place.

The Ninth Chapter

*A work of art reveals more
than it intends.*

PENELOPE HAD MADE IT HALFWAY to the faculty lounge
before realizing that she had forgotten to choose a
bedtime book for the Incorrigibles. She raced back
to the library, but it was too late. The librarian was
gone, the room was locked, and a sign on the door
read THE LIBRARY IS NOW CLOSED. WILL REOPEN AFTER
THE CAKE. HAPPY READING!

"Oh, the CAKE! Oh, my speech! Oh, blast!" she
cried aloud to the empty halls. In the whole sticky-
fingered, dessert-filled history of humankind, had

anyone ever dreaded anything called CAKE as much as Penelope did at that moment? The mere sight of the word made her teeth ache. No doubt it was a significant discovery that Quinzy was really Edward Ashton, and that his wish to gain access to the letters of Agatha Swanburne might be the very needle in the haystack that Miss Mortimer had voiced suspicions about—yet what use would any of that be the next evening when she had to stand in humiliation before the entire student body, faculty, and honored guests, with not one intelligent thing to say?

"Woe!" she thought, for woe is what she felt full of. "O, woe! What shall I do?" Ought she lie, and say some horrible fate had befallen her speech, thus rendering it unspeakable? Perhaps it had been lost in a comical mix-up involving two identical sheaves of paper, in which Penelope's notes were mistakenly swapped for, say, a collection of soup recipes. Or, perhaps, a dog ate it. Or, perhaps, the finished speech had been left unattended by an open window and was carried off, a page at time, by strangely aggressive birds.

But none of these excuses would do. For one thing, she had no soup recipes, only the recipe for Hungarian goulash that Cecily had sent her. Nor were there any badly behaved dogs at Swanburne. There were only the clever and well-trained ones kept by Dr. Westminster, and they were never allowed inside the school because of Shantaloo, who was no great fan of dogs, or really any sort of creature other than herself. (Those of you who are familiar with cats will have no trouble recognizing this type of personality.)

And even in her current desperate state of mind, Penelope had to admit—for a speech to be stolen by birds seemed highly unlikely. Some birds, such as parrots, are known to be good talkers, but to Penelope's knowledge there had never been a great orator among them. Whether a wing'd and feather'd Cicero might someday hatch from an egg was an intriguing question. But it did not matter, for in her heart, Penelope knew she could not and would not deceive Miss Mortimer.

She paused at the top of the stairs to catch her breath. "There is nothing to do but confess my lack of preparedness to Miss Mortimer," she thought. "I am heartbroken and ashamed to fail her on such an important occasion, but alas! Circumstances have conspired against me, just as they did on that long-ago day in the milk bath. . . ." Indeed, there had only been one time during all Penelope's student days in which she had been unable to complete an assignment, and the memory of it still made her itch. It was during her bout with the chicken pox, when she dropped her painstakingly researched art history paper into the milk bath while attempting to proofread it. Tearful, feverish, and scratching, she had to explain to her teacher why "Damp and Spooky: The Depiction of Grottos in Ominous Landscapes" would not be handed in on time.

Luckily, the teacher was sympathetic; she even tried to cheer Penelope by showing her how to write invisible messages using milk for ink. These messages could only be revealed by letting the milk dry and holding the paper over a candle flame, whose heat soon made the milk turn dark enough to read. Cecily had also been sick with chicken pox (unsurprisingly, since they still shared a cot at the time), and the two friends spent the rest of their illnesses writing secret messages to each other from their respective milk baths. It had been a most welcome distraction.

Thinking of those notes in invisible milk ink might have made Penelope smile had she not felt so pained about disappointing Miss Mortimer. "Still, she may be intrigued by what I have learned about Edward Ashton," she told herself, scraping together the last bits of optimism she had left, much the way children will lick the final drops of cake batter off the mixing spoon. "He must have believed that some information of great worth would be contained within Agatha Swanburne's letters. And it seems that with the discovery of the existence of the cannibal book, he has found what he was seeking—or thinks he has, anyway."

Her brow furrowed in concentration; anyone who knew her would recognize it as a sign that her powers of deduction were in use. "But what valuable secrets could lurk inside that strange diary, which is still hidden in the bottom of the armoire beneath my rolled-up stockings, where no one would ever think to look? I wish I could read it and find out, but the pages are so faded from sun and sea as to be indecipherable. If only Simon were here! More than ever, I long to know what his great-uncle Pudge said about that ill-fated voyage to Ahwoo-Ahwoo so many years ago."

The door to the faculty lounge was before her. "And to think I was invited back to demonstrate the accomplishments of a true Swanburne girl," she thought ruefully. "Instead I can only serve as an example of what a Swanburne girl should not be. I have broken my promise, disappointed my headmistress, failed my alma mater in her time of need. . . ." She pushed open the door.

"Friends, Romans, countrymen," Beowulf shouted from atop the faculty dining table. "Lend me your ears!"

Straight-faced, Alexander and Cassiopeia pretended to take off their ears and hand them over. All three Incorrigibles were costumed in the style of ancient Rome. Their Ghostly Postal sheets had been draped and knotted into togas, and there were wreaths of greenery circled 'round their heads. (In Roman times these wreaths would have been made of bay laurel leaves, but the resourceful children had fashioned theirs out of the same ivy that had overgrown the entrance to Swanburne.)

"Hail, Miss Lumley!" Mrs. Apple was likewise wrapped in a toga, although the Swanburne emblem embroidered in the corners of the fabric suggested use as a tablecloth in the recent past. "What imaginative pupils you have! Would you like a wreath? We made extra."

"No, thank you." Penelope looked around. "Where is Miss Mortimer?"

"After our tea and biscuits, we visited the art studio. The children left their paintings to dry. Miss Mortimer just went to gather them up. Meanwhile, our studies of ancient Rome have kept us busy." Mrs. Apple struck a pose in the manner of a Roman consul about to address the senate, much to the delight of the Incorrigibles. "Children, please proceed."

Mrs. Apple struck a pose in the manner of a Roman consul about to address the senate. . . .

Beowulf jumped off the table, and the three Incorrigibles arranged themselves in a row. Cassiopeia's wreath kept slipping over her eyes.

"In honor of the great orations of antiquity," Alexander intoned.

"And Lumawoo's speech," Cassiopeia added, pushing her errant wreath into position.

"And Mr. Gibbon's book, too." Beowulf held up the volume, although it was too weighty a work to keep in the air for very long.

"We have made three *tableaux vivant* of ancient Rome," Alexander finished. "First *tableau*: The Assassination of Julius Caesar."

The children sprang into position. Alexander played the part of Caesar, which was evident by the noble way he held one hand to his temple, as if his mind were filled with thoughts of empire. Moments later, his siblings snuck up behind him, bearing imaginary daggers. With many sharp cries they ran him through.

"Et tu, Beowulf?" he groaned as his brother pretended to stab him once more. Then he crumpled, his toga flapping dramatically on the way down.

After a moment of reverence for the fallen Caesar and a round of applause from Penelope and Mrs. Apple, the three children readied themselves for their next *tableau*. This time Beowulf announced the title. "Second *tableau*: The Roman Colosseum."

The Incorrigibles joined hands and formed a circle, as you might do to play ring around the rosy. In this way they meant to show the great open-air stadium in which the popular entertainments of Rome were held. These included high-speed chariot races, armed gladiators who fought to the death, and the feeding of unlucky people to hungry lions. Evidently, the Romans' idea of what constituted a good show involved a great many gruesome ends.

"Your Colosseum is colossal," Mrs. Apple said approvingly.

Now it was Cassiopeia's turn. Grandly, she proclaimed: "Third and last *tableau*: Fall of Rome!" Whereupon all three children collapsed to the ground, laughing uproariously at their own joke.

"Children, this is excellent work." Penelope glanced at the door. There was still no sign of Miss Mortimer.

Cassiopeia jumped to her feet and tugged at her governess's sleeve. "Your turn! Speech all done?"

"Speech all done! Speech all done!" the boys chanted, still in high spirits from their success with the *tableaux*. In fact, they could not help but reenact the Fall of Rome several more times, as it was great fun to keep collapsing and getting up again.

Penelope could barely make herself heard over the noise. "Well . . . not exactly . . . that is to say . . . when Miss Mortimer returns, I will explain. . . ."

And then, just as in one of those marvelous old stories in which you only have to say the magic words to make the genie in the lamp appear, no sooner had Penelope said "Miss Mortimer" than the kind headmistress herself swept into the room, the children's paintings balanced on her outstretched arms. "Good news, Incorrigibles," she called out gaily as she carefully put the artwork on the table. "Your watercolors are dry as a bone."

"Miss Mortimer!" Penelope said again, and not because she imagined she could make a second Miss Mortimer appear by repeating the name (although that would have been an unexpected plot twist, to be sure). Rather, it was because she feared if she waited even one second more to tell the truth about her speech, she might lose her courage altogether and start spouting nonsense about soup recipes, thieving birds, or worse. "Miss Mortimer, I have something important to tell you. In fact, I have a confession to make—"

But then she stopped, for behind Miss Mortimer stood Baroness Hoover, and behind the baroness was

Edward Ashton. His glasses were on, and a handkerchief was still tied 'round his face.

The baroness smirked. "I would like to hear this confession of yours, Miss Lumley. Do go on."

The children growled, which was extremely rude, as they well knew. Miss Mortimer smiled and patted their heads. "How adorable you three are! But alas, I have no actual bones to give you. When I say your paintings are dry as a bone, it is merely a figure of speech. Like mad as a hatter." She looked at Quinzy. "Or sober as a judge."

"Or mean as a baroness," Alexander suggested.

"Ugly as a baroness." Beowulf crossed his eyes and stuck out his tongue, until his expression was ugly indeed.

"Or smelly!" Cassiopeia wrinkled her nose in disgust. "Smelly as a—"

"I have not heard any of those before," Miss Mortimer interrupted brightly. "But new figures of speech are invented all the time. Shakespeare invented dozens. Ah, Penny dear, you have returned. Perfect timing! Much as I enjoy their company, I must give the children back to your care now. Judge Quinzy and the baroness have some urgent business to discuss with me." She turned to them with a tight smile. "Is it about the dinner menu for tomorrow? The kitchen has been asking, but with so many important guests coming, I simply cannot decide—"

"Lumawoo, look!" Like most children, Cassiopeia did not always find grown-up conversations interesting to listen to, and she was too eager to show off her painting to wait any longer. It was a large work, and she had to spread her arms wide to hold it. It featured a large black dot inside a circle, which sat inside another pair of circles, which were themselves nestled together like a pair of rings.

Mrs. Apple peered at the painting. "Let me guess. It looks like a dark pit, filled with some sticky substance . . . tar, perhaps?"

Cassiopeia shook her head. "Nope! Guess again."

"It is about the *files*," the baroness snarled, in response to Miss Mortimer. "The *student* files. Where are they?"

Miss Mortimer held a finger to her lips. "Not now, Baroness. We are in the presence of art."

"Yes, let the child explain herself, Baroness." It was Edward Ashton, but with his thick Judge Quinzy glasses on, his expression remained inscrutable. "Perhaps we will find her answer illuminating."

Cassiopeia pouted. "Is not a luminating. Is a sheep."

The baroness snorted. "How can that be a sheep? I see no wool. Have you any wool?"

"*Is* a sheep!" Cassiopeia insisted. "Sheepy sheepy sheepy!"

Nowadays, of course, people are accustomed to paintings of sheep that look nothing like actual sheep, but simply content themselves with being paintings, full of color and lines and interesting shapes. This type of art is called "modern," and it is well worth a look. But in Miss Penelope Lumley's day, modern art had not yet been invented, and a painting of a sheep was universally expected to show legs, wool, and a fluffy tail. Thus, like the work of so many visionary artists before her, Cassiopeia's painting was met only with awkward silence and puzzled looks, until someone's imagination took the necessary leap.

"Eureka!" Penelope said at last. "It is the eye of a faraway sheep as seen through the telescope in the Swanburne observatory. How clever you are, Cassiopeia! I am quite sure no one has ever thought to draw a sheep in quite that way." Of course, once Penelope explained the painting, everyone could see how good it was, and the little girl beamed to have her art understood and appreciated.

Alexander showed his work next. He too had found

inspiration in the observatory, and had painted an aerial map of the grounds of Swanburne, showing the school buildings nestled among the fields and farmhouses, and edged by the trees that ringed the valley.

"Swanburne Academy, bird's-eye view," he said modestly. Like his sister, he also received praise from his governess, Mrs. Apple, and Miss Mortimer, while the baroness frowned with impatience and Edward Ashton watched in silence.

Next and last was Beowulf. His painting was even larger than the others, painted with swirling brushstrokes in colors so vivid they seemed to leap off the paper. In the foreground was a sandy beach; in the back, palm trees rose like green leafy spires, vibrant against an azure sky. On the beach, people ran in a circle. Some of them held clubs. Some had mouths open, as if singing, or howling, or perhaps screaming. Others rubbed their tummies, signaling hunger.

"That is disgusting," declared the baroness. "What is it?"

"I call it *Sunday Afternoon on the Island of Ahwoo-Ahwoo.* I got the idea from Lumawoo's cannibal book," Beowulf explained.

"Ahwoo, ahwoo," his siblings helpfully repeated.

Ahwoo-Ahwoo? All at once, Penelope felt as if she

were on some ill-fated sea voyage, with a sea-washed deck lurching beneath her feet. She leaned on the table to steady herself.

Edward Ashton took a threatening step toward her. "As I suspected! Miss Lumley, you are a liar, and here is proof."

"Judge Quinzy, I object!" Miss Mortimer blocked his way. "There will be no name-calling at Swanburne, not even from the trustees."

He slithered past her and moved 'round Penelope like a tiger circling its prey. "Do not be so quick to defend your star pupil. The cannibal book that the boy refers to belongs to Lord Fredrick Ashton. He gave Miss Lumley a direct order to deliver the book to me. She did not obey."

Miss Mortimer turned. "Is that so, Penny?"

Penelope swallowed and stared at her shoes. "I thought the book was lost," she mumbled.

"Yet clearly it is not." Ashton stood quite close to Penelope now, but his voice filled the room. "Luma-woo's cannibal book, indeed! You heard the boy. The book is in her possession, yet she denied it to my very face, not an hour ago."

At this, the children began to whimper and growl. Miss Mortimer held up a hand for silence. "Penelope, why have you not handed over the book, as your employer instructed?"

Penelope lifted her gaze from the floor. "Because Lord Fredrick told me to give it to Judge Quinzy, and no one else."

"And am I not Judge Quinzy?" he asked coolly.

"No, sir." She looked him in the eye. "I am quite sure you are not."

The baroness shrieked with laughter. "Poppycock! The child is mad."

Quinzy paled. "Give me the book, Miss Lumley, or I shall personally see to it that you lose your job, and these three pupils of yours will be scattered to the workhouses and orphanages, never to be seen by you, or one another, again."

The children exchanged meaningful glances. After a tense silence, Alexander spoke. "No job losing necessary, please, Your Honorness. We have it here."

Shyly, Beowulf withdrew the cannibal book from the folds of his toga and handed it to Penelope.

"We found it by following the scent of the sea," Alexander explained. "It was in the arm . . . the arm . . ."

But none of the children could remember how to say "armoire," and they finally just shrugged and patted their arms in explanation.

"These wolf children are idiots." The baroness threw up her hands. "Why anyone would waste an education on them is beyond me."

"Give me the book, Miss Lumley." Ashton stood very still, but his hands flexed by his sides, as if it was only an enormous effort that prevented him from snatching the book from her by force.

"No!" Stubbornly, Penelope clutched the diary to her chest. "*You* are the one who is lying to Lord Fredrick, and to everyone else, for that matter. Whatever your reason is for wanting this book, I know it can only be a wicked one."

"I might say the same to you." His voice dropped low. "A book that cannot even be read—is that truly worth losing your position over? Are those indecipherable pages more important than the good of your three pupils? Ask yourself, Miss Lumley: What sort of governess are you?"

They stared at each other for a long moment. Penelope's eyes were the first to drop.

"I shall take that book now, if you please." Ashton held out his hand.

As if she were seeing herself from some strange bird's-eye view high above, Penelope watched herself give Edward Ashton the cannibal book.

The baroness clucked her tongue in mock sympathy. "Poor girl. I think you have put her under too much pressure, Mortimer. She's cracking under the strain."

Edward Ashton turned to Miss Mortimer. "The baroness is right. I suggest you find someone of a more honest character to address the school tomorrow. Miss Lumley hardly seems worthy of the honor."

Miss Mortimer looked from one stern face to the other before turning to Penelope. "You are here at my invitation, Penelope. Would you like to give your speech, or not? The choice is yours."

Her speech! Penelope felt trapped. It was as if all the pluck and hope and optimism in the world had just gurgled down the bathtub drain, and there was nothing left anywhere but gloom.

"It would be best if someone else spoke in my place," she said dully.

Miss Mortimer looked at her for a long moment but said no more.

"Ahwoo-Ahwoo," Ashton crooned, a soft howl of victory. His long, pale fingers wrapped themselves around the cover of the book. "Ahwoo-Ahwoo!"

MOMENTS AFTER ASHTON AND THE baroness left, Penelope became woozy. The room swayed, and her eyelids began to flutter.

Cassiopeia was the first to notice. "Fall of Rome!" she yelled, and flung her arms open to catch the wobbly young governess. The children intercepted her on the way down, but she could not get her balance and sank to the carpet in a daze. Smelling salts were called for and cold compresses applied. When she regained her senses, she could only sit there in a crumpled heap, weeping.

Mrs. Apple ran to get a fresh platter of biscuits and milk, while Miss Mortimer sat on the carpet next to Penelope and stroked her hair. "There, there, my dear. Take deep breaths! Mrs. Apple will speak at the CAKE tomorrow and manage perfectly well; she is quite skilled at giving long talks on short notice. And I can write a note of explanation to Lord Fredrick Ashton. I am sure it was all an innocent mistake."

Penelope shook her head. "But he has the book!" was all she could manage to say.

Puzzled, Miss Mortimer looked at the Incorrigibles. "But the pages were blank, or at least unreadable, were they not? Even the children said that the only part of the book that could be clearly made out was the title."

"Yes . . . that is true," she said between sniffs. She thought of Simon, and how sad she would be to tell him she had lost what was very likely his great-uncle Pudge's diary (although no doubt he would appreciate the unexpected plot twist of the book being seized by someone whom everyone believed was dead). "I know it is foolish to carry on so. I only wish . . ." But she could not finish, for she did not know what she wished anymore.

"Have a biscuit, Lumawoo." Cassiopeia gave her the biggest one on the tray, her eyes wide with sympathy.

"And some milk." Alexander handed her a glass.

"Thank you," she said, grateful for their kindness. She would have preferred tea, personally, but milk and a biscuit did offer some comfort. She took a sip of the cool, creamy beverage—and promptly spit it out all over her new dress.

"Milk!" she cried. "Oh, no!"

"Is it sour?" Mrs. Apple grabbed the glass and sniffed. "Smells all right to me."

"No . . . the book! The book!" she moaned, freshly upset. Could it be? But it made perfect sense. Oh, why had she never thought to hold the pages over a candle?

The children kept tugging at her dress, asking what was the matter.

"The pages of the diary are not blank," she finally said in despair. "I am quite sure they are not . . . and he must have known all along. . . . Oh, never mind. It is too late now."

They offered her more biscuits and milk, but the sight of the milk only upset her, and she could not bring herself to tell them why. More cold compresses were delivered, and a hot-water bottle, and a headache lozenge. But Penelope could not be comforted.

The Incorrigibles felt confused, and responsible, too, for although they did not know all the disturbing details, they quickly deduced that if they had not found the cannibal book in the first place, their beloved Lumawoo would not be so sad. Beowulf in particular was wracked with guilt, for it had been his marvelous painting of the scene at Ahwoo-Ahwoo that seemed to have let the cannibal book out of the armoire, so to speak.

It was when she saw the poor boy gnawing his own lip in an effort not to cry that Penelope finally shook off her tears and composed a brave face, at least long enough to reassure him he had done nothing wrong.

"And your painting is wonderful," she said, squeezing both his hands in hers. "Why, it is as if you yourself have sailed the seas and seen these distant places, just as a brave explorer would. When Simon Harley-Dickinson returns from his adventures, we shall have to show it to him straightaway. I know he will be impressed."

"When is Simawoo coming?" Cassiopeia asked eagerly, for the children liked Simon a great deal. But the question only made Penelope's heart ache all over again, for who knew when Simon might turn up, or where? Not her, certainly.

Miss Mortimer remained silent during this exchange, but when the dinner bell sounded she spoke. "Penny dear, it is getting late, and tomorrow is the—well, tomorrow will be a long day for everyone. I can see you are done in. Let me send the children to supper with Mrs. Apple so that you can rest and recover."

The history teacher stood. She was still dressed in a toga, but it seemed to suit her. "I will personally see to it that the Incorrigible children are fed, bathed, and put to bed properly, with a bedtime story read-aloud and a cozy tucking in. Veni, vidi, vici!" (As the Latin scholars among you may know, "Veni, vidi, vici" is another phrase that was first spoken by Julius Caesar. It means "I came, I saw, I conquered," and Caesar meant it as a pithy description of a battle, which, in a nutshell, he won. Perhaps Mrs. Apple spoke too soon in declaring victory over the Incorrigibles, but anyone who has successfully managed to put three energetic children to bed after a stimulating day would agree that it is nothing short of a triumph, and well worth bragging about.)

Penelope did not argue. "Thank you," she said.

"Perhaps you ought to go to bed as well," Miss Mortimer gently suggested. "I can find a private guest room for you to stay in tonight, if you wish to be undisturbed this evening."

"No, thank you; that will not be necessary," she replied quickly. She would not want the children to feel she was abandoning them, and she doubted she would sleep that night anyway. "I shall take a walk outside to clear my head, and then join the children and Mrs. Apple upstairs when I return."

A walk out of doors is nearly always a good idea, of course, and Miss Mortimer made no objection. A borrowed cloak from the teacher's cloakroom was quickly found for Penelope's use. Impulsively, she gathered the children together for a hug. "Enjoy your supper, Incorrigibles," she said, smoothing each auburn-haired head in turn. "I will see you later, after my walk."

"Where will you walk?" Alexander asked, clearly anxious. "Maybe you should take my map. Bird's-eye view!"

He rolled up his map painting and offered it to her

with a solemn face. She took it, but she had already decided where she would walk and she did not want the children to know, as they would doubtless want to come with her.

"I promise I will not get lost, as I have walked these grounds a thousand times. I will bring the map with me, just in case. Thank you, Alexander. Good night, children." With that, Penelope slipped out the door.

The Tenth Chapter

Penelope learns the value of a
bird's-eye view.

PENELOPE KEPT THE CLOAK WRAPPED close 'round her
and the hood drawn over her head, for she had no
wish to converse with anyone who might see her on
the path. There was already a voice keeping her company as she walked, and a gravelly, enigmatic voice it
was. It lodged in her brain and would not leave, like
the catchy tune of a beloved school song.

". . . And if anything goes amiss, remember . . . you
can always bring 'em to the vet. . . . Sure, if there's any
trouble, young Westminster'll sort things out. . . ."

Old Timothy was a coachman and not a sooth-sayer, of course. But something *had* gone amiss, just as he had warned, and now there was trouble indeed. Edward Ashton had the cannibal book, and the very depths of his desire for it made her surer than ever that it must be central to some dark purpose of his. Had he already known it was written in invisible ink? Was that mentioned in Agatha Swanburne's letters as well? And what connection could there possibly be between the Ashtons and the wise old founder of Penelope's alma mater?

It was a tangled maze of mysteries, and Penelope could not seem to find her way out. In such a pickle, Old Timothy's inscrutable advice was better than none, so in search of Dr. Westminster she went. From the kind Swanburne veterinarian she had learned everything she knew about how to soothe frightened animals. His low, cooing voice, slow movements, and gentle demeanor might be just what she needed to help ease her own troubled heart.

She owed him a visit in any case, if only to tell him how well his training techniques had worked on all sorts of unexpected creatures: a runaway ostrich, for example, or a sweet-natured if none too intelligent squirrel, or even three bright and curious children who had had a rather . . . *unusual* upbringing. . . .

"Yet it is strange that Old Timothy mentioned him at all," she thought as her feet crunched along the graveled path. "And why did he call him 'young Westminster'?" To Penelope, Dr. Westminster had always seemed neither old nor young, but permanently middle-aged. (Of course, children easily lump anyone over the age of seventeen or so into the category of "grown-up," with a second category of "old person" reserved for the truly wizened and silver haired. But to grown-ups themselves, the difference between being, say, thirty-two and fifty-six is immense. This has nothing to do with the tricky sevens and eights of the multiplication tables, and all to do with how *tempus* seems to *fugit* ever more swiftly the older one grows, a truth you will doubtless someday learn firsthand.)

She knew all his usual haunts in the barns and fields, but Dr. Westminster's office was in the chicken coop, and that is where she went first. It was no ordinary coop, mind you, for the clever doctor had designed and built it himself. From the outside, it looked like a gingerbread cottage from a storybook, much to the delight of the littlest Swanburne girls. Inside were rows of nesting boxes in which the chickens laid their eggs, and an incubator room with its own woodstove, so the room could be kept warm for baby chicks. Dr. Westminster's book-lined office was in the back, with extra windows for ventilation (for even the cleanest and most well-run chicken coop is bound to smell rather strongly of chicken).

Dr. Westminster was in the middle of a training exercise. The chickens were out of their nesting boxes, lined up in a row. They regarded him with blinking, none-too-intelligent stares.

"All right, my chicks, let's try it again. Right foot, in!"

He demonstrated, stepping forward on the right. The chickens, after a moment of ruffled-feather confusion, did the same.

"Right foot, out!" This time they snapped back into position as a unit.

He clucked approvingly. "Well done, clever hens. Now turn, and shimmy, and shake your tails. Shake 'em all about!"

Dr. Westminster flapped his bent arms like wings, whirled in a circle, and wiggled his bottom as if it were a tail. The chickens followed suit, *buck-buck-buck*ing all the way.

"Perfect, perfect." He dug into his trouser pockets and came out with fistfuls of grain, which he scattered on the ground. The eager chickens broke formation and pecked hungrily at their well-earned treat.

Penelope had watched from the doorway, unwilling to disturb this remarkable scene. Now she applauded with vigor. "Dr. Westminster, you never cease to amaze me!" she exclaimed, and stepped inside, lifting her cloak high off the ground so as not to sweep the grain away from the birds.

"Dr. Lumley, is that you?" The dear man had always teasingly referred to her as Dr. Lumley, ever since she was a tiny girl and had volunteered to assist him in his work, with her serious face, little piping voice, and knack for taming wild things. After that, she spent every moment that was not dedicated to her schoolwork helping him care for the animals of Swanburne, and the neighboring farms of Heathcote, too. "Allow me to present my colleague, Dr. Lumley," he would announce to a lame horse or a colicky calf. "Between the two of us, we'll have you fit as a fiddle in no time."

In spite of her worries she smiled. "Yes, your partner in medicine has returned. But I am a governess these days, and no longer a doctor—at least, not a practicing one."

He reached out to clasp her in a fond hug. "Well,

well," he said, and seemed too choked up to say more.

Penelope too had a full heart, and the two of them stood there for a moment. "I see you are training the chickens," she said at last.

Dr. Westminster grinned. "Most people think chickens are simpleminded, but a bit of patient instruction goes a long way, as you well know. This group can perform three different synchronized dance routines in contrasting rhythmic patterns. Let me show you."

Following his cues, which included subtle hand gestures and some *buck-buck-buck*ing in pitches high and low, the chickens stepped and bobbed their heads in rhythm. First they scratched out a *ONE-two-three, ONE-two-three* beat, as one might do when waltzing. Then they pecked a polka. As a finale, they formed two lines and performed a simple reel. It lacked the energetic skipping and twirling one would find in, say, a schottische, but the birds managed to switch partners and hold their positions as each couple waddled its way to the end of the line.

(To put the chickens' achievement in context, consider that in the whole entire history of the Imperial Russian Ballet, not once has even the greatest prima ballerina ever succeeded in laying a single egg. It is not for lack of trying, either. When a dancer attempts to lay an egg, it is called a *grand plié*. When a chicken attempts to dance, it is simply called a dancing chicken. As Agatha Swanburne once remarked, "Some things just sound better in French.")

"These dancing chickens are remarkable," Penelope said, for she knew from personal experience how challenging it was to learn complicated dance steps. "With their well-developed sense of rhythm, these birds could easily learn poetic meter. In time, perhaps you might teach them to scratch out a sonnet."

"Chickens with a knack for iambic pentameter? Dr. Lumley, I think you're on to something. *Ba-BUCK, ba-BUCK, ba-BUCK, ba-BUCK, ba-BUCK!*" Dr. Westminster's expression altered to one of deep concentration. One eye opened a bit more than was usual, and the other closed halfway; he cocked his head to the side and tugged fiercely at his chin.

It was a peculiar expression, yet one that Penelope found familiar. Impulsively, she said, "Dr. Westminster, there is a fellow at Ashton Place who serves as head coachman. He goes by the name of Old Timothy. I believe he may be an acquaintance of yours?"

Dr. Westminster's eyes darted this way and that. "If he's a coachman, perhaps I've tended to his horses at one time or another," he said uneasily.

Penelope's curiosity made her press on. "He mentioned you by name, just before I left for Swanburne. He called you 'young Westminster.' But he did not say how he knew you."

"Didn't say how, eh?" Dr. Westminster cocked his head to the other side; the opened eye narrowed, and the closed one opened wide. "Since he didn't say, I'd guess he'd prefer to keep it private. I'll respect that decision for now, if you don't mind."

"Well! That is an enigmatic reply," Penelope said, hoping to draw him out further.

Dr. Westminster reached into his pockets and busied himself scattering feed on the ground. "There are questions with no answers, and answers with no questions," he muttered. "And yet sometimes the truth of a thing is as plain as the nose on your face. Or the hair on your head." He stopped, and looked at her meaningfully. "Dr. Lumley, what do your friends call you?"

Puzzled, she answered, "Penny. Short for Penelope."

"Mine call me Timmy. Short for Timothy." He tossed the last of the feed on the ground. "The nickname was given to me as a boy, so people wouldn't get me mixed up with my father."

Penelope's thoughts raced like a thoroughbred at

the Epsom Derby. "So, the enigmatic coachman at Ashton Place is Old Timothy. And Dr. Westminster is also named Timothy, but nicknamed Timmy, to distinguish him from his father, whose name, therefore, must also be—"

"Eureka! Young Westminster!" she cried, understanding. "Old Timothy and Young Timmy! Why, the two of you are father and—"

Buck-buck-buck!

Buck-buck-buck!

All at once, in a blizzard of flying feathers and tasty, furiously beating wings, the chickens rose into the air. This took enormous effort, for although chickens are not, technically speaking, flightless birds, like ostriches or dodos, nor are they known for their ability to easily "lift off," as we say nowadays. But they did somehow all end up in the rafters.

"Sorry about that," said Dr. Westminster, blank faced. "I seem to have accidentally given the 'chickens, up!' command." He crooked his pinkie finger to demonstrate. "They like a bird's-eye view, you know. Gives them a fresh perspective on things."

Penelope's heart took a minute to slow. "I did not even know chickens could fly," she gasped.

"It takes practice and determination. No complaining

and no quitting." He covered his mouth with a hand and whispered, "I'd say it takes pluck, but they hate that word."

DR. WESTMINSTER WOULD NOT SAY any more about Old Timothy, and soon they bid each other farewell. It had been a pleasant visit, but this chicken coop (like most others) was a strong-smelling place, and Penelope was grateful to get back into the fresh air.

Once outside, she huddled in her borrowed cloak and stamped her feet against the chill, first the right foot, then the left. Then she laughed. "I am doing the same step as the chickens," she thought. "What remarkable birds! There they were, dancing and flying, though few would expect that a chicken could do either. Most people underestimate chickens, it seems. It reminds me of something Agatha Swanburne once said: 'Never underestimate a Swanburne girl, for a Swanburne girl never underestimates herself.'"

She stopped and let her gaze sweep across the field to the buildings beyond, and then up again to where the observatory tower rose above the school, tall and slender, like a fountain pen poised to write across the sky.

"Yes, indeed," she thought. "I imagine Edward

225

Ashton thinks I have quite given up." Then she broke into a run.

No one saw the cloaked figure make her way through a little-used side entrance to the main building and then up the twisted stairs to the observatory. Here Penelope was quite alone, like a maiden in a tower from some fairy tale of old. It was silent, too, except for the wind that whistled all around.

She gazed out the narrow windows. She did not know what she was looking for, exactly, but if a bird's-eye view could lend a fresh perspective to a chicken, imagine what it might do for an educated young lady with a decent grasp of geography! Still, she did not have much time. The setting sun balanced on the rim of the valley in a fiery red blaze. Soon all would be plunged into shadow.

"Never underestimate a Swanburne girl," she repeated uncertainly, "for a Swanburne girl never underestimates herself." Already her faith wavered. To think that some creaky old saying, too long even to stitch onto a pillow, had the power to solve her problems! Even at sixteen, was she nothing more than a child still, believing in the power of magic words?

"Yet some words do matter a great deal—like the

unreadable words in the cannibal book." She paced in a circle inside the tower, to keep herself warm and help her think. "The book must say something terribly important, or else Edward Ashton would not want it so badly. But what? If only I had thought of the invisible milk ink earlier, when I had the book in my own two hands!"

Despair lapped against her heart like a tide rising against a bulkhead. "Perhaps if I gaze through the telescope, things will come into focus," she thought, and put her eye to the eyepiece. But the sun had already dipped below the horizon. In the valley, night fell all at once. The rosy glow faded before her eyes, and soon it was too dark to see anything but shadows.

She let the telescope go and sank to the floor. A deep fatigue washed over her. "Tonight could well be the last night of the Swanburne Academy for Poor Bright Females," she thought, curling into a ball. "Tomorrow my alma mater will become the School for Miserable Girls, and there will be no singing of the school song, ever again. I expect Baroness Hoover will make a rule against dancing chickens, once she discovers that they exist. Edward Ashton is up to no good, and I have failed to stop him. . . . It is all . . . my . . . fault. . . ."

Exhausted by self-pity, and swaddled tightly in her

227

cloak like an infant, Penelope fell into a deep, dreamless sleep. By the time she awoke it was night. Was it ten o'clock? Midnight? Two in the morning? She had no way of knowing.

Certainly, the Incorrigible children had long since been put to bed. She knew she ought to return to their room at once and relieve poor Mrs. Apple of the children's care. Instead she stood, shivering, and peered out the narrow windows of the observatory. Now she could see quite easily, for the moon was only one night shy of full, and the sky was crisp and clear, an expanse of black velvet pinpricked by stars. It was nothing short of magical, and restored her spirits even more than sleep could.

"Here is a fresh perspective, indeed," she whispered to the night. Once more she looked through the telescope. "What a remarkable device this is! A long tube, some simple glass lenses, and a basic understanding of optics, and voilà: faraway things come impossibly near, and without the inconvenience of a long train ride, either."

She swiveled the telescope this way and that. "I wonder what has become of Cassiopeia's sheep. No doubt it is out there somewhere, chewing away. It must have a marvelously strong jaw, stronger even than

Demosthenes! That sheep would make a fine orator, if it had anything of interest to say, that is." She heaved a deep sigh of understanding. "For memorizing all the great speeches of history is of little value if one cannot find words to speak the truth of one's own heart."

Hindsight, indeed! Why was it all so obvious, now that it was too late? Clearly, the bird's-eye view was having its desired effect. "It is too bad, really, the way things have turned out. Now I feel I could have given quite a wonderful speech in praise of Swanburne, and without much preparation at all, for I know the subject well, and it is quite dear to me, too. My, my! It is not easy to wipe away tears of regret while one's eye is pressed to a telescope!" she thought as she attempted to do just that with the edge of her sleeve.

She swiveled the telescope elsewhere; anywhere would do. She surveyed the empty fields and tried to peek into the shadowy folds of the forest. She looked at the craters of the moon and watched falling stars streak through the skies.

She tried to get a glimpse of the chickens—were they still in the rafters, or had they returned to their roosts for the night?—but the windows of the chicken coop were at the wrong angle to catch the moonlight. Instead she peeked into a large, high window on the near side of the cow barn. There, with a few quick turns of the focus knob, she was able to bring the tender, moonlit eye of a calf into close-up view.

"What a fine chocolaty-brown eye that is," she said aloud, though there was no one there to hear her. "And so intelligent looking, for a cow. It sparkles with the promise of wit, and at the same time seems to shine with a steadfast, loyal glow. Why, that eye positively gleams; there is no other word for it. One might nearly call it a gleam of genius— Wait!"

Frantically, she adjusted the knob once more, to get a broader view. There it was: the delicately arched eyebrow, the waves of brown hair cascading poetically over that intelligent forehead. . . . No doubt he was busy thinking up plot twists even now. . . .

"That is no cow!" she cried. "It is Simon! Simon Harley-Dickinson!"

HE COULD NOT HEAR HER, but "Simon!" she yelled nevertheless. She raced down the stairs and through empty halls until she was outside once more. Her cloak billowed after her like a wind-filled sail.

The earth was muddy with dew, the stone paths slippery and wet. Still she ran, and did not pause until she reached the barn. She undid the rough iron latch with trembling fingers. With her full strength, she pushed the doors open.

"*Moooooo,*" the startled cows objected, for it was much too early for milking.

"Simon, where are you?" she called. Then she realized: he must be in the hayloft! For that was the only high window through which her telescope could have spied. She made her way past the sleepy cows and shed her cloak at the base of the ladder so she might scurry up without getting tangled.

A moment later she peeked over the top of ladder. The loft was empty! Had she dreamed it? But no; among the tied bales nearest the window, there was one particular pile of hay that seemed to be breathing. A lock of wavy hair poked through.

She stepped off the ladder and into the loft. "I may be searching for a playwright in a haystack, but I think I have found him, nevertheless. Simon! Simon Harley-Dickinson!"

Her words were met with a poetic snore.

"Simon!" She pushed the hay aside until a boot-clad human foot emerged. "You were only just awake. I saw you looking out at the stars."

"Harr!" he moaned, dreaming. "Avast, ye hearties! Who's there? Have we been boarded?"

She kicked the bottom of his boot to rouse him. "You are not at sea, but on dry land, or dry hay, at least. Improbable as it may be, you are in the hayloft of the cow barn at the Swanburne Academy for Poor Bright Females."

He turned over and grunted. "Females! Careful, they're bad luck aboard ship."

Penelope rolled her eyes. "Nonsense; that is mere superstition. There have been many competent lady sailors, and even notorious lady pirates. Not that being a pirate is anything to brag about."

Simon flipped onto his back. "I was dreaming I was in the crow's nest . . . my turn as lookout," he mumbled. "Thought I saw an enemy ship in the moonlight, a glint of light off the starboard bow. . . ." He sat up abruptly and gave his head a shake, like a dog coming in from the rain. Then he spat a piece of hay out of his mouth and looked around. "Penelope!" he exclaimed, awake at last. "I mean, Miss Lumley! I mean— Well! This is unexpected, to say the least."

"I am rather surprised to find you here as well," she replied. That it was a happy surprise to them both was clear enough by the looks on their faces, and did not need saying.

Simon rubbed his head. "You're just the person I

came to see, but it seems you found me first. Have you acquired skills of prognostication, like our friend Madame Ionesco?"

"I did make use of a telescope," she confessed. "And how did you know to find me at Swanburne? Surely there was a crystal ball involved."

He smiled. "Sure, there was. One named Old Timothy."

Old Timothy, again! But there was no time to wonder about that now, for her mind flooded with questions. "Simon, I am eager to hear of your adventures, but first I must ask: Did you ever make it to Brighton to see Great-Uncle Pudge? And, if you did, was he really the cabin boy who wrote the diary of that doomed voyage to Ahwoo-Ahwoo? And, if he was, did you find out what happened on the island? For I have reason to think something did happen there—something terribly important—"

His face darkened. "I did, and he was, and I've got plenty to say about the rest, never you fear. But perhaps it's best if I start at the beginning and tell you all that's happened since last we saw each other."

Simon arranged some hay bales in the shape of a seat for her and tucked loose hay all around her legs, too, so that she might sit near him and listen in warmth and comfort. He spoke quietly, for he did not want to disturb the cows. Even so, Penelope could only marvel at his incredible tale, which started shortly after she had last seen him, when the two friends parted at the Ashton train station. . . .

"I could tell you about the trip to Brighton, and all the interesting people I met on the train, and what the weather was like, and what we had for lunch," he began, "but the gist of it is that I got to Brighton on schedule and made my way to the old sailor's home where Great-Uncle Pudge is spending his golden years. The Home for Ancient Mariners, it's called. Not a bad place, really. The residents are always swabbing the floors and keeping things shipshape out of habit, so it's clean as a whistle. On Sundays they serve hardtack and moldy potatoes for dinner, as a bit of a treat."

Penelope made a face, and he explained, "It reminds the fellows of their days aboard ship. Anyway, old Pudge was glad to see me, and we passed the time as we usually do: him teaching me to sing old sea chanteys, me emptying his rum bottles into the drain. After lunch I suggested a stroll on the boardwalk. That's where I planned to ask him about the diary."

"Yes, the diary!" Penelope could barely contain herself. "Did you find out what it says?"

"I'm getting to that part. Well, the boardwalk at Brighton goes on for miles. I pushed Uncle Pudge in a wheeled invalid chair, as it'd be much too far for him to walk, his legs being just as old as the rest of him. Along the way I broach the subject. 'Pudge,' I said—I call him Pudge, and he calls me Pip, ever since I was a pipsqueak—'Pudge, when you were just a boy-o, and first aboard ship, did you ever land on a place called Ahwoo-Ahwoo?'

"Oh, you should have seen his face! 'I did, Pip, I did!' he answers, turning pale as a ghost. 'I rue the day I set foot on that curséd isle!' Then he starts to tell me the tale. But just as we reach the end of the boardwalk, we were accosted! A gang of salty hooligans jumped us from behind. Miss Lumley—I mean, Penelope—you'll never guess. I was kidnapped by pirates!"

"Pirates! Oh, no!" she cried, for truly, she could think of nothing worse, plus it interrupted the part about the cannibal book, which she was desperate to hear. "How dreadful it must have been!"

He shrugged. "It was a bit rough in the beginning. There was talk of ransom, until I explained that I was a playwright. Even a bunch of pirates knew the life of a

235

"Penelope—you'll never guess. I was kidnapped by pirates!"

bard is scarcely worth the cost of a half-price ticket to a children's matinee. But then a storm kicked up, and we were blown off course. We were lost at sea!'"

By now Penelope was perched on the edge of her hay bale. What a storyteller he was! Although she did wish he would get back to the cannibal book soon. "Please, go on," she begged.

"Well, not to boast, but we Harley-Dickinsons have a knack for navigation. But I was locked in the brig! Night and day I told them, 'Let me out, and I'll steer us safe to shore.' They thought my offer was a trick. The days passed. We grew short of food, then drink. At last they had no choice. They let me out on one condition: that I be sworn into the crew by taking the pirates' oath, which is as solemn and unbreakable as an oath can be."

"You mean you became a pirate?" she said, astonished.

"I did." He looked bashful. "I sent you a message in a bottle every day, until we ran out of bottles. You didn't get them, by any chance?"

She shook her head. "I am afraid we are rather landlocked at Ashton Place."

"Huh. Didn't think of that." He frowned. "You must have been worried, not hearing from me for so long. You must have thought I'd forgotten you. Did you?"

"No," she said firmly, realizing it was true. "I never truly believed that. Not deep down." Now it was her turn to feel bashful, and she tried to steer him back to his tale. "Imagine, you being a pirate! I hope they did not force you to be too . . . piratical. Although it would hardly be your fault if they did."

"You know the old saying: 'When in Rome, do as the Romans do.' But a man has to have his principles. I learned more than I'd care to know about being a knave and a rascal and committing roguery of all sorts, but minding our longitude and latitude was enough to keep me busy. Still, what plots I have now! I could write a hundred pirate stories without breaking a sweat. Don't worry, I'll finish telling this one first." He grinned. "After what seemed like an eternity at sea, we sighted a fishing boat bound for Manchester. The *Wise Flounder* was its name. I took the chance to escape. Oath or no oath, I had a previous engagement on land that I fully intended to keep."

"With whom?"

"Why, with you! I set a course as the crow flies to Ashton Place. When I arrived, I discovered that you and the children had left the day before to visit your alma mater. I was penniless, mind you—I'd left my share of pirate treasure behind when I jumped ship;

it seemed only fair. But that curious old coachman, Timothy, gave me cash for a train ticket out of his own pocket, and said to come straight to Swanburne and no delays. 'But, Old Tim,' I said, 'what sort of welcome do you think I'll get at a girls' school?' 'Never mind,' he said. 'When you arrive, go see the vet. Tell him I sent you. He'll know what to do.'

"Well, I got in late, well after dark, and found Dr. Westminster in the chicken coop, just as Timothy said I would. The good doctor settled me in the hayloft for the night. He said I was just in time for cake, too. You don't happen to have any, do you? I'm a bit peckish, to be honest."

"'The CAKE is not until tomorrow—or, later today, if it is past midnight, which I imagine it must be." Penelope was ready to jump out of her skin. "Simon, I hate to rush you, for your mastery of suspense is beyond compare. But if you could please, please, tell me: *What does the cannibal book say?* I have reason to think that your great-uncle Pudge's diary is far more important than any of us realized."

"You're right about that. Do you have it with you?"

She blanched. "I did have it! But Edward Ashton took it."

"You mean Fredrick Ashton, don't you?"

"No, I mean Edward. Dead Edward. The one whom everyone thinks drowned in a tar pit. The one who has changed his appearance and now goes by the name of Judge Quinzy."

"So Quinzy's dead Edward, eh? Just as Madame Ionesco foretold." He stroked his chin thoughtfully. "Well, here's what I learned from old Pudge, before we were so rudely interrupted by pirates. Pudge *did* write that diary. He says it tells the tale of everything that happened. The storm at sea, the shipwreck on Ahwoo-Ahwoo, and much more. It's all in there."

She gave a shiver of horror. "It must have been awful. Cannibals!"

"He said they spent the first night on the island sitting around a campfire on the beach, in the light of the full moon, singing old sea chanteys with the admiral. The admiral had a tuneful voice, apparently. Pudge tried to teach me one of the songs. It was too complicated for me! Lots of rhyming words and harmony parts."

Penelope was so anxious to hear what happened next that her voice was reduced to a squeak. "And—but—so—what then?"

Simon shrugged. "He wouldn't tell. It's all in the book, he said. 'Read it for yourself, Simon, lad!' Bit of a joker, that Pudge."

Penelope thought she might scream with frustration. "But why could he not simply tell you the story?"

"He said he's sworn to secrecy. The only person he'll talk to about it is Admiral Ashton himself. That's who made him swear."

"But the admiral is long dead."

Simon nodded. "I told you, his brain's a bit addled. At least it's all in the diary. Except there's one problem . . . well, two problems, I suppose. First, you don't have the book anymore. Second—"

"It is written in invisible ink!" she blurted.

Simon whistled admiringly. "Your cleverness never fails to amaze! How on earth did you know?"

Her face fell. "I wish I were twice as clever. I only realized it after the book had fallen into Edward Ashton's hands. Is it written in milk?"

The word "milk" prompted some mournful *moo*s from below. Simon lowered his voice to a whisper. "Milk's fine for household secrets, but it washes away at sea. This diary is written in pirates' ink. That's the best invisible ink there is. It's foolproof and waterproof. We pirates use it for treasure maps, secret oaths, and other confidential documents."

It was odd to hear Simon say "we pirates," but Penelope supposed she would get used to it in time. "Pirates' ink," she mused. "Do you know how to read it?"

"Harr, matey, I do!" he said, quite convincingly. "My adventure at sea, though unpleasant in some ways, left me with valuable skills. For one thing, my navigational expertise is twice what it was before. For another, I am now an expert brewer of pirates' ink. It has two parts: the ink itself, and the visibilizer."

"The what?"

"The visibilizer. It's what you pour on the pages to make the invisible ink visible again. Concocting the ink is easy, but the visibilizer . . . well, that takes talent. And a long list of ingredients, too."

"Is there any chance that Edward Ashton knows how to make the visibilizer?"

"Not unless he's ever been a sworn member of a pirate's crew. Both recipes are secrets of the pirates' brotherhood. I myself have taken an oath not to reveal them, unless it's to another pirate who's also under oath." At Penelope's dismayed expression, he added, "Don't worry. I'm allowed to cook up a batch of the visibilizer for personal use, as long as I don't share the recipe with a landlubber. No offense."

Penelope chewed on a piece of hay, concentrating very hard. "So Quinzy has the cannibal book but cannot read it. And we have the visibilizer, or will, once you prepare it—but no book." She looked up. "Simon, how accurate is your great-uncle Pudge's memory?"

He shrugged. "I wouldn't trust him for the day's headlines, but the tales of his boyhood seafaring days are clear as a bell."

Penelope would have shouted "Eureka!" but she did not want to frighten the cows. "Simon, consider this: If the details of Pudge's story are accurate, that means that when they arrived at the island, the admiral did not yet suffer from the curse that plagues the Ashton men during the full moon. For if he had, he would have been howling and barking around the campfire, not singing intricately rhymed sea chanteys in complex harmony parts."

Simon stroked his chin. "I think I see what you're driving at, Miss L. Something changed on that island. Something happened."

"Indeed—and it was something so shocking that Pudge could only write about it in invisible ink, and was sworn to secrecy by the admiral, too." Penelope thought of the unanswered questions surrounding Edward Ashton and the Incorrigible children . . . Agatha Swanburne and her auburn-haired portrait . . . Miss Mortimer and the hair poultice . . . Old Timothy and Dr. Westminster . . . and the Long-Lost Lumleys, too. So many mysteries! Somehow they all seemed inextricably linked. But all she said was, "It would explain the curse on the Ashtons—and perhaps much more, as well."

The almost-full moon poured its pale, cool light through the window of the hayloft, like fresh milk into a pitcher. It would be light enough to read by, easily. All that would be needed was a book.

"I wonder what happened on Ahwoo-Ahwoo?" Simon said softly, and they both gazed out at the star-studded sky.

"There is only one way to find out." Her voice was quiet and cool as the moonlight itself. "We must steal Pudge's diary back at once."

The Eleventh Chapter

*Something criminal is
planned for the CAKE.*

"A Swanburne girl may borrow with permission, and quote with attribution, but she absolutely, positively does not steal." No doubt Agatha Swanburne said something along those lines at one point or another. Indeed, under normal circumstances, a rule against stealing would be one that all right-thinking people ought to follow. But these could hardly be considered normal circumstances, could they? For, in addition to all the other shockingly out-of-character things Miss Penelope Lumley had done recently—telling half-truths to a person in a position of authority, for example, or walking out of a library without a single book in hand, not one!—never before, in the whole history of the Swanburne Academy for Poor Bright Females, had any Swanburne girl spent the night in a hayloft with a pirate, planning an elaborate theft.

The novelty of her situation was not lost on the plucky young governess. "Well, I suppose if no one has ever done it before, then it is high time someone did," she told herself, and stuck another piece of hay in her mouth. She and Simon had already spent hours working out the details of their intended crime, and Penelope had chewed on hay the whole time. It focused her mind wonderfully, and she began to understand why Beowulf found gnawing on hard objects so appealing.

Plotting the theft of the diary had also proved enjoyable. However, it was her first attempt at burglary, and she had little to compare the experience with, other than a thoroughly depressing book she had once encountered, years before, when she was not much older than Cassiopeia. It was about a man who steals a loaf of bread and ends up in prison for many years. After his release, he is hounded mercilessly by an unhappy policeman. More bad things happen, tragedy ensues, and nothing ends well, for anyone.

(The literary-minded among you may have already guessed that this dismal tale must have been *Les Misérables*, by Mr. Victor Hugo. That story also involves a man, a loaf of bread, and an unhappy policeman. But in Miss Penelope Lumley's day, Mr. Hugo's masterpiece had not yet been written. The book she was thinking of was actually a children's picture book called *Pierre et la Baguette*, which translates loosely as "Peter and the Loaf of French Bread." Whether a little French boy named Victor Hugo also read *Pierre et la Baguette* and was inspired to write a similar tale years later, we will never know, but the truth is that grown-up writers cannot help but be influenced by the books they read as children. Someday you, too, may decide to write a novel that touches upon subjects you read about as a young person. Pirates, perhaps. Or dancing chickens. Or even some combination of the two.)

As for dishonest Pierre, with those telltale crumbs down the front of his *chemise*: One would think his grim fate would be enough to put anyone off stealing, but alas, *Pierre et la Baguette* was written in French, and little Penelope could scarcely understand a word. Whatever cautionary value the tale may have had was thus lost, and now here she was, in a hayloft with a pirate, and rather pleased about it, too.

First they devised a way for Simon to reveal the ingredients for the visibilizer without breaking his pirate oath of secrecy. He did this by making an exceedingly long list that was full of red herrings. (A red herring has nothing to do with fish. Rather, it is a false clue, intended to trick would-be solvers of mysteries into shouting "Eureka! I've got it!" when, in fact, they have not.) It was a clever solution, for even if someone found the list, no one but Simon would know which were the real ingredients and which were the fakes, and the recipe would thus remain secret.

Penelope wrote it all down on the back of an empty feedbag, using a pencil stub she found lying in the barn. Most of the items would be easy enough to obtain. However, Simon did specify a rather large quantity of paprika, much more than the Swanburne kitchens were likely to have on hand (paprika not being the sort of spice an English cook would typically stock in bulk).

"It's stretching the bounds of my oath to say so, but the paprika's essential," he explained when she hesitated. "The visibilizer won't work without it. And I should warn you—once I have all the ingredients, visibilizing the book will take some time. There's a bit of mixing involved, and the book has to simmer for close to an hour. It smells pretty foul, too."

"The 'fowl' smell can be concealed by confining our preparations to the chicken coop." Penelope was unable to resist the pun. "So, let us estimate a quarter of an hour for mixing, and three-quarters of an hour for simmering. Add another half hour to locate and steal the book in the first place, plus travel time. . . ." She added quickly in her head. "That means I will have to keep Edward Ashton thoroughly occupied for one and three-quarter hours."

Simon whistled. "You'll have your work cut out for you. And how will we find the cannibal book? Edward Ashton might have hidden it anywhere. It'll be like searching for a needle in a . . . well, you know. Say, look at those stars! It's a navigator's dream out there tonight."

He sounded almost nostalgic and gazed out the hayloft window for a long minute before turning back to Penelope. "My pirate crew were a ruthless, bowlegged lot, but they taught me all a fellow needs to know about thievery. Let me have a crack at stealing it."

"Simon, I have no doubt that you are an excellent thief, and a dreadful knave, and a rascally rogue as well. But you would be far too conspicuous in an all-girls' school. You could never move about unnoticed." Especially now, she might have added, after surviving

249

his manly shipboard adventure: He was suntanned and lean muscled, and hummed sea chanteys under his breath in the moonlight. . . .

She pushed these distracting thoughts from her mind. "Besides, you must prepare the visibilizer, for you are the only one who can."

"All right." He tugged at that poetic forelock and frowned. "But if I'm cooking the visibilizer, and you're keeping Edward Ashton otherwise engaged, who's going to find the cannibal book?"

"The Incorrigible children will find it," she said, after a moment.

"How?"

Penelope chewed upon her hay and smiled. "By following the scent of the sea."

THEIR SCHEMING COMPLETE, SIMON OFFERED to walk Penelope back to the school. She refused. Even in the dark she knew the way better than he did, and she thought it essential that Simon's presence not be discovered, given their unlawful plans for the day to come.

By feel and by memory, she padded silently along the paths. Already the night was less inky than before, and the earliest of the early birds had taken to the treetops and were chirping their sunrise songs. Soon the people and animals of Heathcote would rise and stir. The day of the CAKE had come at last.

She paused when she reached the side door of the school, and looked up once more at the fading stars. Tonight the moon would be full. That meant that somewhere—locked in his secret attic, perhaps, or outside, stumbling alone through the dark woods that bore his name, and the name of his curséd ancestors, too—Lord Fredrick Ashton would be barking and scratching and baying like one of his own hunting hounds, helpless to stop himself.

"Poor Lord Fredrick! The Howling Elimination Program will have to wait awhile longer," she thought. Nearby, a rooster crowed, and Penelope stifled a yawn as she slipped unnoticed through the door. "Yet if our plan to visibilize the cannibal book succeeds, I may soon know the true cause of his affliction. I only hope there is a cure—and that he does not fire me before I discover what it is."

"CAKE DAY! CAKE DAY! THE best day of the year!" The Incorrigibles chanted at high volume as they marched around Penelope's cot. And then, "Where are your pajamas, Lumawoo?" Cassiopeia asked, frowning. For their governess always scolded them if they fell asleep in their clothes, but there she was, asleep in bed and still wearing her new dress, although it hardly looked new anymore. It was muddy and rumpled and stuck all over with bits of hay. It smelled suspiciously of cow barn, too, although the children were too polite to mention it.

Penelope sat up with a groan. "Good morning," she croaked. Her eyes felt glued shut; she had to hoist them open by lifting both eyebrows as high as she could. This gave her a look of shocked surprise. When she forced a cheery smile, she took on the appearance of a badly painted marionette.

Three sensitive noses wrinkled in distaste. "Your dress is a mess," Beowulf said, whereupon his siblings teased him for having written a poem by accident (as you may know, he was quite good at writing them on purpose, too).

"You are right, Beowulf. I ought not to have slept in it." Penelope yawned widely and stretched. She had meant to take an hour's catnap and be up well before her pupils, but the Incorrigibles had risen much earlier than usual, as children are apt to do on any long-awaited holiday. "You were asleep when I came in. I did not want to wake you by rummaging about for my nightclothes."

"Why did you come back so late?" Alexander asked, sounding rather stern.

"It was not that late. Mere moments after you three went to bed. I must have just missed Mrs. Apple's bedtime story, by . . ." She winced and pulled a sharp length of hay out of the back of her dress. "By a straw's breadth," she said, tossing it aside.

At the sound of her name, the history teacher stirred. She too had slept in her clothes; she was sprawled in an armchair, with her feet propped on an ottoman and a blanket draped over her. "Oh, Charlemagne!" Mrs. Apple murmured. Her dreamy smile dissolved into a snore. Penelope whispered to the children that they ought to let Mrs. Apple sleep, but they were wide-awake and much too excited to stay quiet. In the end she had no choice but to bring them along on her morning's errands.

And so, at an hour past dawn on the day of the Celebrate Alumnae Knowledge Exposition, Miss Penelope Lumley found herself in the kitchen of the Swanburne Academy for Poor Bright Females, persuading the cook to make Hungarian goulash for dinner. The Incorrigible children sat happily in the corner, trying to find a lid for every pot.

As it turned out, the cook had once seen a lovely

picture postcard of Budapest, and the beauty and blueness of the Danube River had left her curious about Hungarian cuisine ever since. She was most grateful for the goulash recipe and promised to prepare it for the celebratory CAKE dinner that very night.

"I trust you will be able to obtain the paprika in time?" Penelope asked innocently.

"I'll send a few girls to the spice market in Heathcote straightaway," the cook replied. "Perhaps your pupils would like to go with them? It's full of interesting smells."

The children's noses twitched in hope, but Penelope shook her head. "My students must stay at Swanburne today, for they have important responsibilities concerning the CAKE. Might I suggest you have the girls purchase twice the specified amount of paprika? This goulash sounds so delicious, you will surely be asked to prepare it again within a fortnight. No sense making another trip to the market." (Of course, her true intention was to guarantee there was enough paprika on hand to prepare dinner correctly and mix the visibilizer. No sense skimping on the goulash. After all, she was going to have to eat it, too.)

"What important responsibilities?" Alexander asked after they had left the kitchen. The idea of having some pleased him greatly, for he was that sort of child.

"They will be a happy surprise, just as my birthday party was a happy surprise," Penelope replied. "You shall hear about it all soon enough. Now, our next stop will be—no, not breakfast, for the dining hall is not yet open. First we must go see Miss Mortimer." She clapped her hands three times, *clap clap clap*, and the children lined up, ready to march. "There has been a small change of plans regarding the CAKE. "

It was too early for Miss Charlotte Mortimer to be in her office. They found her in the Swanburne Apartment, a small suite of rooms on the far side of the school. It was called the Swanburne Apartment because Agatha Swanburne had lived there during her years as headmistress, until Miss Mortimer took her place. (Before becoming headmistress, Miss Mortimer had been a poetry teacher at Swanburne. It was she who had first taught Penelope about iambic pentameter, which the eager girl practiced by writing earnest sonnets in praise of fictional ponies: "O, RAINbow, HOW you PRANCE and FLICK your TAIL," and so on.)

Miss Mortimer glanced up as they entered. She was in her dressing gown, her fair hair loose around her shoulders. She sat near the French windows that overlooked the gardens. A pot of tea was on the table in front of her; a cup had already been poured, and the early edition of *Heathcote, All Year 'Round (Now Illustrated)* was opened to the puzzle page. Only the quick rise of one delicate eyebrow, which then floated back down slowly, like a downy feather caught in the breeze, revealed her surprise at seeing them.

"Good morning. You are just in time to help with the puzzle," she said pleasantly. "A six-letter word meaning 'chaos.' I wonder what it could be?" She sniffed and made a face. "Children, have you been walking in the cow pastures? I fear you may need to clean off your shoes."

"It's Lumawoo's dress," the children explained, not unkindly.

Penelope looked down, embarrassed. The kitchen had been so full of strong cooking smells that no one had remarked upon her barnyard scent, but here, in the spotless surroundings of the Swanburne Apartment, it was impossible to miss. "I apologize for my aroma," she said. "I know I am rather unkempt at present. But never fear, I shall be sure to bathe and change before giving my speech."

Miss Mortimer put her pencil down. "Your speech?"

"You are just in time to help with the puzzle."

"Yes." Penelope sat on the love seat, which was unfortunate, as it was upholstered in ivory silk that had been unblemished until that moment. "I have thought about it a great deal, and I would very much like to give my CAKE speech, as originally planned."

The children wriggled with joy at the news, for they had been looking forward to hearing their governess speak, but the headmistress of the Swanburne Academy merely asked, "Are you sure?"

"Completely sure. In fact, it is essential that I be allowed to speak." Penelope gave Miss Mortimer a meaningful look. "As it turns out, I have a great many important things to say."

Miss Mortimer picked up her spoon and stirred her tea with exquisite slowness. Then she spoke. "Children, do you see my bookshelves—yes, those shelves, on the other side of the room? Could you do me a great favor and put the books in order? Thank you so very much."

The children happily obeyed. Miss Mortimer waited until they were busy with their task before quietly replying, "Penny dear, you have my full support as ever. If you wish to speak, you shall. But I must warn you: After what happened yesterday, Judge Quinzy will not be pleased to see you at the podium. Will you risk provoking his anger? I know how much you value your position at Ashton Place."

Penelope held back a smile. Little did Miss Mortimer know just how much "Quinzy" would be provoked by day's end! "As there is no such person as Judge Quinzy, whether he is pleased or not makes no difference to me," she answered. "As for Edward Ashton—for reasons we do not yet know, he has gone to a great deal of trouble to fake his own death and conceal his existence. He has threatened to have me fired, but I believe he is only bluffing. The risk of me exposing his true identity to his son is too great."

It was Simon who had convinced her of this, during their long night of scheming. "There's not much to do on a becalmed ship but play cards," he'd said. "I learned a thing or two about bluffing, believe you me. Edward Ashton's got a full house, perhaps—we'll call it a house full of Ashtons! But you've got four of a kind." When she looked at him blankly, he added, "That means you win."

"But Lord Fredrick would never believe me without proof. And I have none," she had protested.

"That just means you're bluffing, too," he'd answered. "Now you know why people find card games interesting!"

Miss Mortimer looked uneasy. "Certainty is not proof, Penelope," she cautioned.

"Yet I am certain." Penelope leaned forward. "Quinzy *is* Edward Ashton, and your theory about the haystack was correct. His true purpose has nothing to do with school songs or jam budgets or overgrown ivy."

"What is it, then?"

"To gain access to the letters of Agatha Swanburne."

Miss Mortimer's spoon slipped from her fingers and landed on the saucer with a *clink*. "The letters . . . of course! How foolish that I did not realize it—yet the baroness has kept me so distracted with all her interference, I have scarcely had time to think." She frowned. "This is troubling news, Penelope. Has he already read the letters, do you know?"

"He has. How Agatha Swanburne knew so much about the contents of the Ashton Place library is a question I would dearly like to investigate! But right now, I have bigger fish to fry." Penelope stood and did her best to brush the grime off the love seat. "Thank you, Miss Mortimer. One more thing. Might I have your permission to organize a game for the Swanburne girls, as part of the CAKE festivities?"

"Cake Day! Cake Day! The best day of the year!"

The Incorrigibles had decided to sort Miss Mortimer's books by color, thus making an attractive rainbow pattern on the bookshelves. Now they debated what kind of cake would be served for breakfast. Oatmeal cake was a tolerable idea, but the possibility of kipper cake made them gag. (A kipper is not a red herring, but a smoked herring that is eaten whole, with its eyeballs staring up at you from the plate. That some people willingly eat kippers and eggs for breakfast is a fact that others may find hard to swallow. However, as Magistra Grimsby would say, *De gustibus non est disputandum.*" This is Latin for "You can't argue about taste," an insight that is just as true today as it was in ancient Rome. On the other hand, "Not everything should be baked into a pie," as Agatha Swanburne once cautioned, particularly if it still has eyeballs.)

Miss Mortimer's graceful fingers drummed on the table. "Mayhem," she said at last. "It is 'mayhem.'"

"Where?" Penelope looked around in a panic but saw only three children having a no-blinking contest by pretending to be kippers.

"A six-letter word for 'chaos.'" Miss Mortimer rose abruptly, leaving her tea and her puzzle unfinished. "A game, certainly. Do what you think best. But you must excuse me. It is the day of the CAKE, and there are a great many details I must attend to." She sniffed. "Best if you change clothes before breakfast, dear."

PENELOPE TOOK HER HEADMISTRESS'S ADVICE and led the children back to the Incorrigible dormitory for baths and fresh clothes. Mrs. Apple was gone, her blanket neatly folded on the chair. Briefly, Penelope wondered if she ought to find her and tell her that her speech-making services would not be needed after all, but there was no time to go searching.

"Busy, busy me!" she thought as she lowered herself into the bath. (It would have been a perfect opportunity to measure her own volume in the manner of Archimedes, but alas, that "eureka" would have to wait until another day.) "I always assumed that thieves must be shady characters, dishonest and lazy. But now that I have embarked on a life of crime myself, I see it is no mere walk in the park. It requires careful planning, nerves of steel, and a strong work ethic, too." She thought of Cassiopeia's drawing of the sheep eye. "As the wise founder once said, 'All things look different close up.' Very true . . . now where did I put the soap?"

Soon she was clean and dressed in an everyday frock she had worn countless times before. The dress was nothing if not governessy, and brown as a nutshell, too, although it was too big to be crammed into one. However, it had been recently laundered and smelled only of fresh air and lilac water. Penelope was greatly cheered by putting it on.

Seeing her governess change clothes made Cassiopeia want to change as well. Shy as a mouse, she asked if she might wear a real Swanburne uniform in honor of the day. It was easy enough to find one in her size among the clean uniforms stored in the closets. Once she was dressed, Penelope braided her hair into two thick pigtails, just the way Cecily used to wear hers. The sight of her littlest pupil looking like a proper Swanburne girl warmed Penelope's heart, and Cassiopeia was so proud she twirled in circles, auburn pigtails whipping 'round and 'round, until she was dizzy and had to stop.

Not to be left out, Alexander and Beowulf ran to their suitcases and took out their Postal Tyger uniforms, soup-bowl hats and all. Penelope knew better than to object. "It is the day of the CAKE, so any sort of festive attire ought to be suitable. And they are only children, after all," she thought. "Now, if I could make them understand that there will not be cake for breakfast! I hope they will not be disappointed."

But no one could be disappointed with the CAKE day breakfast, except perhaps those few hardy souls who prefer porridge over any other meal. "*Pan*cake, of course!" the Incorrigible children exclaimed in delight, smiting their foreheads; how could they have failed to guess? There was a pot of jam on each table, and plenty of honey, too. Before long, even the solemn Swanburne girls began to talk and giggle among themselves, with nearly the same freedom and merriment Penelope recalled from her own days at school. Many of the girls threw occasional nervous glances at the door, but there was no sign of the baroness. At least, not yet.

The unexpectedly happy breakfast made Penelope feel even more confident in their scheme, and she took it as a sign that the day would go exactly as she and Simon had planned. When the students were nearly done eating, she climbed upon a bench. "Friends, Romans, Swanburne girls, good morning!" she announced. "I am Miss Penelope Lumley, a proud graduate of this fine school. In honor of today's CAKE, and with permission from your headmistress, Miss Charlotte Mortimer, I would like to propose . . . a treasure hunt!"

The girls cheered and stamped their feet, for there

had not been a game announced at breakfast in quite some time, not since the new trustees had taken over. The dormitories quickly formed teams, and Penelope gave each one a list of treasures to find. The girls were so excited that not one of them thought to ask why the lists were written on scraps of empty feedbags.

The Incorrigibles wanted to play, too, but Penelope explained that they would help choose the winner and must therefore stay behind and eat second helpings of pancakes in order to maintain their neutrality. "Like Switzerland," she explained, heaping their plates with food. The children were satisfied with this and busied themselves with the jam.

When all was in order, Penelope climbed back atop the bench. "Attention, treasure hunters! You have your instructions. Find as many items as you can, and be back in the dining hall at precisely eight o'clock, one hour from now. The winning team shall receive a valuable prize. Ready? On my mark . . . get set—and *go*. The treasure hunt is on!" she added as an afterthought, but the girls were already off.

Ga-dong! Ga-dong! Ga-dong! Ga-dong! Ga-dong! Ga-dong! Ga-dong! Ga-dong!
The teams returned all at once, noisy and punctual

265

as the trains of the London and North West Railway screeching into Euston Station during the morning rush hour. The last team slipped in breathlessly between the sixth and seventh *ga-dong*s. By the eighth, all the girls were lined up, their treasures heaped in front of them.

Penelope strode up and down like a general, inspecting each pile and assigning a score, which the Incorrigibles carefully noted down. There were some surprises. For example, "Something soft and squeezable" she thought would be easy to find, given how many embroidered pillows were scattered along the school's many window seats, but the girls of Dormitory C had rounded up poor Shantaloo, who was now imprisoned in a wicker laundry basket, hissing to be set free.

"Ten points for Dormitory C!" Penelope declared. "I suggest you let the cat out of the basket now, though."

The Incorrigibles added up the points. All the teams had done well, but thanks to their capture of Shantaloo and the fact that they were the first (and therefore, only) team to obtain the sheet-covered portrait of Agatha Swanburne from Miss Mortimer's office, the girls of Dormitory C had scored the most. As littlest and loudest, Cassiopeia was given the job of announcing the winner.

"C! C! C is for 'cake!'" she yelled. The girls of Dormitory C cheered, and were congratulated warmly by all the others.

"What is the prize?" someone asked.

But Penelope had not thought of a prize. Anxiously, she patted her pockets. "Yes, of course! It is a wonderful prize . . . no, not this old poetry book, hold on. . . . Eureka! Here it is: a lovely fountain pen."

The winners were thrilled and promised to share the pen fairly among them and write many prompt thank-you notes with it. But the Incorrigibles looked stricken.

"Lumawoo! That is your birthday pen!" Cassiopeia protested.

Penelope put a comforting hand on her shoulder. "And I have enjoyed it a great deal, and written some important things with it. Now it is someone else's turn to use it." To the Swanburne girls, she said, "Time to go to your classrooms! The alumnae will be arriving soon for the CAKE, and they will want to see the Swanburne girls hard at work. I understand the cook has something special planned for dinner, too."

One of the girls raised a hand to speak. "Miss Lumley, shall we put away the treasures first?" Indeed, the dining hall looked more like a junk shop now, with all the items stacked in piles—there were Bunsen burners, dirty socks, tinned herring, a box of salt. . . .

Penelope smiled. "No, that will not be necessary. Now, off you go!" *Clap clap clap!*

SHANTALOO'S PRIDE HAD BEEN WOUNDED by her brief captivity in the laundry basket. Now she was hiding behind the portrait of Agatha Swanburne and would not come out, no matter how sweetly the children called or how many tasty pancake crumbs they offered on their fingertips.

Leaving the children to soothe the embarrassed kitty, Penelope went to work. Quickly, she sorted through the treasures and put the important items to one side. "Measuring spoons, castor oil—*blech!*—a large cooking pot with a tight-fitting lid, moldy apples, goose fat, rinds of cheese . . ." Everything on Simon's list was there except, of course, the paprika. That would not be available until later, when the girls sent to buy it returned from the spice market.

"The paprika can be delivered last," she thought. The rest of the items had to be brought to the chicken coop right away for safekeeping. But there was a great deal to carry, and as she did not know which were the true ingredients for the visibilizer and which were the red herrings, nothing could be left behind.

"Postal Tygers, I require your help," she said. "These treasures must be delivered by tyger post. Are you up to the task?"

"Postal Tygers, at your service!" The boys saluted, then growled. They swatted their tyger paws about and lashed their imaginary tyger tails. Cassiopeia joined in as well, for she saw no reason she could not be a Swanburne girl and a Postal Tyger, not to mention a star of the Imperial Russian Ballet, a brave explorer of parts unknown, and perhaps the Queen of England, too.

Following Penelope's instructions, the children found three empty bushels and packed them full of treasures; the lighter objects they placed in the wicker basket, which was smaller and easier for Cassiopeia to carry. They were so busy that they did not even hear the dining-room doors swing open.

"Will *some*one *please* ex*plain* this *fright*ful *mess*?" Baroness Hoover roared.

"Iambic pentameter!" the children shouted in answer, and returned to their work.

The baroness seemed unimpressed by their mastery of poetic meter. "This is a dining hall, not a flea market," she snapped. Already she was at Penelope's elbow. The mere mention of fleas made the children squirm and scratch.

"Now, now. Just some young people having a bit of fun, eh?" It was the baroness's husband, the baron. He scurried behind her like a shadow, looking thoroughly cowed. (Just as red herrings have nothing to do with herrings, looking cowed has nothing to do with cows. It simply means that the baron had the look of someone who had been bullied and scolded a great deal, and who felt perpetually nervous and ashamed as a result.)

"Good morning, Baroness. And to you as well, Baron Hoover." Penelope curtsied, as was only polite. There was nothing particularly likable about the baron, but she found him far preferable to his wife. "The Swanburne girls had a treasure hunt this morning, and these are the treasures. As you see by our bushels, we are tidying up right now." She smiled the innocent smile of a master criminal at work. "Surely, you have taken part in a treasure hunt, Baroness? In your youth, perhaps?"

"In her youth she was out hunting barons, har har! Caught one, too. Just my luck it was me." Baron Hoover chuckled, and the baroness fired him a sideways look that was sharp enough to cut rope. She turned to

Penelope, waving a sheet of paper.

"Miss Lumley, I have just reviewed the updated CAKE agenda. It appears you intend to make a speech today after all."

"Cake for breakfast! Cake for lunch! Cake for tea! Cake for supper! Even cake for dessert!" The children joined hands and spun in merry circles around the baroness, who did her best to ignore them.

"All speeches must be approved by the DODO. And by the DODO, I mean me." She held out a hand. Her fingers unfurled dangerously, like the slow unsheathing of claws. "Give me a copy of your speech, if you please."

Penelope shrugged in apology. "I am afraid I cannot, Baroness. My speech is committed to memory, not paper. Did you know that all the great orators spoke from memory? Why, in the days of ancient Rome—"

"Fall of Rome!" the children squealed, and tumbled to the ground.

The baron slapped his leg in delight. "Fall of Rome, that's clever, what? Ah, to be a child, all games and giggles! Life is never so simple again, once you grow up to be a big old serious baron, with all your baron responsibilities. What I wouldn't give for a day off . . ."

His wife's furious gaze remained fixed on Penelope. "In that case, Miss Lumley, you will have to recite your speech to me *immediately*. In fact, I may need to hear it several times, just to be sure."

Uneasily, Penelope replied, "That will take some time, Baroness. And as you see, the children and I have a great deal of work to do."

The baroness sneered. "Without the DODO's prior approval, you will not be permitted to speak."

"Dodo!" the children squawked. Still on the ground, they writhed in mock agony and made their dying dodo noises.

Penelope frowned. What to do? The ingredients for the visibilizer had to be delivered, and the sooner the better, but the baroness clearly intended to monopolize the rest of her morning. Dare she trust the Incorrigible children to go to the chicken coop alone? It seemed she had no choice. At least their tummies were stuffed full of pancakes, she reasoned. Surely they would not be tempted by all that plump, tasty poultry . . . or would they?

"Very well, Baroness," she said. "But the children must finish their chores. As Agatha Swanburne said, 'This and that left here and there means a trip and a fall every now and then.'" Penelope knelt and spoke softly to the Incorrigibles. "Postal Tygers, it appears you shall have to make this important delivery without me, for I have some business with the baroness. Are you up to the task?"

"Postal Tygers, at your service," they cried, jumping to their feet.

"To whom should we deliver?" Alexander saluted so crisply it nearly knocked the soup bowl off his head.

"Dr. Westminster. His office is in the back of the chicken coop, and that is where you will find him." Penelope gave them each a stern look. "However, under no circumstances are you to bother the chickens. Understood?"

"We will not bother them," Alexander said firmly. His siblings nodded in agreement. As an afterthought, he said, "Does nibbling bother them?"

"Yes, it does." Penelope glanced at the baroness, who had turned pale with fear and was gesticulating wildly at the baron. A strange yowling sound was coming from the portrait of Agatha Swanburne, and neither she nor her husband could discover why. "Nibbling bothers them a great deal. Biting does, too."

"No nibbling and no biting," Beowulf declared. "Can we eat them, though?"

"No, no, no." She thought quickly. "Some chickens

are for eating, true, but these particular chickens are not. They are trained dancers, for one thing, and it would be a pity to waste all that talent. . . . Eureka!" she blurted, for the answer had come to her. "Do not think of them as chickens. Think of them as precious baby dodos."

That seemed to do the trick. The Incorrigibles began saying *ooooh*, and *awww*, and *oojie-woojie-dodo-woo*, as anyone would in the presence of an adorable baby who might be the very last hope of a soon-to-be-extinct species.

"Who would ever suppose that three fierce tygers could make such soothing noises?" Penelope said encouragingly. "Now, as to the location of the chicken coop . . . proceed out the main door of the school, over the rise of the hill, down a short pebbled path, then make a left at the shrubbery. . . ."

"Do not worry, Lumawoo." Beowulf sniffed deeply. "We will follow the smell of chickens."

"He means baby dodos," Cassiopeia corrected.

"Baby dodos smell just like chickens. It is a remarkable coincidence." Penelope stood. "Off with you to Dr. Westminster, then. Come straight back to the Incorrigible dormitory when you are done. Remember, you will have important responsibilities to attend to later! Careful with your bushels, please."

"Westminstawoo," they repeated to one another so they would not forget. The boys each balanced a bushel on their soup-bowl helmets; the third bushel they carried between them by its handles. Cassiopeia had no helmet, but her pigtails, tied in a knot, provided ample cushioning for the wicker basket. They began to march and sing.

"Our tyger feet
Are quieter than most.
We can't be beat
Delivering the post."

Penelope joined in their singing, her voice high and pure.

"We eat our peas,
But cake we like the best.
We say, 'More, please!'
And gobble up the rest.
A-woof, ahwoo, a-woof, ahwoo!"

"*Woof, ahwoo, a-woof, ahwoo!* Catchy tune, what?" the baron said, tapping his foot. "Reminds me of something I heard in the theater once. Can't think what it was, though."

The yowling that seemed to emanate from Agatha Swanburne's portrait joined in the singing, too.

"Meow, meow, meow, meow!"

"It is haunted!" The terrified baroness extended a shaking hand toward the sheeted painting. "This painting is haunted. Take me away from here immediately!"

"Are you not even curious to see who might be haunting you?" Penelope snatched away the sheet, and there she stood: Agatha Swanburne, clear gray eyes, striking auburn hair, and that look of calm amusement on her face. . . .

The baroness gasped. "Agatha Swanburne! Agatha Swanburne!" Then she fainted dead away.

THE TWELFTH CHAPTER

The children are given
important responsibilities.

THERE WERE NO SMELLING SALTS among the treasure-hunt spoils, but a single drop of castor oil drizzled on her tongue was enough to revive the baroness. She came to in seconds, sputtering and frantically wiping her mouth to get rid of the horrendous taste. Once back on her feet, she was even more cross than before. "The nerve of that Swanburne woman! I refuse to be intimidated by the ghost of some long-dead headmistress," she said. Then she demanded that Penelope immediately present her speech in full for the DODO's approval.

But Penelope had not gotten an A in her Great Orations of Antiquity class for nothing. The speech she gave for the baroness was like something out of one of those modern frozen-yogurt machines they have nowadays: sprinkles of Cicero were ladled over chunks of Demosthenes, and Queen Elizabeth's speech before the battle with the Spanish Armada swirled together with spoonfuls of *Julius Caesar*. In the chill of an empty classroom in which no one had bothered to light the hearth, the young governess babbled on and on, while Baroness Hoover struggled to stay awake. (The baron made no such effort, and took the opportunity to put his feet up and doze.)

While Penelope recited and gestured, she worried about the Incorrigibles. Had she erred in trusting them to go to the chicken coop alone? Would her instruction to think of the chickens as baby dodos be enough to prevent mayhem? And ought she have given Dr. Westminster some warning about the . . . well, *unusual* traits of her three pupils? Most of the time they were exceptionally well mannered and pleasant, of course. But there were those rare occasions. . . .

"The worst that might happen is that they try to feed and burp the chickens, or tell them bedtime stories before putting them down for naps," she thought, stubbornly optimistic (whether she was being optoomuchstic remained to be seen). "For all I know, those dancing chickens would enjoy a bit of coddling. And who does not like to hear a good story?"

She paused for breath and surveyed her audience of two. The baron sagged limply in his chair, his chin lodged on his chest. The baroness looked drowsy; she had given up taking notes, and when her pencil rolled to the floor she had not bothered to pick it up. But her eyelids fluttered every now and then, and her nodding head was stubbornly propped up on one fist.

"I shall have to do better," Penelope resolved, "which is to say, worse. Much, much worse." Practicing the opposite of all that she had been taught, she wove together the most boring, dull, tedious, and uninteresting bits of every speech she knew. She talked too fast, and then too slow. She garbled her words and flattened her voice to a mind-numbing drone. Before long both the baroness and baron snored contentedly in their chairs. She let her voice grow quiet, then trail off . . . silence. They were out cold. Success!

The sheet of paper with the day's agenda lay coiled in the baroness's hand. The old Penelope would never have taken it without permission, but Penelope "Sticky Fingers" Lumley, master criminal and friend to pirates, had no such hesitation. She slipped the paper out of the baroness's sleep-loosened fist with perfect stealth. "I believe I could teach a class on Great Bore-ations of Antiquity," she thought, quite proud of herself. "Now out I sneak, on my tyger feet," and indeed, she was quieter than most as she tiptoed out of the room.

Once safely away, she paused to look over the schedule. The guests were to arrive at half past twelve. At one o'clock, Miss Mortimer would deliver a brief welcome. The afternoon would be devoted to classroom demonstrations. Then, dinner. "And look, just after dinner: Important Official Announcements, followed by Prepared Remarks by Miss P. Lumley, Distinguished Alumna." Even with so much on her mind, it gave her a tingle of pleasure to see her name in print.

A glance at a hall clock revealed that it was half past noon exactly. The school would soon be overrun with visitors—and where were the Incorrigible children? Back in their room by now, she assumed. She went to find them straightaway.

But there was no sign of them in the Incorrigible dormitory, or anywhere else in the building. Worried, Penelope broke into a trot and did not slow until she arrived at the main entrance to Swanburne. The guests were already arriving in swarms. Old schoolmates who had not seen each other in years squealed and embraced. "You have not changed one bit," they cried, or "You are so changed, I scarcely recognize you" or "How has it been so long?" or "It feels like only yesterday we recited the multiplication tables together!"

Luckily, the welcoming committee of Swanburne girls was prepared for all the happy tears being shed, and handed each arriving visitor the gift of a commemorative handkerchief. These had been embroidered with the word "hope," which of course was a reference to the Swanburne motto, still buried beneath the ivy above the door.

Penelope spotted some old schoolmates of her own among the throng, but she could not stop to exchange greetings now, not with the children unaccounted for. "Pardon me, I must get to the chicken coop. . . . Excuse me, I beg your pardon. . . ." Politely but firmly, she tried to elbow her way through, but alas, she was but one little herring swimming against a mighty tide of Swanburne girls.

"Look! It's Miss Lumley, our distinguished alumna," one of the girls cried, and the rest circled 'round in excitement. After the morning's treasure hunt, even the girls who had not previously heard of Penelope thought of her as a celebrity.

"Would you sign my composition notebook?" one of the girls from Dormitory C asked, holding out the prized fountain pen.

"I shall be happy to, as soon as time permits." Penelope grew frantic, for now she was even more trapped than before. "First I have to find my pupils. . . ."

"Ahwoo!"

"Ahwoo!"

"Ahwooooo!"

"Did you hear that? Sounded like wolves," someone remarked. Quickly, the news spread. "Wolves! Wolves at Swanburne!"

If this had been an ordinary crowd, one could easily imagine the terrified stampede that might have ensued. But these were Swanburne girls, through and through, and they had been well trained not to panic. It was Penelope's heart that thumped with fear.

"Let me pass," she pleaded, shouldering her way through. "It is only the children! I assure you, they are not dangerous—not to people, I mean. Oh, those poor chickens!" With a heroic shove, she pushed her way out of the crowd. She could not help but assume the worst and pictured a gruesome mess of flying feathers, and a distraught Dr. Westminster, too.

But the Incorrigibles had already flown the coop,

so to speak. They were a little ways down the path, where they had set up a demonstration of their own.

"Lumawoo, look!" Beowulf called out happily when he saw his governess approaching at full speed. "Trained baby dodo tricks!"

"Trained—what?" She stopped short. Each of the children held a chicken. On a flat patch of grass, Alexander had made a simple obstacle course by putting the soup-bowl helmets on the ground. At his "ready, set, go" signal, which was two short *awhoos* followed by a long one, the birds were to run around the first helmet, jump in and out of the second, and then pass through the climactic curtain of Cassiopeia's swinging pigtails. If they completed the course successfully (as all three birds had just done), they were given a cuddle and a treat and the chance to do it all over again.

"Dodos are really the smartest birds," Alexander said with pride, for he had done most of the training himself (with some help from Dr. Westminster, of course). "And these are only babies. Dodos back on the ground, please! Now, watch. *Ahwoo! Ahwoo! Ahwoooooo!*" he called, and they were off.

A crowd of curious alumnae quickly gathered. All were amazed at this demonstration, and at the sight of the baby dodos, too, for everyone knew that dodos were long extinct. The birds' resemblance to ordinary barnyard chickens was deemed remarkable, and many commented upon it.

"Can I stop now?" Cassiopeia asked unsteadily. Waggling her upside-down head from side to side to keep the pigtails in motion had caused her to feel a little green.

Beowulf tugged at Penelope's sleeve. "Postal Tygers made our delivery," he said. "But guess who we saw in the chicken coop? It was Sima—"

"*Ahwoo!*" Penelope interrupted, for she did not want any mention of Simon's presence to be overheard. "*Ahwoo! Ahwooooo!*"

At the sound of their cue, the chickens began another round of the obstacle course. Cassiopeia was too dizzy to swing her pigtails, so the birds finished by doing a few of the dance steps they had learned from Dr. Westminster. At the end they bowed (they dipped their beaks, to be accurate) and waited for their treats, as before.

The dancing made the crowd cheer and clap, which attracted even more onlookers. Clearly, the situation had to be nipped in the bud, for any change in the day's schedule risked throwing off the careful precision of the plan Penelope and Simon had devised.

"The dodo babies are tired; that is all the tricks they can do for now," she announced. "Girls of the welcoming committee, please escort our guests inside. Did everyone get a handkerchief?"

Efficient as sheepdogs, the girls soon had the alumnae proceeding cheerfully into the school. Penelope made a mental note to tell Miss Mortimer what a good job the welcoming committee had done. Then she turned to the Incorrigibles. Each of them now cradled a sleepy, clucking dodo baby. "Children, it is time for the CAKE," she said. "You shall have to bring the chickens—I mean, baby dodos—back to the chicken coop. Understood?"

"*Oojie-woojie-dodo-woo,*" the children crooned to their little feathered friends. "Nap time for dodos!"

"Right away, please." Penelope used her firmest voice, for she could sense some resistance from the Incorrigibles about parting with their new pets. "Inside a school is no place for dodos."

"But how else are they to learn?" Alexander said. His siblings nodded, and all three cooed to their dodos even more adorably than before.

This strange yet tender scene was interrupted by a late arrival to the CAKE. She stomped along the path to the school with tiny, angry steps and anxiously twirled her parasol.

"Oh, how I dislike arriving in strange places all alone! It is enough to make one forget who one is. I keep glancing in my pocket mirror for reassurance." Lady Constance Ashton prattled without stopping, as if she were trying to keep herself company. "Yet I suppose I am still the same person I have always been. Unless acquiring a new name turns one into a different person! Does it? Before I married my husband, I was Miss Constance Barbey, youngest of the Barbey children, and dare I say the favorite, but since my wedding day I have been Lady—*chickens?*" At the sight of the children, she stopped. "Why are you holding chickens? I thought this was the Sunburne School, not a poultry academy."

"Good morning, Lady Chickens," some girls from the welcoming committee chanted melodiously. One of them offered Lady Constance a handkerchief. She accepted it with suspicion.

"I am *not* Lady Chickens," she retorted. "I am a lady who is surprised to *see* chickens."

"Dodos," Cassiopeia corrected. Then she remembered her manners. "Good aftawoo, Lady Ashton," she said, and curtsied.

Lady Constance brightened. "Well, at least *somebody* around here knows who I am! And what is your name, small person?"

"I am Cassiopeia Incorrigible," she answered, confused. "Don't you know?"

Lady Constance smiled indulgently. "What a peculiar coincidence! There is a little girl who lives in my house with that exact same name. But she is nothing like you, for you are a proper schoolgirl in a starched school uniform and neatly braided hair, and she is a half-savage creature who is as likely to growl and bite as to do what she is told. I wonder: What are the odds against two such wildly different girls being given the same clumsy, unattractive, and frankly unspellable name?"

A growl formed in the back of Cassiopeia's throat, for she was proud of her name and could spell nearly all of it, too. Meanwhile, the boys began to calculate the odds Lady Constance had proposed. It was a difficult problem, as they did not know how many girls were in existence. Swanburne alone was full of them, and that, they suspected, was only the tip of the iceberg.

Penelope stepped forward and put a hand on each of Cassiopeia's shoulders. "Lady Ashton, it is a surprise to see you here," she said. That much was certainly true. "To what do we owe the honor of your visit?"

"I am here for the CAKE, to which Fredrick and I were inexplicably invited." Lady Constance paused. "I hope it is a chocolate cake! I much prefer chocolate to any other flavors of sweets."

Penelope looked around. "And where is Lord Ashton?"

"Fredrick," Lady Constance began, but it came out as a squeak. She cleared her throat and tried again. "My husband is not feeling well today."

"Naturally he is not, for it is the night of the full—" Penelope caught herself. "That is to say, I am sorry to hear that he is ill and had to stay home."

"I wish he *had* stayed home! I wish we both had! But he was the one who insisted that we come." Lady Constance's round, doll-like eyes grew even wider. "He behaved frightfully in the carriage, Miss Lumley. Oh, he was making the most indecent noises! Whimpering and barking and growling. Once we arrived, Old Timothy took him straight inside, through some secret, private entrance that he claimed to know. Now Fredrick is indisposed with what he calls a headache, but I am quite certain it is something worse."

She fiddled anxiously with the handle of her parasol. "As soon as we return to Ashton Place, I will insist that he see a doctor. More and more I find myself wracked with worry about those spooky tales his mother told . . . strange illnesses in the Ashton family tree, gruesome ends, and so on. Fredrick says it is all nonsense. But really, Miss Lumley, what am I to think?" Her voice dwindled to a frightened whisper. "During the ride here, he chewed a hole in the seat leather of the carriage. A *hole*! And scratched himself all over, like a flea-bitten dog! I am no doctor, but that does not sound like a headache to me." She reached into her reticule and took out an envelope. "As if all that was not unpleasant enough, he asked me to deliver this note. To you!"

Penelope's mind raced—Lord Fredrick, at Swanburne! Barking and chewing!—but "Me?" is what she exclaimed.

Lady Constance handed her the envelope. "Yes, you, Miss Lumley. I do not know what it says. As you see, it is sealed. The indignity! I suppose Fredrick imagines I am some sort of postal employee, with nothing better to do than carry letters to my own governess."

Penelope turned the envelope over in her hands. A letter, from Lord Fredrick? Had he already learned of her deception about the cannibal book? Was she being fired after all?

The wax seal was a swirling capital A. She broke it with a fingernail, and read:

> *Bad day today and getting worse by the hour. Is it the moon? Can't find my almanac, blast! Need first lesson tonight, urgently, as soon as the sun goes down. Ask Old Timothy where to find me; he'll know. Must have HEP!*
> *Fredrick Ashton*

Lady Constance was crying now. "It is something dreadful in the letter; it must be! Else why would he not tell me?"

The Incorrigible children put down their chickens and comforted her as best they could. *"Oojie-woojie-lady-woo,"* they said kindly, patting her on the arm. She dabbed at her eyes with the commemorative hand-kerchief, but when she saw the word "hope" it only prompted fresh tears.

Penelope slipped the letter from Lord Fredrick into her pocket. With an urgent wave, she summoned two of the welcoming-committee girls to come near. "Lady Constance, do not fret. There is nothing dreadful, I assure you. It is merely . . . a surprise!"

"A surprise?" Lady Constance blew her nose. "What is it?"

"I cannot tell you, because it is a surprise," Penelope replied, improvising madly, "but I am sure you will find out soon enough. Now, please allow these kind girls to escort you to the CAKE. I promise, all will be well."

Each of the girls offered an arm. "Will it be chocolate cake, do you think?" Penelope heard the sniffling lady ask as they led her inside. "Oh, I hope so! I could use some chocolate right now, in the most desperate way!"

IT WAS PAST TIME TO go in, but the children still had three chickens to deal with. The Incorrigibles wanted the sleepy baby dodos to be put to bed properly in a cozy room, with a glass of warm milk and a copy of *Nursery Rhymes for the Nearly Extinct* close at hand. (There is no such book, unfortunately. The children made up the title for fun, to amuse the baby dodos. Whether they succeeded we shall never know, for even the world's leading chicken experts have a hard time telling when chickens are amused. They are mysterious birds and have even been known to cross the road for no reason that anyone can deduce, though thousands have asked why.)

However, Penelope insisted that the dodos would be happier in the chicken coop, with all their dodo brothers and sisters nearby. "Remember, Incorrigibles: You have important responsibilities today, which you will shortly learn more about. There will be no time for dodo sitting," she said. Reluctantly, the children shooed the birds back toward the chicken coop. Then they followed their governess inside and whispered excitedly among themselves about what their important responsibilities might be.

Penelope kept thinking about the note in her pocket. "I feel sorry for Lord Fredrick's difficulties, but his timing—or rather, the moon's—could hardly be worse. I must give my CAKE speech according to plan, but he surely needs his HEP, too." She ushered the children to their seats in the auditorium, where everyone had gathered for the welcoming remarks. "And how does Old Timothy know about the secret side entrance to Swanburne? Is he truly Dr. Westminster's father?" How curious it all was!

Miss Mortimer clapped her hands three times—*clap clap clap!*—and everyone laughed in recognition, for who could forget those claps? "Good afternoon," she said, full of good cheer. "I will keep my remarks brief and pithy, for that is the Swanburne way. To all of you

I say: 'Welcome!' And to the Swanburne girls among you, let me add: 'Welcome home!' Now, go wander about and enjoy yourselves. See you at dinner!" *Clap clap clap!*

THE CLASSROOM DEMONSTRATIONS WERE A great success. The Swanburne girls celebrated their knowledge, and the alumnae celebrated theirs. Science experiments were performed, Latin verbs conjugated, multiplication tables recited, and spelling bees held. Globes were spun 'round like tops, and the capital cities of midsized European nations were identified with an impressive degree of accuracy, by current and former students alike.

Penelope was glad to greet some old friends among the guests, but there was no sign of Cecily. "I suppose it is a long way to come from Witherslack," she thought, disappointed. "Or perhaps she could not leave her Hungarian lady employer untranslated for so long. Still, I shall be sure to write her a long letter. . . ." Then she remembered she had given away the new fountain pen and sighed.

Late in the afternoon, the halls of the school filled with a delicious and unusual aroma. Everyone sniffed and tried to guess what would be served for dinner.

Penelope said nothing, although inside she began to feel the kind of fluttery, nervous tummy that she supposed every master criminal felt as the moment of truth grew near. Soon, very soon, it would be time to put the rest of the plan in motion.

And where was the chairman of Swanburne's board of trustees during all this? Nowhere to be seen. It was as if he too were written in invisible ink. However, at one point during the afternoon, as they walked from one classroom demonstration to the next, the children complained of a strange, foul smell wafting from a long-unused wing of the school. Classes had not been held in those rooms for many a year, but they still contained some antiquated laboratory equipment—enough to do some mixing and simmering, at least.

"Perhaps Edward Ashton is trying to visibilize the cannibal book himself," Penelope thought. "Luckily, only Simon knows the true formula. I wonder what mystery those pages will finally reveal?"

And, speaking of Simon, between demonstrations the children plied Penelope with questions about Simawoo's unexpected presence in the chicken coop. She convinced them that he was in Heathcote to attend a surprise birthday party, and that it would ruin the surprise if anyone discovered that he was near. They solemnly promised to keep the secret, but naturally, the children suspected that this was the same surprise meant for Lady Constance. Beowulf remarked that Lady Constance already behaved as if every day were her birthday, and all three children grew wide-eyed at the thought of what she might be like on the actual day.

Personally, Penelope was intensely curious to know how Simon's preparations for the visibilizer were going. She longed to take a peek, but alas, because of his pirate oath, his work must be done in secret. In any case, she still had to obtain the final two ingredients, which were, of course, the paprika and the cannibal book itself. And what on earth was she to do about Lord Fredrick Ashton?

"Important responsibilities," Alexander reminded, tugging at her sleeve. "When do we get them?"

"Soon," she said thoughtfully, for his question had given her an idea. "Very soon."

Ga-dong! Ga-dong! Ga-dong! Ga-dong! Ga-dong!

"Iambic pentameter o'clock," the children cried. "Time for dinner!"

And so it was. The guests were as punctual as one would expect a group of Swanburne graduates to be.

Before the fifth *ga-dong* had chimed, they had filed into the dining hall in perfect order and taken their seats. The graduates were full of praise for the school, its teachers, and especially its pupils, who were as full of cleverness and pluck as Agatha Swanburne herself could have wished. And the trustees had not been glimpsed all afternoon.

Only Lady Constance was unhappy with the day. "All that thinking!" she complained as she was led to her seat. "I am utterly worn out from it. And someone, please tell me: *Who* is responsible for inventing the multiplication tables? That person ought to be fired! I have never heard of anything so complicated. Especially those tricky sevens and eights."

Penelope thought she might cheer Lady Constance with a brief history of mathematics, starting with the ancient Babylonians and then on to the Greeks, including Thales of Miletus (the Theorem of Thales is not to be missed by fans of semicircles), Pythagoras, Euclid, and even—eureka!—Archimedes (of whom you ought to think each time you take a bath). Luckily, someone tapped her on the shoulder before she could make the attempt. She turned to see who it was.

"Mrs. Apple!" she exclaimed. At once she felt guilty. "Dear Mrs. Apple, I apologize for not coming to tell you myself. By now you have heard about the change in the speaking schedule, I hope?"

Mrs. Apple merely pointed to her throat and shook her head. "No voice," she mouthed. Not even a squeak came out.

"Mrs. Apple makes very good rabbit noise," Alexander said, impressed (those of you who are expert at animal sounds already know that rabbit calls are inaudible, and therefore quite difficult to learn).

Miss Mortimer swooped in. "There you are! Penny, dear, you and the children are to sit with me at the faculty table. We thought that was appropriate, given your accomplishments as an educator. Poor Mrs. Apple seems to have caught a dreadful cold! She has lost her voice completely. Thank goodness you are able to step in after all." Yet there was something about the twinkle in Mrs. Apple's eye that looked perfectly well. Penelope said nothing, and she and the children followed Miss Mortimer to their seats.

How festive the dining hall was now! Banners hung from the high rafters, each one emblazoned with a different saying of Agatha Swanburne. Chandeliers sparkled overhead, and fires blazed in every hearth. Even so, it was as if a cold wind swept through the hall when Edward Ashton entered, flanked by the baroness and her husband. With them was the Earl of Maytag, another unpleasant acquaintance of Lord Fredrick whom Penelope had met in the past. The other trustees followed nervously as a group, and they sat together at a long table that had been reserved for them.

A reporter from *Heathcote, All Year 'Round (Now Illustrated)* went from table to table asking questions of the graduates: What had been their favorite classes when they were students here? What had they accomplished since graduation? What were their favorite sayings of Agatha Swanburne? Finally, just like everyone else in the hall, the reporter found himself wondering aloud, "What is that tasty smell?"

It was dinner, at last! The soup course was served, and then a fish course, and finally the main dish was brought out in great kettles, piping hot and fragrant with paprika. "Hungarian goulash!" the cry went up. "So *that* was the delicious and unusual aroma we smelled earlier!" The cook had followed the recipe to perfection: chunks of tender stew meat simmered with onions, garlic, potatoes, parsnips, carrots, and tomatoes, seasoned with caraway and, of course, the paprika. Penelope was too nervous to take more than a few bites, but the children gobbled the goulash with gusto once they realized the dish contained no peas whatsoever. When the waiters came 'round to offer second helpings, they could only groan, for they had stuffed themselves at breakfast and now again at dinner, and their tummies were already tight and round as if they had each swallowed a melon.

"Save room for dessert," Miss Mortimer said, dabbing her lips with a napkin. "For how could we have our first annual CAKE without a cake to celebrate the occasion?"

"Cake . . . oh, no!" the children wailed, for they had never been less interested in dessert in their lives. As if on cue, the cake emerged. It was so large that it took two servants on each side and one in the back to push the enormous wheeled trolley that bore this confection out of the kitchen. It had twelve layers, and each one was a different kind of cake altogether.

"Chocolate cake, vanilla cake, carrot cake, sponge cake, coconut cake, marble cake, pineapple cake, mousse cake, nougat cake, cheesecake, pound cake, and Black Forest cake," Miss Mortimer explained. The icing had been applied in thick, painterly swirls. On top, written in a delicate script, was the Swanburne motto: *No Hopeless Case Is Truly Without Hope.*

A cheer went up at the sight of this masterpiece. Penelope kept her eye on the clock. It was twenty

"Cake . . . oh, no!"

minutes past six. The three children stared in horror as great wedges of cake were placed in front of them. Cassiopeia stabbed hers idly with a fork.

"Excuse me," Penelope said, and rose from her seat.

"Be back soon, Penny, dear!" Miss Mortimer warned. "It is almost time for your speech."

She smiled. "I shall return in a moment. Incorrigible children, come with me. It is time for your important responsibilities."

PENELOPE GAZED UP AND DOWN the deserted hallways of the school. It was just as she had hoped. Everyone was inside the dining hall, including Edward Ashton. The Incorrigibles would have the building all to themselves.

The three eager children lined up before her. "Each of you has a different job to do," she explained. "You are to complete your task as quickly as possible and then wait for me among the baby dodos, in the chicken coop. Understood?"

The mention of the dodos made the children even more excited. They nodded eagerly.

Penelope took a deep breath. "All right. Alexander, here is your task: You must find the cannibal book one more time. Remember how you did it before, by following the scent of the sea? It will be even more well hidden now, so you may have to sniff extra hard."

He closed his eyes and sniffed, long and deep. "Salty, briny, fishy . . . I think I have it," he said after a moment.

"Wonderful. Find the book and bring it to the chicken coop. Simawoo will know what to do with it. Wait for me there. And remember, when it comes to the birds . . ."

"No bothering, no nibbling, no eating. Only cuddling." He grinned.

"Correct." She smiled and turned to his brother. "Beowulf, your job is to obtain six and one-half cups of paprika from the kitchen. They will have plenty left over from making the Hungarian goulash. Have the cook tie it up in paper, bring it to the chicken coop—"

"Give to Simawoo, wait there, no nibbling birds," he finished. "Will do!"

"Splendid! Now, Cassiopeia. I had originally intended for you to accompany Alexander and act as lookout, but something else has come up. I fear you have the most difficult job of all." She knelt and took Cassiopeia's hands in her own. "Lord Fredrick Ashton is here at Swanburne, and he is not feeling up to snuff. He has urges to howl and bark, and he wishes to learn how to stop. Can you give him a no-howling lesson?"

The little girl frowned. Her furrowed-brow, thinking-hard expression looked not unlike Penelope's, although Penelope had no way of knowing that, as she was not the sort of person who spent her idle hours staring into mirrors.

"What do you think, Cassawoof?" she urged. "Can you teach Lord Fredrick to stop howling?"

Cassiopeia looked up, her green eyes wide. "Cannot teach him to stop howling. But can teach him to *like* howling."

Penelope sighed; she knew she was out of time. "That will have to do. First you must find Old Timothy, the enigmatic coachman from Ashton Place."

"Follow smell of horses," Cassiopeia said, understanding. "And mysteries."

"Precisely. Old Timothy will take you to Lord Fredrick. And remember, when you are done, meet me and your brothers—"

"In the dodo coop, *buck buck buck!*" She stood straight and gave a crisp salute. "Ten-hut!"

The boys joined the salute, and Penelope nearly cried to see those three brave faces before her. She swept them all into a fond embrace. "You are the best and cleverest pupils any governess could ever hope to have. Now, off with you. You have much to do, as do I." She gulped, suddenly nervous. "It is almost time for my speech."

"Good luck, Lumawoo!" the children said, as each one hugged her in turn. Then the three Incorrigibles ran off to do as they had been told.

The Thirteenth Chapter

Penelope's education proves
its worth.

PENELOPE SLIPPED BACK INTO HER seat at the faculty table. Miss Mortimer gave her a quizzical look, and the speechless Mrs. Apple drew a question mark in the air with her fingertip as a way of asking if everything was all right. Penelope merely smiled and shoved a forkful of cake into her mouth.

Polite as ever, Miss Mortimer waited until Penelope swallowed before asking, "Penny, dear, where are the—"

Hastily, Penelope took another bite of cake. With

her mouth full of food, she could hardly be expected to answer questions, she reasoned. At the Swanburne Academy for Poor Bright Females, good table manners were serious business.

She chewed as slowly as she could manage, but eventually the cake insisted upon being swallowed. The moment it was, Miss Mortimer spoke. "Penny, are the children—"

Penelope gobbled more cake. Miss Mortimer gave a nearly imperceptible sigh of exasperation, but still she waited. Meanwhile, the chairs that the Incorrigible children had occupied during dinner seemed to grow emptier by the minute.

If you have ever tried to make a delicious dessert last an extra-long time (by mashing it into crumbs suitable for the feeding of infant mice, for example, or by forcing yourself to recite the multiplication tables in your mind between forkfuls), you already know that there are only so many teeny-tiny bites one can take before reaching the bitter, cakeless end. So it was with Penelope. The last tasty morsels were already in her mouth. She chewed with exaggerated care. As she did, she ran the side of her fork ever so slowly 'round the edge of the plate, in order to scrape up the invisible traces of icing that might still cling to the rim of the dish.

"Penny! Where are the Incorrigible children?" Miss Mortimer cried at last.

Penelope took a moment to lick the fork clean. "Tummy aches, all three," she answered briskly. "Too much goulash, I expect. They went to lie down. Nothing to be concerned about."

Mrs. Apple and Miss Mortimer exchanged worried looks. "Poor dears," Miss Mortimer said. "Shall I call a doctor?"

"A doctor, for a child's tummy ache? Nonsense. Some castor oil and a hot-water bottle will do just fine." Penelope glanced at the clock. It was six thirty exactly, time for the speeches to begin. "It is not as if they have the plague, after all. Besides, a little suffering is good for them. Builds character!"

"Wh-what?" Miss Mortimer stammered, flummoxed, for this was not the sort of reply one would expect from a Swanburne girl.

"I agree. The more suffering, the better!" With a flourish of her fur-trimmed cape, Baroness Hoover strode by their table. When she reached the podium, she turned. "Assembled guests, good evening. I am Baroness Hoover. At the request of our chairman, Judge Quinzy, I have been asked to report on the operations of the school." Her husband's halfhearted

307

clapping echoed in the otherwise silent room; after a moment he stopped and sat on his hands in shame. "My conclusion is this: The school is undisciplined! Some remedies have already been put in place. I promise you, there will be further improvements."

"What improvements?" an alumna called out in alarm.

"Tighter budgets! Leaner operations! And no more frivolity. Consider that cake, for example." The baroness wiped a bit of frosting out of the corner of her mouth. "A garish, wasteful display."

"The chocolate bits were delectable," Lady Constance chirped. Indeed, she had had an unusually hearty appetite at dinner and had eaten two helpings of everything, including dessert.

Many voices began shouting all at once. Some cried out against the baroness's words, while others agreed with Lady Constance, for truly, the cake had been scrumptious, and there was hardly a speck of it left on anyone's plate.

Miss Mortimer held up a hand for order. "Baroness, rest assured we do not serve cake every day."

"No, but you hold classes every day, and many are as impractical as this cake." The baroness's eyes glittered in triumph. "For example, geography is entirely unnecessary. These girls are too poor to go on holiday, so what is the point of knowing where things are?"

"The capital of Hungary is Budapest!" someone called out hotly from the back of the room. Penelope startled, for the voice sounded familiar.

The baroness ignored the protest. "History, too, must go. The past is over and done with. I see no need to dwell upon it." A yelp of dismay came from near where Mrs. Apple was sitting, but as the dear history teacher had lost her voice, the sound obviously did not originate with her.

"And then there is this business of the school motto. 'No hopeless case is truly without hope.' Ridiculous! Some cases simply are hopeless, and it is no use pretending otherwise. I propose something more realistic. For example, 'Keep quiet and know your place.'" A shocked silence settled over the hall. Baroness Hoover's thin smile twisted into a sneer. "Or this: 'Children should neither be seen nor heard.'"

"I like that one," the Earl of Maytag interjected. "I'd eliminate children altogether, if I could! But I suppose new people have to come from somewhere. They don't grow on trees, eh?"

"I've got one. 'Keep your expectations low, and you'll never be disappointed.' Quite true in my experience, har har!" It was the baron. He forced a chuckle, but it sounded like he was choking.

The baroness silenced her spouse with a look. "These improvements will mark a new day in the life of this slipshod academy. Therefore, it is only fitting that the school itself be renamed. After tonight's official vote by the board of trustees, this institution shall forevermore be known as the Quinzy School for Miserable Girls."

"Quinzy!" Penelope blurted in outrage. "Quinzy!"

Magistra Grimsby handed her a fresh handkerchief. "Gesundheit!" she whispered. "Did you know that Latin has no word for 'sneeze'? And with those drafty togas, too."

An ominous buzz rose from the guests, like a hive of bees preparing to swarm. Miss Mortimer chose that moment to stand. She was the very picture of calm, and she glided to the podium as she spoke. "Baroness Hoover, thank you for your fascinating remarks. Everyone, please remember the trustees have not yet voted; the future, as always, remains unknown. As Agatha Swanburne would say, 'We will hop on that omnibus when it arrives, and not one moment before.' Now, let us proceed with our agenda for the evening."

The baroness seethed. "But I have not yet finished—"

"Tempus fugit, Baroness! We encourage early bed-times here; best not to dilly-dally." Miss Mortimer's gentle smile cast its spell over the hall. "Our next speaker is known to many of you. A former student, she is now a professional governess, currently charged with the education of three remarkable pupils. I expect her thoughts on the value of a *Swanburne* education will be nothing short of riveting." She said the word "Swanburne" with special care, so it could not be missed. "Please join me in welcoming our distin-guished alumna, Miss Penelope Lumley."

"No!" The baroness seized the podium with both hands, as if daring someone to tear her away. "The DODO protests! I have not approved Miss Lumley's speech."

Penelope was already on her feet. "But Baroness, you heard every word."

"And I hated each one! I have never been so bored in my life." She glared at Miss Mortimer. "The DODO demands a different speaker."

"Alas, our only alternate speaker has laryngitis." Miss Mortimer gestured toward the irrepressibly talk-ative Mrs. Apple, who shrugged and pointed to her throat. "Given the circumstances, we shall have to let Miss Lumley take the podium. Once more, may I present Miss Penelope Lumley!'"

The applause was tremendous. The baroness gnashed her teeth as if she planned to bite someone, but the ovation grew until she had no choice but to step down and return to her seat at the trustees' table.

Slowly, Penelope made her way to the podium. Miss Mortimer put a hand on her arm and whispered: "Remember, Penelope. You are a Swanburne girl, through and through. Speak from your heart, and all will be well."

From the heart, indeed! As Miss Mortimer left her standing there alone, Penelope's heart skittered like a bird's. She had no notes to speak from, nor any speech prepared. How could she and Simon ever have imagined this plan would work? But he and the children were already doing their parts. Now she had to do hers.

She turned to face the audience. She smoothed her everyday brown dress and took a deep, calming breath. During that breath she noted the poised pen of the reporter from *Heathcote, All Year 'Round (Now Illustrated)*. She saw the empty chair next to Lady Constance in which Lord Fredrick had been assigned to sit, and the three empty chairs where the Incorrigible children had been. Could she do it? The fate of the school hung in the balance. So did the fate of the cannibal book, and the moon-cursed Ashtons, and perhaps the Incorrigibles, too.

And what of her own fate? Why had Miss Mortimer used the poultice to conceal her among the other Swanburne girls all those years? Was it no more than happenstance that she had ended up at Ashton Place, governess to the Incorrigibles? And were the Long-Lost Lumleys truly lost? Or, like Edward Ashton, had they concealed themselves for some pressing reason that was, as yet, unknown?

The storm of questions threatened to blow her off course before she had even begun. She placed her hands on the lip of podium to steady herself. "I was asked to speak at the CAKE in order to make a good impression on the trustees," she thought. Determination filled her sails like a steady wind. "Well, I am going to make an impression, one way or another. And I cannot take one minute less than an hour and three-quarters to do it."

With a glance at the clock, she began.

"HEAR ME, O MEN OF Athens! And fellow Swanburnians, too," she proclaimed. (The bit about the men of Athens was from a famous speech by Demosthenes. Granted, it was an odd beginning, as there were no

313

men of Athens in the room. But Penelope liked the sound of it, and with an hour and three-quarters to fill, she could hardly afford to be picky about words.) "That is to say, hello, to all current and former Swanburne girls, to the faculty, and to the esteemed board of trustees. Hello, hello, hello! Thank you all, so much, for coming here today."

She looked at the clock. Scarcely one minute! She had best slow down. She took another breath and continued at a measured pace.

"To celebrate alumnae knowledge at Swanburne is no easy task. Nor is it a quick task. In fact, it is a lengthy task, for there is a great deal of knowledge to celebrate." Her eyes met those of Mrs. Apple, whose face shone with unspoken encouragement. "History, for example! A most important subject. In the words of Cicero, 'Not to know what has been transacted in former times is to be always a child.'"

"'If no use is made of the labors of past ages, the world must remain always in the infancy of knowledge!'" Mrs. Apple, suddenly in possession of her voice, shouted the rest of the quote, and earned a smattering of applause for it, too.

"Quite so. If not for my studies of history and the great speeches of antiquity, I might never have even

314

heard of Cicero. And that would be a shame, for Cicero could coin a pithy, wise saying with the best of them." Boldly, Penelope looked at the trustees. "It was Cicero who said, 'A community is like the ones who govern it.' Cicero is not here tonight, of course, for he is long dead. But if he were, he might well ask: Is Swanburne like its current board of trustees? With its strict rules against birthday presents and parties and singing? With its dislike of geography and its objection to the occasional tasty treat?"

"No!" First one voice cried out, then others. "No!" "Hardly!" "Not a bit!"

Penelope scanned the crowd. Each face seemed like a beacon of hope, and she took courage from every one. "To me, Swanburne is more like Miss Mortimer: unfailingly kind and calm under pressure. Or like Mrs. Apple, ablaze with passion for her favorite subject. It is like the Swanburne girls, full of curiosity and mischief and loyal to a fault, with high-leaping imaginations and plenty of good common sense."

She looked up at the banners that swayed above her head like a line of dancers. "Swanburne is like Agatha Swanburne herself—wise and strong, with a fierce heart for justice, and a sense of humor, too."

More voices rang out. "Yes, that's right!" "Quite so!"

"Swanburne forever!" and so on.

In this way, Penelope spoke from the heart, just as Miss Mortimer had advised, and if that were all she had done, her speech would have been a resounding success. She quoted Cicero, and Demosthenes, and Shakespeare. She threw in some wisdom from Cato the Younger, and from Cato the Elder, too. But before long, she had said all she could think of to say on the subject of education, and the minute hand on the clock had barely swept past the half-hour mark.

Once more she surveyed the room. Her audience was rapt, ready to spring to their feet in a thunderous ovation. "My years at Swanburne have given me so much!" she said with passion. "Good memories, good friends, good posture, excellent penmanship, and a deep love of poetry and all its meters. For example, iambic pentameter, which, as you may know, sounds like this: *ta-TUM, ta-TUM, ta-TUM, ta-TUM, ta-TUM.*"

She clapped her hands to demonstrate the rhythm. "Let me offer an example. I HAVE a FURry FRIEND called NUTSaWOO. Might you all say that with me? Feel free to clap if you like."

Puzzled, the audience chanted and clapped: "I HAVE a FURry FRIEND called NUTSaWOO."

Penelope smiled. "Well done! You are natural-born

316

poets, each and every one of you. Of course, iambic pentameter should not be confused with anapestic tetrameter, as I am sure you already know. Would anyone care to demonstrate?"

There was an audible scuffling of chairs. Students and alumnae alike looked worried, as if suddenly confronted with an unexpected quiz in a topic they had never studied.

"Or even dactylic hexameter," Penelope added.

Edward Ashton's voice boomed from the trustee's table. "All right, Miss Lumley, that is quite enough—"

Penelope held up a hand. "Please, save your questions for the end. Now I shall recite the beginning of one of my favorite poems. See if you can guess the meter. It is called 'Wanderlust.'

"I wander through the meadows green
Made happy by the verdant scene."

Nobody volunteered the answer, but Penelope was all too happy to explain. "It is iambic quadrameter, you see? Four *ta-TUM*s per line, instead of five. And a rhyming couplet as well, which hardly bears mentioning, for I am sure you do not need me to point out that 'green' and 'scene' rhyme with each other, as well as with many other words. Like 'string bean,' and 'soup tureen,' and 'Byzantine,' and—well, there are far too many to list. For now, let me simply recite the poem for your enjoyment. No further interruptions, I promise!"

As good as her word, Penelope recited "Wanderlust," and several other poems as well. She analyzed their meter, rhyme schemes, and anything else she could think of. By the time she had finished exhausting her knowledge of poetry, she had been speaking for an hour. Members of the audience were fanning themselves, and she saw a few yawns in the back.

"But so much for my introductory remarks." She leaned against the podium for support. "At last it is time to address the true subject of my talk. It is a subject about which I had scarcely given a second thought before coming to Swanburne. Happily, my education here lit a bonfire of interest within me that burns brightly to this very day."

The candlelight flickered in the lenses of Edward Ashton's glasses as if his eyes might shoot flaming arrows at her. Penelope looked away, so as not to lose heart. "I will keep you in suspense no longer. The subject of my speech is ferns. Ferns!" she repeated, raising one hand in the air as if she were addressing the Roman Senate. "Yes, ferns, or Pteridophyta, as they are scientifically known. A topic about which I think I may humbly call myself an expert."

After a lengthy preamble, in which Penelope talked about fronds, spores, roots, rhizomes, and the impressive knack ferns have for growing in the shade, she began to catalog the varieties. "One of my favorites is the interrupted fern. In this curious specimen, the brown sporangia do not grow from the tops of the frond stalks. Nor do they grow on their own separate stalks, as they do on the ostrich fern. I am sure you will be as shocked and amazed as I was to learn that, on the interrupted fern, the brown sporangia grow right in the middle of the stalk, 'interrupting' the pattern of green fronds, so to speak. Hence, the name."

Penelope looked out at the audience. The normally straight-backed Swanburne girls were slumped in their chairs. Some of the faculty were asleep; others pinched their own cheeks to stay awake. Only Miss Charlotte Mortimer sat upright and cheerful, with her hands calmly folded in her lap. She listened attentively to every word Penelope uttered. At times she nodded, and a secret smile seemed to play about her lips.

"In the early stages of growth, before the appearance of the sporangia, the interrupted fern is easily confused with the cinnamon fern. Luckily, there are several ways the careful observer might tell them apart. . . ."

On and on she went. She spoke of the maidenhair fern, with its striking black stems, and the hay-scented fern that smelled, remarkably, like hay. When she ran out of ferns that were real, she invented fictional ferns: the quilted fern, which died down each winter into a soft and cozy clump. The Dalmatian fern, with its dappled fronds and alert bearing. The earlobe fern, with its pendulous, spore-bearing clusters.

Her imagination took leap after leap, and all the while she kept her eye on the clock. Fern by fern, the minute hand inched forward, until an hour and twenty minutes had passed . . . an hour and thirty minutes . . . forty minutes. . . . Now she was at one hour and forty-four minutes, with only one minute to go. . . .

She paused and took a sip of water from the glass that some kind soul had brought to the podium. She cleared her throat and dabbed her lips with her commemorative handkerchief.

"And so, there you have it: the mighty fern, in a nutshell," she concluded at last. "Any questions?"

MISS PENELOPE LUMLEY DID NOT invent the filibuster, which, as you know, has been in use since the days of ancient Rome. However, she may fairly be credited with inventing the fernibuster. It is not a style of oration that has been often used since (ferns being not quite as popular nowadays as they were in Miss Lumley's day, a frankly inexplicable state of affairs). But on this occasion, a fernibuster was just what the doctor ordered.

It should be noted that Penelope's fernibuster did not plunge all her audience into a stupor. In fact, some of her listeners (all right, two) found it nothing short of riveting. Miss Mortimer seemed enthralled by the performance and approached the podium as soon as the applause died down, which, to be blunt, did not take very long.

"Penny, dear, you have outdone yourself! I had no idea you had grown so expert in the matter of spores and fronds. I only wish you could tell us more. But, as the saying goes, 'So many ferns, so little time.'" (As you may recall, she was here paraphrasing a saying of Agatha Swanburne which originally had to do with cupcakes, but Miss Mortimer was well able to adapt the wisdom of the past to suit her present circumstances, and so should we all.) "Really, Penny, it was a tremendous display of pteridological expertise. I can honestly say I have never seen anything like it. And I am not the only one who thinks so. Here, allow me to introduce Mrs. Diane Worthington, of the Heathcote Amateur Pteridological Society."

Miss Mortimer stepped aside to reveal an elderly lady with piercing blue eyes. Her white hair floated, cloud-like, atop her head, and a delicate pattern of creases fanned across her face like arching fronds, especially when she smiled. The crinkly-eye fern, Penelope could not help thinking.

"How do you do, Miss Lumley?" said Mrs. Worthington, clasping her hand. "Always a pleasure to meet a fellow fan of ferns! I wonder if you remember me. I spoke at Swanburne some years ago, when you were still a student here."

Of course Penelope remembered her. In fact, it was the lecture by Mrs. Worthington that had prompted Penelope's interest in ferns to begin with. It would be a genuine pleasure to renew their acquaintance, but now was not the time, for she had to get to the chicken coop, quick!

"What a thrilling presentation!" the good lady continued. "I wonder if you might be available to address the members of our society at one of our monthly meetings. Your talk was impeccably thorough. I have a few quibbles, mind you. Do you really think the ostrich fern can grow to three meters? I have rarely seen a specimen that big."

"I must have been thinking of actual ostriches. Mrs. Worthington, forgive me; I would be honored to speak to your society, but at this moment I must run to another engagement. Might we continue our conversation by post? And may I say, I will be sorry to miss your upcoming talk on Ferns Under Glass: Tips and Techniques for Indoor Growing. I have long wondered about the effectiveness of Wardian cases."

Mrs. Worthington beamed. "A fascinating topic indeed. We meet the second Wednesday of every month. I shall send a letter proposing some dates."

"Ferntastic." Clearly it would take awhile for Penelope to shake the fronds out of her mind, so to speak. "That is to say, I shall look forward to your correspondence." Giddy with triumph, Penelope made her way toward the door. Her speech was over, and Edward Ashton and his minions had been trapped here in the dining hall the whole time, just as she and Simon had planned. By the time Ashton discovered the cannibal book was missing, they would have visibilized it and read the whole thing twice, at least!

She was nearly to the door when a distinguished-looking woman seized her and kissed her firmly on both cheeks. "Speech good!" she proclaimed, and began to talk rapidly in a language Penelope could not understand. Then she stopped. "Wait," she said. "My translator."

A round-cheeked young lady stepped forward, beaming. Her thick, curly hair was tied in two long braids that hung down her back like ropes. The hair was a glossy strawberry blond, nothing like the drab, dark brown of days gone by. But there was no mistaking who it was.

"Cecily!" Penelope forgot about everything else and squealed in pure delight. "Cecily Longstocking! Oh, look at you! How has it been so long? You have hardly changed a bit!"

Cecily hugged her so hard her feet left the ground. "Penny Lumley! I was so afraid we'd miss you! We suffered a broken wheel on the road from Witherslack, so we had to wait for a change of coach. But we made it just in time for a bit of dinner and your speech. Goodness, Penny, you gave me a workout! All those ferns! I couldn't think how to say 'spores' in Hungarian, so I kept calling them 'crumbs.' Close enough, I guess. But what on earth is a widget fern?"

"I wish I knew," Penelope said, laughing. "And is this lady your employer? How kind of her to accompany you to the CAKE."

"Well, she has business here as well. She's one of the trustees. She likes to keep her charitable causes quiet, though. Otherwise there's no end to people asking her for money. It's because of her the school has so many language teachers. She always insists on having a Swanburne girl as her translator."

Cecily spoke rapidly in Hungarian to her employer; Penelope thought she heard her own name in the stream of words. Cecily turned back to her. "Miss Penelope Lumley, I am honored to present you to Her Grace, the Archduchess Ilona Laszlo, third cousin to Prince Franz-Fritz Spitz-Wilhelm, Count Palatine of the Spotted Cavern of Dalmatia."

At hearing her title, the archduchess stood straight and clicked her heels together. Then she replied to Cecily, who listened attentively before explaining, "She wants you to know that dinner was excellent. Very rarely does she taste an authentic Hungarian goulash in England. She says it was nearly as good as the one she makes herself."

That the dinner had been made from the archduchess's own recipe seemed like a revelation best saved for another day, so Penelope said only, "Thank you," and curtsied deeply.

"Good goulash makes good school," the archduchess declared. "I vote no change."

Cecily's smile faded. "Yes, what's this about changing the name of the school? They're not serious, are they?"

Penelope's face fell. The vote! In her relief at surviving the fernibuster she had forgotten about that. "Perhaps it is too late now," she said, hoping against hope. And indeed, Miss Mortimer was trying desperately to dismiss everyone, with handshakes all around and many exclamations of "Good night now, sleep well, sweet dreams!"

"Silence!" It was the baroness, forcing her way back to the podium. "Nobody leaves this room! I don't care about your early bedtimes. The board of trustees must vote, and vote we will, despite having to endure that exhausting display of expertise! Trustees, gather at the front of the room!"

The seven trustees came forward as requested. Penelope gasped with surprise to see Mrs. Worthington take her place among them. She was the first to speak and declared, "Any school that could produce such a well-rounded aficionado of ferns must be doing a superb job. I vote to keep Swanburne Swanburne!" Her face crinkled wonderfully as she smiled, and all the girls cheered.

326

Next was Mr. Felix Trundle, a well-off solicitor from Heathcote, and as it happened, an amateur singer of light opera. "When I heard there was to be no more singing, I thought, 'Well, that is not going to sit well.' And why have we not heard the school song tonight? It's very catchy, in my opinion." In his rich bass voice, he sang, "All hail to our founder, Agatha!" Some of the girls started to join in, but the baroness shushed them.

The third vote came from the archduchess. "Good goulash, good school!" she said, as she, too, voted in favor of keeping the school as it had always been.

That made three votes in defense of the school, and everyone looked hopeful. But Baroness Hoover and the Earl of Maytag voted firmly in favor of changing the name to the School for Miserable Girls. So did the chairman, from behind his bandit's kerchief. Now there were three for, three against.

"And how do you vote, Baron Hoover?" Edward Ashton asked, his voice so smooth as to sound indifferent.

The baroness checked her watch, as if the whole business would soon be over. But Baron Hoover did not answer straightaway; he hemmed and hawed and cleared his throat. When he did speak, he kept his eyes downcast, as if he were talking to the carpet. "Well, I must say, I keep thinking about that motto. 'No hopeless case is truly without hope.' I remember feeling rather like a hopeless case at times, when I was a lad. Still have dark days, to tell the truth! Could use a true friend or two, but people lack sympathy for your problems when you have a title and an estate and pots of money. As if a rich fellow never gets the toothache or misses his mum!" He looked up from his shoes. "It's not my fault I was born a baron. I'd have made a good gardener, I think. Flowers are so cheery."

The baroness glared. "Stop wasting everyone's time. You will vote the way I do. We are married, after all."

The baron tugged at his collar. "True, true. Still, it seems as if I might sometimes feel differently than you do about this or that. Thinking for myself, what? Well, it's possible!"

But not on this occasion, it seemed. Held captive by his wife's temper like an insect stuck on a pin, the baron squirmed and blushed until he finally turned to Edward Ashton.

"Quinzy, old chap, I hate to cause trouble. I shall have to recuse myself. I abstain! In fact, I find it rather tedious to be a trustee. I don't much like telling other people what to do. Count me out, if you please."

Edward Ashton's voice took on a decided chill. "Do I take it you have resigned from the board?"

"Quite right, Quinzy, quite right!" Relieved, the baron sat in the nearest chair and tried to wipe his face with a handkerchief. It was one of the commemorative Swanburne handkerchiefs. At the sight of it, his wife snatched it and flung it to the ground in anger, and the poor man had to make do with a dinner napkin.

"Well, well," oozed the Earl of Maytag. "Three for, three against, one abstained. Seems we have a tie, Quinzy."

"According to the bylaws, there must be seven trustees in order to conduct any official business," Miss Mortimer said quickly. "We only have six. That means bedtime for all!"

Ashton held up a hand. "A minor inconvenience. As chairman, it is well within my powers to appoint a new trustee. Fortunately, we have a perfect candidate right here. I appoint Lady Constance Ashton."

Penelope's heart sank. Surely Lady Constance would vote however she was told. And Simon and the children still waited in the chicken coop!

Lady Constance stood and clapped her hands with delight, for she dearly loved to be the center of attention. "Me? A trustee? If only Fredrick were here!"

The baroness stepped forward. "Enough squealing, Constance. Vote and let us be done with it."

"I will be honored to cast my vote, Baroness. But first, I must make up my mind. Let me think. Hmm!" Lady Constance seemed in no rush to decide, for now everyone hung on her every word. "I have the utmost respect for Judge Quinzy, even when he is dressed in a bandit costume, as he is now. If he says the students here need a firm hand, I am sure he is correct." She frowned, and her pretty eyebrows furrowed together, like twin arches of gold. "On the other hand, I have had a devil of a time learning the name of this school. But after Miss Lumley's speech about poems and ferns, I believe I have it at last." She looked at Penelope. "Swan*burne*. Rhymes with 'fern.' Isn't that correct?"

"Fern, yes!" Penelope said encouragingly. "Or 'stern,' or 'learn,' or 'nocturne,' or—"

"Do not confuse me, please! Swan*burne*, rhymes with 'fern'; that is all I need recall. Now, despite my total lack of responsibilities I am an extremely busy person, and I know I shall never have time or patience to learn a new name. Therefore, I vote to keep things exactly the way they are." She trilled a little laugh. "You must admit, it is much simpler that way."

The baroness loomed over Lady Constance. "You silly, spoiled little doll! Wherever did you get the notion that we wanted you to think? Quinzy, do something!

330

She is obviously not qualified to be a trustee. She must be replaced! Remove her and appoint someone else—" But her protest was interrupted by a dreadful sound.

"Ahwoooooo!"

"Ahwoooooo!"

It was deep, ragged, desperate howling, followed by a higher, sweeter, more piping sort of howl.

"What is that horrible noise?" The baroness sounded afraid.

"Farkas," said the archduchess knowingly. "Sharp teeth!"

"Farkas is Hungarian for 'wolf,'" Cecily explained. "Sounds like a papa wolf and a cute little wolf cub to me."

"Or perhaps it is Lord Fredrick Ashton and Cassiopeia Incorrigible," Penelope thought—and then she had an idea. "Yes!" she cried. "It *is* wolves! Packs of them. Vicious and dangerous wolves." She turned to her friend and spoke in her ear. "Cecily, I need your help. I have urgent business in the chicken coop. I would prefer if no one noticed my going. Can you create a bit of mayhem? A diversion? Something along the lines of the haunted hay maze, perhaps?"

Cecily's eyes sparkled. "The hay maze! That brings back memories. Don't worry, I'll keep everyone occupied here for as long as I can."

Without further delay, Cecily threw back her head and screamed.

"Ahhhhhhhhhh!"

What a scream it was! Nowadays it would be featured in the sound track of a horror movie. It was an eardrum-piercing, bloodcurdling nightmare of a scream, petrifying enough to make even a Swanburne girl forget all her antipanicking skills.

"Wolves!" Cecily yowled. "Wolves! Wolves at Swanburne!"

"Wolves! Wolves at Swanburne!" Others picked up the cry. Fear crackled dangerously through the crowd, like a brushfire snaking through a drought-stricken field.

"Wolves!"

"Wolves at Swanburne!"

"Ahwooooooo!"

"Ahwooooooo!"

"Ahhhhhhhhhh!"

Cecily's lung power had only improved with time. She screeched like the brakes of a Bloomer steam engine pulling into the station. She moaned like the ghosts that haunt other ghosts. She wailed as if she were the headmistress of the Banshee Academy for Hair-Raising Wails. "Wolves at Swanburne! *Run for your lives!*"

"Wolves at Swanburne! Run for your lives!"

"Stop!" yelled the baroness. "Back to your seats! We must appoint a new trustee and conclude our vote!" But no one listened. The dining hall had turned into a free-for-all of chaos. Miss Mortimer stood placidly in the middle of it all. Clearly, there would be no more voting that night.

"Wolves! Danger! Mayhem!" yelled Penelope, getting into the spirit of it. "Now, to the chicken coop!"

The Fourteenth Chapter

In the chicken coop, blurry
things come into focus.

PENELOPE SLIPPED OUT OF THE chaos of the dining hall
unnoticed. "It may not have been a Great Oration, but
at least there was plenty of it," she thought with pride
as she trotted toward the chicken coop. Had the fernibuster bought enough time for the Incorrigibles to
accomplish their tasks and for Simon to prepare the
visibilizer? Were all their questions about the mysterious events on the island of Ahwoo-Ahwoo about to be
answered?

"*Ahwoo! Ahwoo!*"

"Ahwoooooo!"

The odd, wolfish duet floated through the air: this time it was a pair of high-pitched, girlish howls, followed by a deep and manly one.

"Lord Fredrick's lesson seems to be going well," Penelope thought. "Clever Cassiopeia! She will have the makings of an excellent governess someday." Quietly, she opened the door to the coop. Once inside, she wrinkled her nose, for the smell was much worse than usual. It was as if someone had made a goulash out of spoiled fish, sprinkled it with pungent cheese, and then served it in an unsanitary shoe.

"Boo!" Alexander and Beowulf jumped out from the shadows. "Lumawoo, look! Boo!" The boys' faces and hands were scarlet with paprika. The pair of chickens that pecked and strutted at the boys' feet were also covered with the stuff. The red paprika dusted over white feathers had turned them a most unchickenlike shade of pink.

"We are the Crimson Postal Ghostlies, with our Spooky Baby Dodo Pets," Alexander explained. "This one is named Pinky."

"This one is named Pinky Too," said Beowulf. The boys were in high spirits. The chickens seemed pleased as well (although if they understood that they

336

had been seasoned, rather than merely decorated, they might not have felt so, well, plucky).

Penelope lifted her skirt and sidestepped past the rosy birds. "I see the paprika was successfully obtained. Good work, Beowulf."

"The cannibal book, too. I followed my nose and the scent of the sea, all the way inside Quinzawoo's room, under his bed, and into the secret compartment of his hidden suitcase. Easy!" Alexander inhaled deeply to demonstrate his sniffing powers, but the paprika made him sneeze. *"Ah-choo!"*

"Gesundheit!" Simon's voice rang out from the back of the coop. "I'm in Dr. Westminster's office. The visibilizer is simmering like mad."

Penelope and the boys ran to the office, with Pinky and Pinky Too *buck-buck-buck*ing close behind. Simon looked up from his improvised laboratory. "It's all right; you can come in. The confidential ingredient mixing is finished. Now I'm just cooking it up."

With a pair of kitchen tongs, Simon lifted the cannibal book from a vat of bubbling liquid that sat upon a makeshift stove, fashioned out of Bunsen burners from the Swanburne laboratory. He held up the book for all to see. "Someone's tried to visibilize it already, but they obviously didn't have the right formula. See the faded letters peeking through here and there?"

The smell was so overpowering Penelope could barely speak. "Will it work?" she croaked.

"Oh, it'll work, never you fear. My formula's fool-proof. Another ten seconds or so should do it." He lowered the book into the vat and sniffed. "Miss L, it was awfully clever of you to suggest we brew it in here, among the chickens. You can hardly smell the castor oil, or the rancid cheese, or the unwashed socks— Oops! Forget I said that. Here, let's have another look." Once more he lifted the dripping book from the vat. This time he laid it flat on a nearby bed of straw.

"If you want a book, why not read Mr. Gibbon's?" Beowulf asked helpfully. He and his brother seemed untroubled by the stink, but of course they had spent much of their early years in forests and caves and so on, and were accustomed to all sorts of gross and mushroomy smells. "Why cook a book?"

"This book is special." Penelope kept her eyes fixed on the diary. "It may tell us how to cure Lord Fred-rick of his difficulties, and possibly much more as well. Poor Lord Fredrick," she said, in a burst of sympathy. "Imagine, to be left howling and scratching every four weeks, with no explanation, and a father who simply—"

"Abandoned ship," Simon finished. "Aye. Look! I'm

starting to see some letters! Although the prose looks a bit odd . . ."

"That is because it is written in verse." Penelope leaned closer. "At first glance, it appears to be rhyming quatrains in iambic heptameter."

"Poetry! Who knew old Pudge had it in him?" Simon angled the book toward the window so it caught the fading light better. The four of them crowded around.

Penelope read quickly, her finger hovering over each stanza. "This first part tells of the voyage. There are lists of provisions, a description of the crew and the ship."

"And here's some admiring bits about the admiral: stern of jaw, broad of shoulder, never blinks at danger. Sounds like quite a chap." With great care, Simon turned the sodden page. "Now he's standing on deck, cursing the wind or lack thereof, and praying for a breeze. Looks like his prayers are soon answered, for a storm kicks up and blows them hither and yon."

Again he turned the page, and his eyes grew wide. "Here comes a plot twist! The storm leaves them shipwreck'd on an unmapped island, somewhere south of the equator."

"Like 'Wreck of the Hespawoo,'" Beowulf said.

"Quite so, and the 'The Wreck of the Hesperus' is

written in quatrains as well, four lines to a stanza."
Penelope could not help adding this tidbit of information, for with so much going on, the children had been
woefully short on lessons.

Simon read:

> *"Night after night, the moonlight fell*
> *As soft and pale as wool,*
> *'What cursèd place is this,' we cried,*
> *'Whose moon is always full?'*

> *"'Ahwoo-Ahwoo!' the answer came*
> *From creatures, nearby, prowling.*
> *'Ahwoo-Ahwoo! Ahwoo-Ahwoo!'*
> *How fearsome was their howling!"*

As Simon read, Penelope's skin turned all goose
bumpy. ("Chicken bumpy" would also be a logical way
to describe it, for chickens, too, have bumpy skin when
plucked, as would any bird. However, "goose bumps"
is the usual term, and that is the one we shall use.)
"How strange! An unmapped island with a moon that
is always full."

"And woofs, too," Alexander said, using his sister's
word for wolves.

"They'd have to be unusual wolves, to live on a tropical island. It's all quite strange. Let's see what happens next." Once more, Simon turned the page and read.

> "'Show yourselves!' the admiral boomed.
> (It was a manly roar!)
> 'Ahwoo-Ahwoo!' The monsters fled,
> And left us as before.

> "'These mocking wolves, these savage beasts
> Shall know my wrath anon.'
> The admiral's fury sealed our doom:
> 'Ahoy! The hunt is on!'"

"The hunt is on. . . ." Penelope felt as if a eureka were brewing someplace inside her, if only she could put all the pieces together. "That is what Madame Ionesco said, too, when she first met the Incorrigible children. The wolf babies, she called them."

"We are not woofs," Beowulf protested. "Or babies."

"I believe the good soothsayer was speaking metaphorically. You remember what a metaphor is: when one thing is used to describe another—" But Penelope's explanation was cut short by a rhythmic sound.

Ta-TUM, ta-TUM, ta-TUM, ta-TUM, ta-TUM!

"Iambic pentameter?" Alexander said, his voice quivering. The sound grew closer by the second.

Penelope grabbed both boys by the shoulders. "It is hooves, at a gallop. Someone is coming, and quick! Everyone, hide!"

IF YOU HAD DROPPED BY the chicken coop a scant moment later, you would have seen nothing out of the ordinary. True, there were traces of red powder scattered on the otherwise clean-swept dirt, and the stink was more foul than fowl. But rows of fat hens roosted contentedly in their roosting boxes, with their red-combed heads nestled into their plump bodies. No doubt they dreamed happy chicken dreams, of tasty feed and egg-filled nests, and perhaps the occasional dance step, too.

Outside was a far less peaceful scene. There was the snorting protest of an overridden horse and the anxious stamping of hooves, followed by a thud as of a man leaping from the saddle. Still the chickens did not stir, not even as the heavy tread of boots on dirt approached. The door to the chicken coop swung open.

"I have had quite enough of your games, governess!" Edward Ashton roared. (One could fairly call it a manly roar. Perhaps it was a talent he inherited from his grandfather, the admiral.) "Reveal yourselves!"

The rustling of feathers and some mild squawking was the only answer he received. He lowered his voice and tried again. "I know you are in here, Miss Lumley. And I know you have my book. Give it to me now, or suffer the consequences. Prison . . . orphanages . . . workhouses . . . the choice is yours."

Silence.

Taking one slow step at a time, Ashton surveyed the coop's inhabitants. The birds were drowsy and contented, with their feathers fluffed around them like pillows. Down the rows of snowy-white and dappled-brown chickens he walked, yet not a creature stirred; one would think nothing unusual had ever happened in this chicken coop in the entire history of chickens. Then he arrived at the end of the row, where Pinky and Pinky Too sat, pink as a pair of flamingoes.

"What pretty pink chickies," he cooed. "Please, pretty chickies, won't *you* tell me if someone is hiding in this stinky, stinky coop?"

Alas, Alexander's good manners got the best of him; the man had said please, after all. "Apologies, but there is no one here. Except for us chickens, of course.

Buck-buck-buck," he added, but it was too late.

"As I thought," Ashton snarled. "Come out at once, all of you!"

Heads hanging in defeat, the two boys, Penelope, and Simon emerged from their hiding places, covered with hay and feathers. Edward Ashton loomed before them. He wore no glasses. There was no putty concealing his long, sloping Ashton nose, nor was there a handkerchief tied 'round his face. He bore little resemblance to the portrait in Lord Fredrick's study, for his plumpness had dwindled to a lean and catlike frame, and his hair was as black as if it had been dyed with India ink. But those eyes were unmistakable—dark as twin smudges of pitch, dangerous as a pair of bottomless wells.

He surveyed the guilty foursome. "One is missing," he said. "Where is the girl?"

"Cassawoof is giving howling lessons," Beowulf said with an edge of pride.

Ashton let out a bark of a laugh. "Howling lessons? That is even more impractical than poetry. But this ridiculous school is no longer my concern; I have learned all I need from it. Miss Lumley, for the second time in two days, I command you: Give me my book!"

"It is not your book and never will be," Penelope retorted.

Ashton took a threatening step closer, but Simon blocked his way. "Simon Harley-Dickinson, at your service." He extended his hand, which was ignored. "Last time we met you were someone else! Say, Edward— I'd call you Lord Ashton, but it seems a bit formal for a dead person—that diary you're so keen to get your hands on was written by my great-uncle Pudge. Surely, that makes him the owner, wouldn't you say? Him being the author and all."

"The cabin boy Pudge was in service to my grandfather when he wrote his account of their voyage." Ashton sniffed deeply and swiveled his head, as if searching. "It was the admiral's property then, and it is my property now."

He sniffed again and turned once more to the chickens. Following his nose, he stopped in front of Pinky (it might have been Pinky Too, actually; they were not easy to tell apart). His hand darted out so quickly that the chicken scarcely had time to *buck-buck-buck* in protest, as Ashton reached underneath and extracted the diary as if it were some precious egg that the pink bird had just succeeded in laying.

"I, too, have a keen sense of smell, at least during

345

the full moon. A talent left over from the howling days of my youth." He opened the book, and his eyes grew wide as he read aloud.

"Night after night, the moonlight fell
As soft and pale as wool . . ."

He looked up. "What happened to the invisible ink?"

"Simawoo cooked it in the visibilizer. Now you can read it fine," Alexander bragged.

Ashton smiled. "Simon Harley-Dickinson, at my service, indeed. It appears you have done me a great service, although, I assure you, I would have solved the riddle of the ink myself, eventually. I am nothing if not patient." He closed the book and cradled it in his arms like a child. "Poor Fredrick! It was never my desire to pass my affliction on to him. But thanks to this volume, his suffering will soon be over."

"Surely, your cruelty is the true cause of his suffering," Penelope said sharply. "You let him think you were dead, all these long years!"

"My cruelty? Perhaps. Yet everything I have done, I have done for my family. Do you think it has been easy for me to stand in the shadows as my son grew to manhood? To know that, moon after moon, year after year, he hides himself away in the attic in shame? And all because he is an Ashton. That is the proud lineage that I gave him, along with its curse! It is my duty, my purpose—my obsession, if you will—to undo the harm my ancestors have wrought. Renouncing my name, my very existence, was a small price to pay. What I have had to do, and may have yet to do, I cannot do as Edward Ashton. Let Judge Quinzy bear the blame for my misdeeds! I will not bring more shame upon my family."

His words rained down, sharp as hailstones. "Do not speak to me of cruelty, Miss Lumley. Better Fredrick believe me dead than to think I abandoned him willfully. You of all people ought to know how it feels to be left behind."

As if on cue, the howling duet in the distance resumed. It sounded much closer than before.

"Ahwoo! Ahwoo!"

"Ahwooooooo!"

Ashton cringed. "Listen to my son, Miss Lumley. Listen! And imagine the gruesome end that awaits him, and me, if this curse is not ended." He held up Pudge's diary. "I believe the answer is contained in this book, for it was on this voyage that the curse upon my family began."

Simon and Penelope exchanged a look. "But surely you already know what it says," Simon interjected. "Didn't your father tell you? It was your admiral grandpa who got the whole mess started, after all."

Ashton's face clouded. "I was a boy, no bigger than this one"—he nodded at Beowulf—"when I first heard rumors of the curse's existence. Mind you, I was its victim already. My earliest memories are of me howling in misery at the moon, helpless to stop myself, as my mother held me and wept. My father denied everything. 'Curses are poppycock,' he said. 'You just need willpower, that's all.' Oh, the humiliation of it! My father ordered me not to speak of it or to complain. He told me to take up hobbies to distract myself, as he had done—hunting, oil painting, and so on. He even installed a secret attic apartment at Ashton Place so that I might suffer in privacy. Still, I would not give up. Eventually, he confessed the truth: Yes, there was a curse on the Ashtons, but one that could only be ended in the next generation of our lineage—my son's generation, not mine. He promised he would tell me more when I was older. Before he did, he met a gruesome end."

"The Honorable Pax Ashton, pecked to death by murderous pheasants." Just saying it made the back of Penelope's neck grow cold.

Ashton nodded. "My mother, Wilhelmina, was never the same afterward. She lived out her days hidden in those very attic rooms, railing against the evil of birds. Years later, it always pleased her when her little grandson, Fredrick, would bring her a pheasant he had shot. After my father's death, I, too, became obsessed. I consulted soothsayers, and sought out the world's experts on curses and the lifting of curses. Most were charlatans, liars, fakes, and phonies, but the ones with a true gift all had the same vision: a family tree split down the middle, like an oak after a lightning strike, sap running from the wound like blood."

Once more, Penelope thought of Madame Ionesco's vision of the wolf babies—but the old soothsayer had said nothing about a tree. "A bleeding tree . . . what does it mean?"

"That is what I asked as well. Always I received the same answer. 'The hunt is on.' That was my clue—my only clue. Still, I thought I understood. Four times I have tried to break this curse! Four times I have failed. Fredrick's affliction remains; if anything, it grows worse. There must be more to it, I realized—more than my father had told me, more than the soothsayers could see. I would have to go to the source. Luckily, the school was in need of money; it was a simple matter for a wealthy and generous man like Judge Quinzy to charm his way onto the board of trustees."

"Buy his way on, you mean," Simon said sharply.

"Most people find money irresistibly charming. I'm sure even my so-called friends, the Baron and Baroness Hoover, and the Earl of Maytag, would lose much of their affection for me if my wallet were suddenly to run dry. For now, though, they do my bidding without question and accept my lavish gifts with glee. Their votes were worth every penny I paid.

"Still, I did not want my research to draw attention. I knew the baroness to be stingy, rigid, and mean—the perfect temperament to throw a well-run school into turmoil. I gave her free rein. I counted on her small-minded interference in the day-to-day running of the school to keep attention diverted elsewhere, while I searched for the information I needed." He shook his head. "What a tiresome ordeal that was! Most of the Swanburne letters were useless to me. All that cheerful correspondence, full of sound advice! I read through hundreds, perhaps thousands, before I found what I was looking for."

Penelope was lost. "But what does it mean, to 'go to the source'? What do the letters of Agatha Swanburne have to do with the curse upon the Ashtons?"

350

A slow smile snaked across his face. "An excellent question, and one I will leave you to puzzle over in your own time. Suffice it to say, the letters confirmed that some record of the admiral's doomed voyage still existed. The ship's log was lost in the shipwreck, but the cabin boy's diary in invisible ink had been saved. What delicious irony to discover it had been hidden at Ashton Place all along! When Fredrick could not find it, I nearly despaired—until you and the children delivered it right into my hands. A kindness for which I am truly grateful."

The boys growled at this, but Ashton paid them no mind. "Once in possession of the diary, the ink proved more stubborn than I expected. Again, you have provided a solution when I had nearly given up." He rubbed his nose quickly, as if he had an itch. "It seems the Swanburne motto is proven correct: No hopeless case is truly without hope. I will read this diary, and I will learn the origins of this curse upon my family . . . ah—ah—*choo*!"

"Feather up your nose?" Alexander asked, and offered a handkerchief.

Ashton ignored him, though his nose twitched uncontrollably. "I will end this curse, Miss Lumley. No matter the price, to me, to you, or to those wolf children of yours. I will end it! *Ah-choo!*" He looked around, wild-eyed. "*Ah-choo!* Has someone let a cat inside?"

"A cat in a henhouse?" Simon scoffed. "That'd be ill-advised."

Simon was correct, and yet a glimpse of something small and tiger striped flitted through the shadows.

"*Meow!*" it said fearfully. "*Meow!*"

"Shantaloo!" the boys cried, delighted.

"*Ah-choo!*" Edward Ashton sneezed so loudly the walls shook and the chickens *buck-buck-buck*ed in alarm.

He turned and bolted for the exit. Before he could reach it, the door to the chicken coop flew open violently, as if kicked. Lord Fredrick Ashton burst inside, panting and sniffing. "Kitty, *ahwooo! Woof! Woof!*"

"No no no, Your Howling Lordship! Kitty is *not* for chasing!" Cassiopeia's piping, scolding voice was like a puppet version of Penelope's. She pushed her way past her runaway pupil. "Tigawoo, come here at once!"

With the bored indifference that cats exhibit even when they are doing as they have been told, the feline troublemaker moseyed over to Cassiopeia and allowed herself to be picked up. Safely imprisoned in the girl's

Lord Fredrick Ashton burst inside, panting and sniffing.

arms, the cat stared at Lord Fredrick. The tip of her tail twitched with scorn.

Meanwhile, Lord Fredrick Ashton, lord and master of the vast estate that bore his name, and one of the richest men in all of England, hunkered on all fours on the dirt floor of the chicken coop, whimpering like a dog that has just been scolded.

"*Ah-choo!*" Edward Ashton's reddened eyes blazed with shame and fury. "Behold my son and heir, pride of the Ashton family tree!"

"Father?" Fredrick Ashton squinted in his direction. Of course Edward Ashton looked nothing like how his son might have remembered him, but then again, Fredrick's eyesight was notoriously poor. "Fathawoo?" he howled tentatively.

"*Ah-choo!* Forgive me, Fredrick," Ashton said, backing his way to the door. "Next time we meet, this torment will be over. I swear it. *Ah-choo!*" He shoved the cannibal book into his coat pocket. Then Edward Ashton wheeled and dashed outside.

"Stop! We must stop him!" Penelope cried, for she could not bear to see the cannibal book spirited away before they could finish reading it—not after all they had done to find it, and steal it, and visibilize it, too! She raced outside in pursuit. Simon followed, but

Ashton was already on his horse. Stubbornly, Penelope grabbed hold of the reins.

"Out of my way!" Ashton roared. Still she hung on. The frightened horse reared and pawed its massive hooves in the air, perilously close to Penelope's head.

"Watch out!" Simon grabbed her and pulled her to safety. She strained against him and shouted at Edward Ashton.

"But why not share the information in the diary? Perhaps we could help each other untangle its meaning."

"Step aside, governess, I warn you!"

This time, Simon stood in Ashton's way. "She's right, Edward old chap! The diary is written in verse. Miss Lumley is an expert in the poetic-meter department, and I'm a bit of a bard myself. Perhaps we could sort out the mystery together."

A gust of cold air swept through the valley. The clouds skidded across the sky, and the glowing face of the full moon was revealed. It bathed them all in its ghostly light.

"Help each other? But the hunter cannot help his prey." The horse gave a pained whinny as Edward Ashton pulled it hard around. "How shocked you look, governess! Surely you ought to have figured it out by now."

He urged his mount forward until Penelope and Simon had no choice but to step aside or be trampled. "I am no gardener, but I do know this: When a tree splits down the middle, one side must be pruned away for the other to survive. How providential that you and those children came under my very roof! It is almost enough to make one believe in fate."

"It was Miss Charlotte Mortimer who sent me to Ashton Place, in response to a job advertisement!" Penelope had to shout to be heard over the howl of the wind. "And what do the Incorrigible children have to do with it?"

Edward Ashton laughed. "Geneology, Miss Lumley! A wonderful hobby. I highly recommend it." He leaned forward in his saddle and kicked the horse sharply in the sides.

Penelope and Simon watched helplessly as horse, rider, and long-lost diary galloped away, *ta-TUM, ta-TUM, ta-TUM, ta-TUM, ta-TUM.*

The Fifteenth and Final Chapter

*A generous donation comes
from an unexpected source.*

The CAKE was finished, and left a queasy feeling
of regret in its wake. Edward Ashton was gone, and
Great-Uncle Pudge's diary with him. It was bad luck
as far as Penelope and Simon were concerned, for they
had dearly wanted to finish reading the cannibal book.
Alas, Edward Ashton had interrupted them before they
had gotten to the "good part," as one might say nowadays, and the diary's contents would be known only to

him, and to Great-Uncle Pudge, too, since he was the one who wrote it. But Pudge was sworn to secrecy, and the Harley-Dickinsons took their oaths seriously. This Penelope had seen for herself.

Yet all was not lost. As Agatha Swanburne once observed, "Luck is only luck; the bad is often merely the good in disguise." The bad luck was that Edward Ashton was gone, but the good luck was that so was Judge Quinzy. Now, one member short and without a chairman to appoint a replacement, the board of trustees of the Swanburne Academy was stripped of all its power.

"It is an unexpected turn of events, but rules are rules," explained Miss Mortimer, who sounded cheerful as a lark in spring as she announced the mysterious disappearance of the chairman at the next morning's assembly. "I have consulted the school's bylaws, and they are clear as can be: In the absence of a duly appointed chair, the board's responsibilities will fall to the holder of the Swanburne Seat," she said, reading from a yellowed document. "That person will remain in charge 'until things settle down and life gets back to normal.' Once again, our wise old flounder—I mean, founder—has provided a sensible solution, and written in plain English, too."

"And who on earth is the holder of the Swanburne Seat?" the baroness demanded.

"As it happens, I am," Miss Mortimer said with an enigmatic smile. For a moment she looked as if there might be more to say on this topic, but if there was, she kept it to herself.

Penelope, slumped in the first row of the auditorium, yawned and dozed until the children had to poke her awake. The ordeals of the CAKE had quite worn her out, and their evening in the chicken coop had not ended with the sudden departure of Edward Ashton, either. She and Simon had scarcely had time to exchange tragic looks over the loss of the diary when Lord Fredrick Ashton, still in the grip of his wolfish curse, had finally noticed all those delicious-looking chickens (as you know, his eyesight was very poor).

"No no no!" Cassiopeia scolded as he licked his lips. Recall that she had been unable to stop Lord Fredrick from chasing Shantaloo from the observatory to the chicken coop (they had gone to the observatory to practice howling at sheep who were too far away to mind it, Cassiopeia later explained, but the curious cat had followed them and proved to be Lord Fredrick's undoing). Likewise, her stern instruction now was unlikely to help him resist the chickens.

This was no reflection on Cassiopeia's skill as a teacher, of course. Willpower, self-control, stick-to-itiveness—call it what you will, but like most other skills, the knack of doing what one must and finishing what one begins, rather than being distracted by every tasty-looking bit of poultry that comes along, takes a good deal of practice to master. The Incorrigible children already knew this, but Lord Fredrick Ashton had not had the same careful training in how to resist temptation. Especially the kind posed by small, twitchy animals. Like squirrels, for example. Or cats. Or even—

"Chickens, woof!" he barked, forgetting all about Shantaloo. "Chick*ahwoo*!" He began to drool.

"Now, now, keep your paws off my birds, if you please!" Thankfully, the ruckus in the henhouse had summoned Dr. Westminster back from his rounds; he came jogging in just in the nick of time. Old Timothy arrived moments later, moving a bit slower but in hot pursuit of his runaway master.

Another unexpected father-son reunion in the chicken coop? Truly, what were the odds? But there was no chance for Penelope to share this plot twist with Simon, for Lord Fredrick whimpered with hunger for the chickens, and the situation needed to be addressed at once.

After hearing a brief explanation of Lord Fredrick's condition from Penelope, and a description of the first lesson in his Howling Enjoyment Program from Cassiopeia, Dr. Westminster stroked his chin. "A fascinating case, Dr. Lumley and Dr. Incorrigible, and far from hopeless, too. I'd say some HEP is just what the gentleman needs. The full-moon business complicates things, but I see nothing here a bit of training couldn't improve, at least." He frowned and patted his coat. "I'll need some treats that will suit his tastes. What does he like?"

"Billiards at the club?" Alexander suggested.

"Glass of port?" Beowulf offered.

Dr. Westminster emptied his pockets. "Blast! All I have is chicken feed."

"I've got it!" Old Timothy pulled one of Lord Fredrick's favorite cigars out of a pocket and offered it to his scratching, drooling master. "Here you go, Freddy. A fresh El Regente, imported from Habana. It's your favorite." He used the same soothing tone of voice that Penelope had learned from Dr. Westminster (who, it now appeared, may have learned it from his own father!).

It took some persuading, but "Cigawoo," the Lord

of Ashton Place finally conceded. He took the cigar, and Old Timothy helped him light it. Before long he was puffing away, which at least kept him from barking at the birds. The chickens settled down to roost, Shantaloo fell asleep in Cassiopeia's lap, and the aromatic scent of the hand-rolled Cuban all but erased the stink of the visibilizer from the chicken coop. For once, Penelope had been glad of the strong cigar smell.

Miss Mortimer tucked her yellowed copy of the bylaws out of sight. "I believe those are all the announcements I have, so let us get on with this glorious day. Oh! There is one more thing: All that business about wolves at Swanburne turned out to be a false alarm. In other words, much ado about nothing."

"Shakespeare!" cried the Incorrigible children.

"Correct! And that concludes the morning's assembly," Miss Mortimer said. *Clap clap clap!* "Girls, grab your gardening shears. We have a great deal of work to do to put things right."

"All hail to our founder, Agatha!
Pithy and wise is she.
Her sayings make us clever,
And don't take long to tell.

When do we quit? Never!
How do we do things? Well!"

It was wonderful to hear the Swanburne girls singing the school song with spirit, and just as wonderful to see them working together to cut down the ivy from the entrance to the school. They snipped and chopped in time to the music. Soon the motto was revealed once more, in all its optimistic glory.

"No hopeless case is truly without hope," Penelope read, and fell silent.

Simon noticed her thoughtful look. "It's a perplexing business, isn't it?" he said. "What with the moon curse, and 'the hunt is on,' and Ahwoo-Ahwoo, and all the rest. I wish we could have read a bit more of that poem Pudge wrote."

"As do I." She turned to him. "But I was thinking about how easily the former board of trustees was bamboozled by that fake Judge Quinzy. One could have hardly found a worse person to put in charge of the school. It reminds me of the old saying—"

"A flounder saying?" Cassiopeia piped up. The boys had buried themselves in a heap of shorn ivy, but Cassiopeia stood next to Penelope and Simon, with Shantaloo curled in her arms. The fussy little cat had not left her alone since being rescued from Lord Fredrick. One moment it wriggled to get down; the next it yowled to be picked up and petted. Cassiopeia had been kept busy as a nursemaid with a newborn baby, although she did not seem to mind.

Penelope shook her head. "It is a much older saying than those of Agatha Swanburne. It may even be older than the pithy wisdom of Cicero. It goes like this: 'Don't set a fox to guard the henhouse.'"

"Or a Lord Fredrick to guard a henhouse," Cassiopeia said solemnly, scratching Shantaloo between the ears. "Or a tyger kitty."

Alexander poked his head out of the ivy. "Or a Nutsawoo to guard an acorn."

"Or an Incorrigible to guard a piece of cake!" Beowulf added. That made them all laugh.

Magistra Grimsby, who had been listening, leaned in. "In Latin we say *'Ovem lupo committere.'* 'Don't set a wolf to guard the sheep.'"

No one could argue with that.

WITH THEIR LEADER GONE AND the board dismissed, the rest of the foxes—that is to say, Baroness Hoover and the Earl of Maytag—had no reason to linger among the hens. The baroness packed her bags and left in a fury right after the morning assembly. All her husband's attempts to calm her had been in vain, and the words she uttered upon hearing the girls' full-throated bellowing of the school song would have made a sailor blush (but not a pirate, for as you might guess, pirates are not so easily shocked).

The Earl of Maytag did not care one way or the other about the singing, but he was deeply annoyed by Quinzy's disappearance. "Never would have wasted my time on a girls' school if Quinzy hadn't made such a fuss about it! I'd rather be out hunting grouse. Well, now he's run off. When he turns up again, I'll give him a piece of my mind. At least the dinner was worth the trip. That was a tasty goulash, what?"

It was the newest trustee, Lady Constance Ashton, who did something utterly unexpected. Early in the morning on the day after the CAKE, she paid a private visit to Miss Charlotte Mortimer and made an extremely generous donation to the school. "Use it for whatever the girls require," she said briskly. "New uniforms, perhaps. Something with a bit of lace around the collar would be nice. And hire a staff of gardeners, if you please! There are not nearly enough flowers along the paths. Tulips are impractical for such a large area, but daffodils should do quite nicely. It would be a pity to let all that sunlight go to waste."

Even Miss Mortimer, who was rarely flummoxed by anything, was taken by surprise. "We are so grateful, Lady Ashton," she said. "To what do we owe your extraordinary kindness?"

Lady Constance trilled a nervous laugh. "I cannot explain it myself! For some reason, being around so many young people has made me feel somehow—what is the word?—maternal?" At this admission, her cheeks blushed pink as two fresh-bloomed roses. Truly, the always pretty Lady Constance did look unusually radiant, despite all the cake and screaming of the previous evening.

"Children do have that effect on the heart," Miss Mortimer said warmly. "I hope you will visit us again in the spring to see the gardens we will plant in your honor."

Lady Constance's pale hands fluttered around her tummy like birds. "Well, I may be busy in the spring; who knows? But we shall see, we shall see!"

Mr. Felix Trundle, the singing solicitor, had to return promptly to his business in Heathcote (although not before adding a booming bass line to the formerly all-girl arrangement of the school song, which everyone found quite thrilling). But the Archduchess Ilona

Laszlo chose to spend the afternoon at Swanburne, so she might catch up with her friends in the languages department. Naturally, they all spoke fluent Hungarian, so Cecily's services were not required and she had the afternoon free.

Penelope was overjoyed, for it meant she could spend some time with her old friend. It also gave her the chance to introduce Cecily to the children and, of course, to Simon. (Simon proved to be a source of fascination to all the Swanburne girls, especially the older ones. Perhaps it was his pirate's swagger, or that poetical shock of hair that fell in his eyes. He did not seem to notice the girls' interest, however, and spent most of his time discussing advanced navigational techniques with Alexander, and teaching sea chanteys to Beowulf, and letting Cassiopeia wrap herself 'round one leg to make him limp as he walked, as if he had a peg leg.)

The pleasant afternoon flew by, and at last the time came for Penelope and Cecily to say their farewells. They hugged for a long time, and Cecily whispered in her ear, "I think that Simon is sweet on you. It's not every day a fellow writes notes in a bottle and throws them in the ocean!"

"But—but I did not even receive the notes," Penelope stammered. "Ashton Place is nowhere near the sea."

Cecily pressed her hands to her heart and swooned. "Still, he took the time to send them. And while imprisoned by pirates, too! That's awfully romantic, don't you think? Do you like him, too?"

"I think . . . that is to say, I admire his talent a great deal. His hair has a pleasant wave to it, to be sure. And have you noticed the gleam of genius in his eyes?" Penelope blurted, a bit too eagerly.

"Sure, there's an awfully nice gleam in there." Cecily grinned and tossed her braids from side to side. "Wish we had such charming playwrights in Witherslack. But who knows? Maybe one'll wash ashore someday."

By THE NEXT MORNING IT was Penelope who had lost her voice; all her fernibustering had caught up with her, and she could scarcely utter a croak. Miss Mortimer brought her cups of soothing tea laced with honey, and the children laughed and clapped to see her acting out all her thoughts, rather than speaking them. Luckily, Penelope had always been good at charades, and she found she rather enjoyed the challenge.

When the girls of Dormitory C learned of her condition, they insisted that she take back her fountain pen. "You will need it to write down your words," they explained. Penelope tried to refuse, for they had won it

368

fair and square, but it was hard for her to be convincing when all she could do was shake her head and mouth the word "no." In the end the good-hearted girls had their way, and the pen was back in Penelope's possession, along with a fresh new pad of paper to write her thoughts upon.

"The generosity of the staff at Ashton Place, and now the kindness of these girls, shall make this pen a reminder of what is truly important," Penelope thought (luckily, even the worst case of laryngitis does nothing to prevent one from thinking). "I resolve to use this pen, and often: to write to the Swanburne girls and to Cecily, to Miss Mortimer and Mrs. Apple, to Dr. Westminster and even Mrs. Worthington, and to all the other people who are important to me, and to not let time and miles come between true friends."

She twirled the pen between her fingers. It felt good to have it in her hand once more, she had to admit. "Perhaps I shall write some verse, as well. I rather liked the sound of those rhyming quatrains. . . ."

SIMON TOO SPENT ONE LAST night at Swanburne. Miss Mortimer offered him a guest room (there were plenty available, now that the trustees and most of the alumnae had gone home), but he preferred to sleep in the hayloft. He liked the view, he said, for it reminded him of the crow's nest aboard ship. "I always feel better when I can see the stars," he confided to Penelope. "It's the navigator in me. I like to know which end is up."

Sadly, the train schedules dictated that he leave quite early, before breakfast. Penelope walked him to the crossroads to wait for the coach. His intention was to go to London to see if he could interest one of the theaters there in a play about his adventures with the pirates. After his business in London was settled, his next port o' call would be Brighton.

You have grown used to being near the sea, Penelope wrote on her message pad. She felt oddly forlorn at his leaving. How could a simple landlubber of a governess ever compete with the lure of the waves and the tides, the tang of the salt air, and the beckoning twinkle of the stars?

He shrugged and shuffled his feet. "It's not only that. I've been awfully worried about Great-Uncle Pudge, ever since I was kidnapped. I hope he made it back to the Home for Ancient Mariners all right. That troubled me a good deal while I was stuck at sea with the pirates. I'd like to think some Good Samaritan on the boardwalk at Brighton wheeled him back to the HAM."

Penelope gestured in the air with her pen, as if to ask, "Why not write him a letter?"

He understood at once. "Oh, I've written him plenty, but I've no return address for him to send a reply to. I'm no more likely to get an answer than you are to find all those bottles I tossed into the waves. I'll have to go back to Brighton and see for myself."

He tilted his head to one side, in the precise way that made that unruly lock of hair tumble across his forehead. "Say, Miss L, now that I've got my land legs back, I feel a bit silly about sending all those letters from the briny deep. What was I thinking, throwing bottles overboard and imagining they'd somehow reach you on a landlocked English estate? But when you're at sea, it's hard to remember what dry land is like."

Penelope could only shrug. Bravely, she wrote, *The bottles may turn up yet.*

He grinned. "That'd be a stroke of luck, wouldn't it? Funny thing, luck. You can't tell if it's good or bad until well after the fact. Why, if I'd never been kidnapped by pirates, I'd never have learned to make the visibilizer. . . ." His smile dissolved, and he looked glum.

"And then Edward Ashton would never have been able to read Pudge's diary. Well, we got a piece of it, anyway. Pity old Pudge can't simply tell us what he wrote! But an oath's an oath."

Penelope could not answer, of course, but there was no need for a reply. They both knew the oath of a sailor—and of a Harley-Dickinson, no less, steadfast, loyal, and true!—would not be easily broken.

AFTER WATCHING SIMON BOARD THE coach (when he was gone she dabbed the tears from her eyes with a commemorative Swanburne handkerchief, for who knew when she would see him again?), Penelope arrived at the dining room just in time for the morning's meal. And what a meal! It was a breakfast worthy of all the birthdays in the world. There were heaping plates of pancakes served with warm honey, and sliced peaches cooked in butter and sugar, and platters of fluffy scrambled eggs, tender and lemon yellow. The hens had been laying particularly well in recent weeks; perhaps it was all the dancing.

Miss Mortimer and Mrs. Apple sat with the Incorrigible children at a table crowded with happy Swanburne girls, but the seat next to Miss Mortimer had been saved for Penelope. Naturally, Mrs. Apple was in the midst of giving a speech.

"And speaking of ancient Rome," she said, waving a fork in the air, "do you know the story of Romulus and Remus? They were twin brothers, and their father was Mars, the Roman god of war. He had many enemies, as one might expect, given his line of work. To protect his sons, the babies were put in a basket and set adrift on the River Tiber. Eventually, they were found and cared for by a kindly she-wolf."

"Mama Woof!" Cassiopeia's mouth was full of pancake, but her excitement was evident from the way she bounced up and down in her seat.

Mrs. Apple nodded. "You could call her that. The boys grew up, as children tend to do. Together they founded a city on the banks of the Tiber. That's when the trouble started, for they both wanted to be its ruler. They argued terribly. *Tsk, tsk!* If you went through all the history books and tore out the parts where people squabble over who gets to be king, there'd scarcely be one slim volume left! But when your father is the god of war, I suppose you're bound to have a quarrelsome temper."

She speared another pancake and put it on her plate. "Anyway, the brothers fought. In the heat of anger, Romulus killed Remus with a rock. And thus was Rome founded! For if Remus had killed Romulus instead of the other way 'round, it would have been the Reman Empire, instead of the Roman."

The children seemed fascinated by the bloody tale, but Penelope gently cleared her throat. It was not the nicest story to tell a trio of siblings, after all, especially at such a pleasant breakfast.

"Well, it is only a legend, of course," Mrs. Apple said quickly. "Such an unlikely tale could not really be true. Imagine! Children raised by wolves!"

Mrs. Apple was puzzled at first by the children's uncontrollable laughter, but eventually she simply laughed along. "Yes, all hail to the Roman flounders, quite right! Pass the peaches, please!"

Miss Mortimer remained quiet and thoughtful throughout this exchange. Penelope took the opportunity to pass her a note. *The Swanburne Seat???* she wrote, with extra question marks, for she was intensely curious to know what it was.

Miss Mortimer read the words and smiled. "The Swanburne Seat is written into the bylaws of the school," she replied. "It is a hereditary position with no real duties, except for the rare occasions when circumstances demand otherwise."

Penelope tried to write *Hereditary???* on her paper,

but quickly lost patience with sorting out which vowels went where. She put down her pen. "You?" she mouthed.

The headmistress leaned close. "Agatha Swanburne was my grandmother. Few people know that, Penny, dear. I would be grateful if you kept it to yourself."

EPILOGUE

THERE ARE LAWS OF PHYSICS and laws of mathematics. Schools have bylaws and marriages have in-laws. Even the jungle has a law, although following it may make one the kind of person whom no one is particularly eager to sit next to at parties, for fear of being eaten.

And then there is the Law of Coming and Going, which states: When traveling round-trip, the fact that the distance from here to there equals the distance back again in no way guarantees that the journey home will not be a tedious torment of endless miles that somehow feel ten times as long as they did before.

Plucky and cheerful though they most often were, the Incorrigible children were no exception to this law. The return to Ashton Place seemed to last forever. The novelty of staring out train windows at sheep-dotted meadows had long since worn off, and the books they brought to read on the train had already been read to exhaustion.

Starved for entertainment, they begged Penelope to recite poetry, tell jokes, anything—but she could not, for her voice had not yet returned. *Too much CAKE speech!* she wrote on her pad by way of apology. This made the children wild with curiosity about what their governess had actually said at the podium (recall that all three of them had been attending to important responsibilities during her remarks, and had therefore missed them completely).

It was yet another example of how good luck and bad luck can be two sides of the same coin, for if Penelope had not had the misfortune of losing her voice, the Incorrigibles would have surely demanded an encore presentation of the entire fernibuster—spores, rhizomes, and all. Luckily, she had lost her voice, and she could only smile and shrug and wave her arms gracefully, like fronds, as the children tried to guess what sort of charade she was enacting.

In the end they concluded their governess had given a long and heartfelt speech about the Imperial Russian Ballet, and that was close enough.

LADY CONSTANCE AND LORD FREDRICK Ashton had traveled home by private carriage, driven by Old Timothy. Although the carriage was slower than the train, they had left a day earlier, made no stops, and did not have to be picked up at the station, and so they arrived at Ashton Place not long after Penelope and the children did.

The usually no-nonsense Mrs. Clarke made an uncharacteristic fuss over Lady Constance. "My lady ate too much cake while she was away, I think! Look at her, growing plump as a partridge," she said approvingly.

Meanwhile, Lord Fredrick Ashton was in a strangely cheerful mood. He even turned up in the nursery after dinner. Penelope could not recall him ever visiting the nursery before. Mrs. Clarke escorted him, as he might not have found it otherwise. Ashton Place was a very large house.

Penelope feared he might demand an explanation for the strange man in the chicken coop who had claimed to be his dead father, but he did not. He had come, he said, to let her know that he no longer needed any HEP.

"Do you believe yourself to be cured?" she croaked; indeed, for a moment she wondered if Edward Ashton had somehow already succeeded in his quest.

Lord Fredrick snorted. "Oh, I doubt I'm cured! Next full moon will tell. But I learned something important, thanks to my little instructor over there. The truth is, I don't mind the howling. It's nice to blow off steam, so to speak. And I'm used to it, too. I might even miss it if it stopped."

Cassiopeia gave a *woof* of agreement. He looked down his long nose at her, and the expression in his blurry eyes seemed almost fond. "I've never howled with anyone before. It's more fun that way. Afterward, I realized it wasn't the howling itself that bothered me. It was that I felt so alone and ashamed about doing it. But when you know there are others like you . . . well, that's different."

His voice grew stern again. "Even so, I don't want to put a child of mine through all this. No children, and that's that. I just have to figure out how to tell Constance. She's got babies on the brain lately."

Mrs. Clarke overheard this and frowned but said nothing.

"And why does she keep asking me when she gets her 'surprise'?" he added as he was leaving. "I suppose I ought to find out when her birthday is. Blast! I hope I didn't write it in the almanac. It's a slippery book, that almanac, always wandering off. . . ."

WITH PERMISSION, OF COURSE, CASSIOPEIA had borrowed her Swanburne uniform on what Miss Mortimer called an "open-ended loan." This meant that there was no due date, as there would be with a library book. Rather, the kind headmistress had assured her that in no time at all she would outgrow the uniform altogether, at which point she could simply wrap it up and return it by post, so that one of the "little" girls could wear it.

The thought of handing down her Swanburne uniform to an even littler girl made Cassiopeia feel thrillingly grown-up. It also made her want to wear the uniform as much as possible while she still could, for after hearing Miss Mortimer's words she now imagined herself doubling in size overnight with no warning. She had worn the uniform for traveling and had kept it on all afternoon their first day back at Ashton Place, and now she wanted to sleep in it.

It was not Penelope's usual practice to let the

children sleep in their clothes, but with hardly any voice to argue, she could only raise her eyebrows and hold up one finger.

"Yes, one time. Just for tonight." Cassiopeia hugged her governess around the legs (for she was still really rather small, on the outside, at least). "Thank you, Lumawoo!"

Before bedtime the children wanted to play at the fall of Rome, which was their new favorite game. They joined hands and spun and declined and fell until they were dizzy, and then they rose and did it again.

Watching them, Penelope could not help thinking of Romulus and Remus. That siblings could be hidden from danger by being left in the care of wolves was a wild and improbable story, just as Mrs. Apple had said, but this was one of the great virtues of studying history. If such a thing had happened once, even in the days of antiquity, surely it might happen again. Was it possible that the parents of the Incorrigibles had done the same thing, and for the same heartrending reason?

"If the three of you should end up founding an empire, I hope you will not fight over who gets to be in charge," Penelope whispered hoarsely as she turned down the beds. "Or what to call it."

381

Alexander struck an oratorical pose. "I shall name it Alexanderton!"

Beowulf pushed in front of his brother. "The Kingdom of Beowulf sounds better."

Their sister would not be outdone, of course. "Quiet, subjects!" she bellowed, jumping on her bed. "You have entered the Queenly Realm of Me, Who Is Named Cassawoof!"

The three of them squabbled, and Penelope sighed. "And this is how otherwise reasonable people end up throwing rocks at one another," she thought, and took out her pen. Hastily, she wrote the children a note suggesting that they could choose to work together, take votes to decide points of disagreement, and have sensible, plainly written bylaws so everyone understood the rules in the same clear way.

The children thought this over and agreed that it was a good plan. However, they still had to settle on a name they all liked. They thought deeply. Finally Alexander looked up.

"Eureka! How about the Incorrigible Land? That way no one is left out."

Cassiopeia shook her head. "'The Incorrigible Land, and Lumawoo, Too.' *Now* no one is left out."

That solution was promptly voted on and unanimously

adopted. After a few choruses of "All Hail to the Land Incorrigible," the national anthem that they began making up on the spot, all three children finally declined and fell into their beds.

PENELOPE WENT BACK TO HER OWN room, then. Oh, it was good to be home! As a child she would never have imagined preferring any bed to her narrow, lumpy Swanburne cot, but the truth was that she, too, had grown used to the comforts of Ashton Place. With a grateful heart she looked at the furnishings of her well-appointed room and appreciated each one anew: the pretty leaf-and-ivy pattern on the carpet, the delicate floral wallpaper, even the mushroom-shaped drawer pulls on her mahogany dresser.

Inside the closet hung her new dress. It had become so dirty during her travels that the Swanburne laundry had volunteered to take a whack at cleaning it. Now, after being washed in boiling water and bleach, it was no longer brown at all, but a perfectly lovely, nearly white color, not quite beige, not quite cream. "It is the color of moonlight," Penelope thought, very pleased. She was certain Lady Constance would approve.

Once in her nightgown she slipped under the comforter, which was soft and mossy green as a forest floor.

The mattress contained not a single lump. Contented, she gazed up at the posts of her four-poster bed, each one tall and straight as a tree trunk. Why, it was almost as if she were sleeping outdoors, in a surprisingly cozy forest where friendly animals would keep her safe from harm.

Her thoughts grew dreamy . . . perhaps she, too, had been sent away for her own safety, by loving but frightened parents . . . parents who had only her best interests at heart and who had not forgotten her, not for a single moment. . . .

"My imagination is leaping wildly tonight! Yet family trees do sometimes bear unexpected fruit." She roused herself just enough to blow out the candle on her bedside table. "Think of Old Timothy and Dr. Westminster. And Miss Mortimer and Agatha Swanburne, although I confess, I still cannot see a resemblance between them, at least judging from the portrait. And the Incorrigibles . . . and Lumawoo, too?"

She turned her pillow over and over until it suited her perfectly. "Are we? Could we be? But how? That is to say, what are the odds? And why was Edward Ashton so keen on my taking up genealogy as a hobby, anyway?"

The answers to these questions, like so many

others, remained unknown, at least for the moment. But Penelope felt quite sure they would be discovered at some future date. "And truly, the future gets closer every day," she told herself, "like a train approaching the station, whose whistle can be heard in the distance though the train itself is still many miles off. *Whooo-whooo* . . . I think I hear it now. . . ."

Thoughts of that ilk galloped through her brain for quite some time—*ta-TUM, ta-TUM, ta-TUM, ta-TUM, ta-TUM*—long after a tired governess ought to have been asleep.

The UNMAPPED SEA

Still, that Madame Ionesco might be able to undo the curse was cause for optimism, in Penelope's view. Many things were, of course. Swanburne girls were taught to look on the bright side of things, so much so that they were often in real danger of optoomuchism, a word that means precisely what it looks like it means.

But how to discover the exact wording of the curse? Edward Ashton had run off with Pudge's diary. Pudge was in the Home for Ancient Mariners in Brighton and would only talk to a long-dead admiral. "Blast!" she said aloud in frustration.

Margaret had been ducking sock balls and prattling away this whole time. "'Blast?' You sound like Lord Fredrick! Anyway, as I just said, Her Ladyship has me running errands faster than Bertha the ostrich galloping at full speed. You'd think we were going to the moon, instead of Brighton."

The letter Penelope had just read nearly slipped from her hands. "Did you say Brighton?"

"Haven't you been listening? I just told the whole story! The doctor says Lady Constance must take the sea air for her health, and he knew a hotel that would take us in the off-season, and now we're all going to shiver ourselves to pieces in Brighton."

A poorly aimed sock ball hit Penelope square in the forehead, but she scarcely noticed. "Brighton, England?" she asked, disbelieving.

Margaret sat down, dreamy eyed, and folded her long legs beneath her on the armchair. "Yes, Brighton. It's a shame, really. I've always longed to stroll the pier and the sea walk, and watch all the bathers in their finery, and perhaps get a glimpse of Her Majesty Queen Victoria, taking the air at her summer palace, but in wintertime there'll be none of that. That awful doctor! Why couldn't he have ordered a trip to a nice cozy spa, with hot mineral springs to soak in and a gift shop for buying picture postcards? By the time we come home from Brighton I'll be an absolute wreck!"

Wreck . . . shipwreck . . . Ahwoo-Ahwoo! "Be on guard against hyperbole, Margaret," Penelope said quickly, for a plan was already unfolding in her mind. "There is no need to exaggerate. I daresay the weather in Brighton will be no worse than it is here at Ashton Place. It is not as if you are traveling to the Arctic, as so many brave explorers do. Or even to wildest Canada, among those fascinating Eskimaux and their snow huts and sled dogs."

At the mention of sled dogs, the children dropped their socks and galloped in circles 'round the nursery. "Mush, mush!" they cried to egg themselves on, although, like most children, they hardly needed encouragement to run around making noise.

Margaret stretched lazily; it was rare she got to sit down. "You're right, Miss Lumley. I oughtn't complain. It's just that at the beach you expect it to be warm and sunny, which makes it seem all the colder when it's not." She cocked her head to the side. "But I suppose the ocean is just as vast in January as it is in July, and the horizon just as far. That'll be something wonderful to see! And what will you and the children do while we're away? It'll be nice and quiet around here, I suppose." Even as she said it, she looked doubtful; between alternating cries of "Harr, mateys!" and "Mush, mush!" as the children careened around the nursery, the Incorrigible pirate sled dogs were making a fearsome amount of noise.

"Oh, we will keep busy with this and that," Penelope

replied evasively. "Letters to write, bookshelves to tidy. The children are painting family portraits, too—"

Like a pat of butter tossed in a hot skillet, Margaret's cheerful expression melted all at once. "The poor loves! Painting family portraits, and them with no family but one another, *tsk, tsk!*"

"On the contrary, they have a great many people to paint. Even you, Margaret." Penelope spoke briskly, for she was not in the habit of feeling sorry for the children, who never felt sorry for themselves. "In fact, I was posing for them when you came in."

"As Little Bo Peep? My heart aches to hear it! Taking characters from nursery rhymes and pretending they're family, since they've no real family of their own." Margaret's lip trembled as if she might cry. "So brave these children are, and so lively in spite of their hardships."

The children were lively to be sure, but at present their only hardship had to do with the difficulty of building an igloo out of sock balls. Their sled-dog game had given them the idea to build an entire Eskimaux village out of the materials at hand. Alas, sock balls have a tendency to roll, and this was just as true in Miss Lumley's day as it is in our own. A proper igloo ought to be made of snow, the children wistfully agreed. With deep longing they looked out the nursery window at the powdery white fields below.

Reluctantly, Margaret rose from the chair. "I'd best get back downstairs before I'm missed. I wish you all *arrivederci*!" The way she said it sounded like the peeping of newborn chicks. "That's what Lady Constance says. *Arrivederci!* Soon there'll be a new baby in the house, won't that be exciting? I wonder what they'll name the wee thing."

Empty laundry basket tucked under one long arm, Margaret took a hop, then a skip, and whirled out of the nursery. She really was a charming sort of girl. She walked as if dancing, spoke as if squealing with delight, and sounded merry even when she had cause for complaint. No wonder Jasper was so keen on her.

The children begged to go outside and build igloos, after which they intended to carve some canoes suitable for paddling through Arctic seas, but a look from Penelope reminded them that they ought to tidy up their painting project before starting something new. As they did so, she too gazed with longing out the window.

"So the Ashtons are going to Brighton, and all because of that clever Dr. Veltschmerz," she murmured. "Clever, clever Dr. Veltschmerz! For I believe a winter beach holiday is just what the doctor ordered. . . ."